Praise for Lee Nichols

"Nichols is one of chick lit's brightest lights."
—*Publishers Weekly*

Tales of a Drama Queen

"A delightfully silly, vivacious debut.
This good-natured, irrepressible fairy tale is
better than a box of bonbons; *Shopaholic* fans
may have a new heroine."
—*Publishers Weekly*

Hand-Me-Down

"Nichols' second novel is a delightful tale
about a young woman coming into her own
and finding love in the process."
—*Booklist*

"Nichols' talent for telling stories is enhanced by
her special knack with characters."
—*Romantic Times BOOKclub*

"[Nichols]…delivers a funny, utterly
winning story of family, love and self-discovery."
—*Publishers Weekly*

Also by Lee Nichols

Tales of a Drama Queen
Hand-Me-Down

TRUE LIES OF A
Drama Queen

LEE NICHOLS

RED
DRESS
INK
TM

First edition June 2006

TRUE LIES OF A DRAMA QUEEN

A Red Dress Ink novel

ISBN 0-373-89575-5

www.RedDressInk.com

Printed in U.S.A.

TRUE LIES OF A

Drama
QueeN

chapter

1

The groom is perfect this time. His white Hugo Boss suit is crisp, his gray eyes are solemn and joyful and all mine. The palm trees sway in the Santa Barbara ocean breeze like a heavenly chorus of tall skinny angels with green hair. The nomadic tents match the linen napkins, the silver is antique and the orchids are pale green. Everything is discreet. Tasteful. Flawless.

Oh, and I got a big honking diamond. The thing's like a glass doorknob, I can barely lift my hand. Though somehow, I think I'll manage.

I also got the Luna flatware from Pottery Barn, the lead-crystal Bordeaux glasses, and a year-long subscription to flowering plants from Smith & Hawken. I even got a KitchenAid

Mixer in Majestic Yellow—I never mix, but Maya wants one, and I knew she'd be jealous. (As a married and established matron, I will be less petty…but I remain single for another seventeen seconds.)

The justice of the peace murmurs something about loving and cherishing, and when he comes to the "I do" part, Merrick politely agrees. But I…well, I'm too busy worrying that Maya—best friend and maid of honor—is so poisoned by envy she can't enjoy the ceremony. Okay, actually I'm worried that's she's not envious enough. I won't be happy until she matches the pale green of the orchids. Maya is the sweetest, kindest best friend anyone could want, but if she has a single fault it's that she's so much *better* than I am. She doesn't get petty, she doesn't get jealous, not even now, on my perfect wedding day. Doesn't she know this means I've *won?*

In fact, not only does she lack all human (I mean negative) emotions, but she's chatting away in the middle of my vows. "So we're settled on April."

"What?" I say. "What?"

"We decided April."

"April?"

"What do you think of the song?" Maya asks.

A cruel jolt and my daydream vanishes. There are swaying palm trees and Maya is clearly present, but there is no wedding—not mine, at least. We've met for lunch at Leadbetter Beach on a pristine sunny January day in Santa Barbara, and we sit at one of the tables out back, our bare feet drawing patterns in the sand. Makes me feel like I'm vacationing in Mexico. Maybe after lunch I'll have another margarita and a siesta.

No, after lunch I'll have another client and a headache.

Because my perfect best friend has told me she and her perfect boyfriend, Brad, are getting married. And *they'll* have the perfect wedding and the perfect marriage. And I'll be happy for her. Really. Because I love her. And it's not like this means she won or anything…it's not really a competition. Is it?

"Right," I say. "The song."

"It's Sting," Maya says. "Everyone loves Sting."

"Is it off his first album?"

"No."

"The second?"

"No."

"Then I don't know it."

Maya grimaces. "You could at least be a little more excited. Aren't you happy for us?"

"Of course I'm happy! You know I'm happy. I'm thrilled and happy and…happy! So an April wedding. Where?"

"In Santa Barbara. Brad's parents want us to have it in Vegas."

Perfect Brad's parents had retired to Las Vegas last year and hadn't stopped extolling the virtues of low-cost housing, the senior discount at Caesars and the wonders of the Hoover Dam. They were convinced they could persuade Maya and Brad to move there, if only they explained how really affordable the buffets were.

"Vegas," I say. "Some of those chapels are really nice—they're not all cupid-themed, you know." Plus, I wouldn't be so jealous if she got married in Las Vegas. "I'd get married there in a second."

"Elle, you would *never.*"

"Well, no. What about San Ysidro Ranch?" Because I shouldn't be such a bad friend. "Gwyneth Paltrow got married there."

"Gwyneth Paltrow makes fifteen million a movie."

"I know it's expensive, but you're only going to do this once. You and Brad—" I roll my eyes. "You'll never divorce."

"*Elle...*"

"Who's going to cater?"

Maya shrugs. "There are listings in the Yellow Pages."

"The Yellow Pages," I say faintly. Does she have any idea how long it took me to settle on a caterer when I arranged my almost wedding to Louis? "Well, at least you've got over a year to plan."

"No," she says. "April."

"Yeah," I say. "April."

"*This* year."

A sudden chill rises from the sun-drenched beach. "Maya, that's three months away."

"That's why I'm starting now," she says, clearly pleased with herself.

"You can't plan a wedding in three months."

"Why not?"

"Because it's never been done, not in all of human history. Because it takes a minimum of *four* months to select, buy, write and mail invitations. Because all the caterers and venues have been booked since April of *last* year."

She appears unconcerned. "We'll find someplace."

"Like the Tiki-Tiki lounge at a motel in *Goleta.*"

"Elle, you've gotta get over your Goleta-phobia. That's so early nineties. Goleta's 'The Good Land' now. Brad and I want to buy a house there...if we can afford one."

"If you do, I'll never visit."

"And there are *other* reasons Goleta is wonderful, too."

I make a face, but bow to the inevitable. "Okay, I'll do it."

"Visit?"

"Visit, we'll see. I mean plan the wedding."

I detect a flicker of concern. "Great. That'd be…great."

"Three months!" I say, staying chipper. "This is gonna be fun."

"I mean, if you want to, you could help with the, um…"

"More than help! I'll be your wedding coordinator. Leave everything to me." I beam, thrilled to finally be giving something back to Maya. She's better than I am at virtually everything, but now *I* can finally help *her*. "What are best friends for?"

"Well, I wouldn't want to…I know you're busy with your, um, career?"

Because I am a good friend, I pretend not to hear the question mark after "career" and simply say, "I will organize an elegant, classical, understated affair…" She looks so unconvinced I can't help adding, "I was thinking a Western theme, 'Jackie O meets rodeo.' Or have you considered a Hawaiian luau?"

I'm still in a wedding planning daze—the flowers, the band, the maid of honor dress—so when my client phones, exactly on schedule, I chat on autopilot until the woman tells me she thinks her boyfriend poisoned her.

"And for a free copy of my newsletter," I say, "all you need is—*what?*"

"I, like, think my boyfriend poisoned me."

I dart into the kitchen and throw open drawers, rummaging for my phone book. I need the number for Poison Control. Is there a national number? Why is she calling a psychic when she's been poisoned—she wants to know if she'll live? I have a list of Important Numbers—domestic violence chief among them—but who knew I'd get a poison question? "How exactly did you ingest the poison?" I ask calmly, hurling open a cabinet. "Are you sure you're poisoned? Did he cook something for you?"

"He doesn't cook."

"Make you a drink?" Staying calm, staying steady…but where the *hell* is that phone book? "Bring you a glass of water?"

"Not that I recall. Should he bring me glasses of water? Do they *do* that?"

"Well, relationships are all different, you have to—but you don't sound worried, how are you feeling?"

"I feel fine. Never better."

"So—"

"Except for the puking."

"Eww."

"Yeah, like every morning for the last three weeks. And my boyfriend's acting all suspicious, asking how I feel, if I'm okay, do I want anything. I'm gonna start asking for glasses of water."

"Sick every morning? Like…morning sickness?"

"Exactly! Omigod! There's a *name* for this?"

"Well, it's not so uncommon, many women—"

"Is it girlfriend poisoning? Is he like Scott Peterson?"

"Let's back up a second. How are you fixed for birth control?"

"You mean like rubbers?"

"Exactly like rubbers."

"Oh, yeah, we use them every time, unless we get all, y'know. Caught up in things. You think he poisoned me with a rubber?"

"I think he poisoned you *without* a rubber. Did you have sex prior to feeling sick?"

"Omigod!" she says, seeing the light.

"Exactly."

"He *did* poison me with a rubber."

"Um, no. Let me put it this way—you're pregnant."

A slight pause. "You're *good,*" she says in a low voice.

"Thank you," I say. "But the question is, how are *you?*"

"So he poisoned his pregnant girlfriend? Wow, that's low. That's daytime TV low."

I'm sure my mother would have an appropriate anecdote, as she watches a lot of *Oprah,* but I explain from the beginning. The sex without protection. The sperm and egg. The fertilization. The hormones. When realization finally dawns, she's thrilled, "So *that's* why he keeps bringing home stuffed animals." We spend the rest of the session discussing midwives and pain medication and *Desperate Housewives.* She's amazed when I tell her the child will *definitely* be the same sex as one of the grandparents' children.

Before the phone hits the cradle, I shoot into the bathroom to check that my birth control pill prescription is current. This surge of activity rouses my dog Miu—though she slept through all the banging around in the kitchen. She's a boxer I adopted from the local shelter as a bald and sickly skeleton (her, not me—I have good hair, and can *never* lose those last ten pounds) and is now my official babygirl. She lifts her head and yawns at me and I discover the phone book is half-eaten under her ectoplasmic jowls. She still has separation anxiety sometimes, but I know how that feels, so I don't get mad. Not even when she ate the Marc Jacobs handbag I accidentally bought with my credit card, which led to an uncomfortable conversation with Carlos, my credit counselor. Well, he says he's just my creditor, but I need the therapy.

★ ★ ★

My boyfriend, Merrick, lives perched on a cliff over-
looking the ocean, in a little gem of a house he designed
himself. He's an architect, which is one of the better jobs for
a boyfriend, and has some issues with perfectionism, for
which he claims his treatment is me. At six o' clock, I pull
my car—a BMW, 1974, pumpkin-orange, which Maya says
looks like a Halloween float—next to Merrick's Volvo station
wagon and walk down the lavender-lined stone path to the
front door. I'm a little surprised, when he opens the door,
that he's not wearing Hugo Boss, but kiss his sloppy jeans-
and-T-shirt self anyway.

He steps back when Miu scampers inside, and eyes me.
"You look extra-delicious."

This is a loving lie, I look like I always look: a strong seven
out of ten, with a bit too much chub and a large head, but
good hair and nice eyebrows. If I made enough money to
afford Kiehl's for everyday use, maybe I'd be an eight. If Visa
and Mastercard weren't so shortsighted, and let me buy
Theory, I'd be a strong eight. "On a scale of one to ten?" I ask.

"Ten."

"You're not supposed to say ten," I tell him. "Ten means
you're just making me happy. Nine makes me think maybe
you're telling the truth."

"Then nine. How was your day?"

"A strong seven."

"That's pretty good," he says. "That's the 'sweet spot,' a
strong seven. Anything better, you get spoiled, anything
worse, you've missed out."

And that's why I love him—he thinks I'm the "sweet spot."
I show him my shopping bags from Lazy Acres, the gourmet
grocery. "Then dinner's a really strong six. I got salad."

"Just what every man wants to hear," he says. "Salad for dinner."

"Sorry." I lead him into the kitchen and hand him his box from the salad bar. "Sometimes I forget."

"That I'm a man?"

"Well, at least your salad's bigger than mine. And there's meat in there."

He opens his box. "Baco bits?"

I nod.

"And…" He frowns at the contents. "Pineapple."

"It's Hawaiian themed."

He peeks in my box. "What'd you get?"

I take a heaping bite of tomato, cuke, feta, kalamata and chickpea. "Greek. Wanna trade?"

Merrick only believes in predetermined kinds of salad. There are maybe five salads in his world…a few more, if you add chicken. He'd never dump the entire bowl of Bacos into his salad and heap pineapple on top with the lettuce tongs, but he still takes a tentative bite, and looks surprised. "This isn't so bad."

"You can add it to your salad list."

He takes another bite, and nods, and I'm more satisfied than is psychologically healthy. He cracks two beers and gives me one and I tell him about Maya's wedding, making a short story long. I finish a half hour later with, "And she thinks you can find a caterer in the Yellow Pages."

He sips his beer. "Speaking of which, why did you put my phone book in your bag?"

"I didn't," I say.

"I was standing right there."

"Maybe I'm looking for an architect."

"I'm not architect enough for you?"

"Maybe I'm looking for an architect who delivers."

Merrick puts his beer bottle down and takes a pull of me instead. We go to bed early…I fall into a satiated sleep until a couple hours past midnight, when I wake and nudge Merrick with my elbow.

He says, "What—Wha?"

"Sting!" I say. "What is she thinking?"

"Sting is the new Elton John," he mumbles, and rolls away from me.

I can't decide if this is profound or idiotic. True that Elton and Sting both made all their best music when young, but while Elton appeals to nobody under the age of fifty-five, Sting does well with the prematurely middle-aged thirtysomething crowd. And there is the movie connection: Elton has composed many movie scores and Sting's a regular fixture at the Oscars.

The real question is, who'd want either for their wedding? Maya hasn't dreamed of weddings since she was little—hell, she hasn't even planned a wedding that failed to occur due to the groom marrying someone else. In her world, a wedding is just a big dinner party, you invite a bunch of people and get married. She doesn't know this is an entire industry she's inviting into her personal life. She can't handle this by herself. She needs me, and I'm gonna give her the wedding she deserves, like it or not.

I snuggle happily into my pillow, warm with the glow of good intentions, then sit up again and poke Merrick with my index finger.

He peers at me, sleepily.

"How come you've never married?" I ask.

"What time is it?"

"It's past time you married. You're over thirty, an attractive straight man with an income, you should be married."

He squints. "Do you want to marry me?"

"Is that a proposal?"

"No."

"Then no."

He rolls closer and presses against me and runs his hand along my hip. "Do you want to have sex again?"

"Is *that* a proposal?"

"Yes."

"Then yes."

I normally drift into sleep after sex—I read somewhere that's nature's way of making babies, giving the seamen calm waters in which to find their way to shore. But tonight I'm more awake than I was before we started. Not sure if I should be offended Merrick wasn't serious about marrying me, or relieved. I ponder for half an hour before finally giving up and getting out of bed.

I creep downstairs into the living room where Miu's asleep on Merrick's olive slip-covered sofa. She knows she's not allowed on the furniture, but I'm convinced she sleeps there every time we spend the night. She's lying on her back, doggie paws in the air, three-inch jowls hanging open, revealing the pink glossy skin underneath. She lifts one eyelid at my approach, unalarmed to be discovered. I check there isn't drool leaking from her chops and leave her there.

I open the French doors, step onto the Jerusalem stone patio and stand a moment, smelling the salt air and listening to the surf until my skin goose pimples under Merrick's robe. I pad into his office, looking for something to read. He keeps his books perfectly aligned on built-in shelves. I teased him once that his carpenter—and best friend—Neil made the shelves crooked, and even though he'd known I was teasing, I'd found him in his office later with a measuring tape.

I smile as I run my fingers along the spines of the books. I love this house, the comfortable lines inside and the strong warm exterior. It's so Merrick. I love that he lives frugally so he can afford the ocean view—even if it means, well, that he lives frugally. I love that his books are a reflection of who he is, mostly heavy architectural tomes, with an eclectic collection of nonfiction (English history, contemporary art, biography and nature), plenty of thrillers and a scattering of sci-fi.

I grab a random novel and wander into the kitchen. There's no ice cream, but I find flour tortillas in the fridge and decide to make *buñuelos,* a new favorite, from a cookbook Carlos gave me. I'd asked about his mother's cooking and he'd sent me *Mexican for Gringos.* I butter the tortillas on both sides, toss them in cinnamon and sugar and throw them on a cookie sheet. Not what you'd call authentic, but nevertheless delicious.

I slide them into the oven and Merrick staggers downstairs, disheveled in a pair of USC sweatpants he's had since graduate school, and mumbles a question.

"I was hungry." I grab the novel I'd taken from his office. "And thirsty for knowledge."

He raises an eyebrow at my reading choice, which I now see depicts an enormously buxom woman wearing a skintight suit and a chrome bra with hazard lights for nipples.

"What are those?" I ask. "Do they flash when she breaks down?"

"I've had that since junior high, the subject of many a boyhood fantasy." He brushed his hair with his fingers, always a sign of impending seriousness. "Listen, when you asked—"

I'm afraid of Merrick in his serious moods, that's when he usually tells me I ought to get a real career. "She looks like air-traffic control for extremely jumbo jets," I interrupt.

"When you asked if that was a proposal—"

The timer on the oven dings and I cheerily sing out, *"Buñuelos!"*

"Elle," he says, as I open the oven door and pull out the piping-hot, sugared tortillas, "move in with me."

I startle, and we both scream as the *buñuelos* career off the cookie sheet and splatter Merrick's bare chest.

The old wives' tale says you're supposed to butter your burns, but what if your burns are from butter? I stand over Merrick, an unwrapped stick of margarine in my hand, babbling apologies. "Oh, God, honey! I'm sooo sorry! Ouch—that's all red, I'm so so so sorry…"

He backs away. "What are you doing? Get that away from me."

I wrap the stick and aim for one of the angry red welts. "It's cold, like a cold pack."

"As opposed to ice?"

He opens the freezer, and his ice cube trays are full, of course. In my house, if you want an ice cube, you pour your own and wait forty minutes. He grabs a handful of cubes and holds them against his chest. He's scowling. I don't like when he scowls.

"I never have any ice," I tell him, happy to change the subject.

"I know," he says, tightly.

"These are like ice-on-demand. Just-in-time cubes."

"Get me a napkin."

I fill a cloth napkin with ice and hand it over. "Does it really hurt?"

"Jesus, Elle, I thought you'd be happy."

Tears spring to my eyes. "That I burned you? That's a terrible thing to say! I'm totally—"

He glares. "You know what I mean."

"I do?"

"Is this one of your new psychic theories? Block out anything you don't want to deal with? Pretend it was never said?"

"That's not fair—you've always hated my job."

"You're a fraud psychic, Elle."

"I'm an intuitive counselor," I say in a small voice, and my throat hurts from biting back tears. "Why are we fighting? It was an accident."

"I asked you to move in with me and you hurled hot tortillas at my chest."

"You surprised me! I…I don't know. I mean, I *do* want to move in with you, but I'm all…" I gesture wildly, but manage not to injure Merrick. "I don't want to ruin this."

He says, standing there with an icy rag dripping down his chest, "You won't ruin anything."

I try a watery smile. "What if I break you?"

"You break it, you bought it." He hooks a gentle hand around my neck and pulls me closer. "Will you move in with me?"

I can't.

I moved in with my ex-fiancé, Louis, after three months, and we lived together for six years. Merrick and I have been together roughly four months and he's no Louis. Well, technically, yes, Merrick *is* Louis—that's his first name—but while

Louis was a prickly perfectionist, Merrick is…well he's not prickly. He's a lovely and kind and supportive perfectionist, the kind of guy you see with another woman and think: *Why can't I find someone like that?*

The problem is, he's too good for me, he's got the house and the career and he knows who he is. Louis left me during Stage 9 of wedding planning, and I vowed never again to lose myself in a man. Then came Merrick, who is so delicious I could get lost in him forever and…see, that's the problem, he's too tempting. I'm deathly afraid of clinging, until one day I turn into the Human Cling Wrap, and if Merrick manages to uncling himself before suffocating, he'll run screaming.

Poor Merrick. He probably thought I'd jump at the chance to live with him, like any normal woman. Why can't I be more normal? That should really be my goal. To act like one of the humans. I'm like Pinocchio's long-lost sister. I just want to be a real girl.

I stand there and gape, and the silence lengthens until Merrick tosses the melted ice cubes into the sink. "I'm going to bed," he says, and leaves me standing amid the ruins of my midnight snack.

chapter

2

Merrick is gone the next morning when I roll off the sofa where I'd curled next to Miu to finish sleeping. There's a fresh-brewed pot of coffee, though, which means he doesn't totally hate me. I laze around his house, then clean the kitchen (the sugar got everywhere) and berate myself for my Pinocchio'd state. At least my nose doesn't grow when I tell a lie, which is a good thing, 'cause it'd be eighty yards long. Imagine the potential for clogged pores. Or how much I'd spend on concealer.

I'm about to crack the sci-fi novel when I remember I have an appointment in roughly six minutes. I race through the morning routine and am only twenty minutes late to meet Randy, a healer who practices from his comfortably ramshackle house on the lower riviera. He forgives me, and ushers me into his parlor where he offers a tall glass of iced tea.

"Many people find the practice odd," he tells me, after an introductory spiel that turns my face white. "But this is centuries old—millennia, really—an established Ayurvedic treatment, plus the Aztecs and ancient Chinese both used uropathy. It's even in the Bible."

I refuse the iced tea. "The Bible?"

"In Psalms. 'Drink from your own cistern, flowing water from your own stream.'"

"But doesn't that mean, y'know, the brook in your backyard?"

"A mind is like a parachute," he says, with a scolding wag of his finger.

"Don't jump from a plane without one?" I ask.

"It only functions when open."

I don't tell him that yes, I've seen the bumper sticker, but remain alert and professional. I am Lois Lane in rhinestone flip-flops. This is one part of my career—okay, one of many—I haven't quite come to terms with yet. Four months ago, due to a series of idiot mishaps and happy coincidences, I solved "The Case of the Missing Bitch"—not, as Maya claims, the title of my autobiography, but the story of a female puppy stolen from a breeder's house. I led authorities to the miscreant, and my psychic powers were credited for the criminological triumph in the newspaper and on the local news.

A couple weeks after the attention crested, when I was heading quickly back into total obscurity, I got a call from Teri Clifton, managing editor at the *Santa Barbara Permanent Press*.

"You're exactly what I've been looking for," she'd said, which are words I'd never heard before. "Are you interested in writing a column?"

ﬤ

.vn column. *Sex and the City in Santa Barbara.* Beau-
young girl about town, wreathed in two-thousand-
dollar designer outfits, with her adoring friends and witty
repartee. I'll write about where to go for chocolate martinis,
the eternal hunt for the best shoes and datable men. I inhaled
deeply, to keep from squealing. "Perhaps a small-town *Sex and
the City* approach, with occasional forays to L.A. for Hollywood glamour? Celebrity cameos in every issue, gossipy
insider fashionista—"

"No," she said repressively. "A New Age column—you're
a psychic, not a party girl."

"Well, I *could* be a party girl."

"Each week you'd profile a new alternative healing
business, one week an acupuncturist, the next an aura reader.
Eight hundred words max. Can you do it?"

Aura reading. How cool would that be? I totally wouldn't
have to listen to people talk anymore. "Eight hundred
words…" I said thoughtfully. I wanted to ask how long that
was, but I suspected she'd tell me it's eight hundred words
long. "What's the pay?"

"Seventy-five an article."

One column a week? That's two-seventy, no, almost three
hundred bucks a month. Pretty good for easy work, and how
hard can writing be? All kinds of idiots are writers. "Will
there be a little picture of me next to the column?"

"No."

"Oh."

"Yes or no?" she said.

Being a fake psychic was one thing, but pretending to
know about auras and acupuncture was something else. On
the other hand, my Mom runs a crystals-and-runes store in
Sedona, so I've already built up a total resistance to incense

and the jingling of wind chimes. Plus…an extra $300 a month. "You bet," I said.

For my first column, I covered an acupuncturist, who asked me if my breasts were tender and wanted to see my tongue. I didn't mention that in the column, though, because he stuck pins in my earlobes that totally cured a headache. Then I did an aura reader, expecting to discover that my aura was violet or sage-green, and was crushed to find I'm a "mental tan." I interviewed an herbalist, and someone who makes ear candles—which are *not* composed of ear wax, so don't even ask—and on and on until roughly three months later, I'd run out of ideas.

That's when I'd met Darwin and Adele for lunch at the Natural Café. They were friends from my days working the phones at Psychic Connexion, a cubicle farm of phone psychics where I developed my latent talents until I got fired. Adele suggested a psychic she thought was terrific, but Darwin and I both nixed this idea—didn't want the real deal showing up the fake psychic, though that's not what we told Adele, as she's convinced I have the "gift."

Then Adele suggested Randy, who is now saying, "It's nature's perfect tonic, every molecule custom designed for your body. Ninety-five percent water, with five percent vitamins, minerals, enzymes, hormones, antibodies—"

"And you, um, drink it?"

"Every morning."

I jot "piss" on my notepad as if I might forget that this man drinks his own pee.

"Urine isn't a waste product," he tells me, clearly heartened by my note taking. "It's a by-product of blood filtration, full of healing properties. Your urine's got melatonin, for example—like your doctor prescribes for long flights, but why pay for a pill when you manufacture the stuff yourself?"

Because nobody peed on the pills? "Um…"

"The pharmaceutical companies would lose billions if people started sipping their own nectar instead of popping pills, that's why they suppress the studies. Uropathy helps everything from cancer to HIV—gangrene, heart disease, shingles, gout—I could go on."

"Please don't—I mean, I think I have enough." More than enough, and only six hours before my column is due.

Two bits of good news strike me as I drive home. One, this is the perfect icebreaker with Merrick. Two, I'm *really* glad I didn't try the tea.

Merrick's office is on the first floor of the building I live in—a large pale yellow Victorian a few blocks to the west of lower State Street. I slip into his office and he's standing at his desk, delicious in a charcoal shirt, dark pants, his hair slightly mussed. Makes me smile just looking at him.

"Listen to this," I blurt, before he can say he's still mad. "No, wait—this is good. Apparently drinking your own pee leads to clear skin and lustrous hair. Can you imagine drinking your own urine?"

Merrick turns slowly from me to the older couple sitting in the antique Chinese chairs at the coffee table. Early sixties, she's got ropes of pearl, a Fendi handbag, and breeding, and he's tweedy in an over-respectable super-wealthy sort of way.

Somewhere in the distance, a cricket chirps.

"*That*…was not what it sounded like," I say. "Ha ha! Almost sounded like I said urine, didn't it? What I actually said was, uh, 'Can you imagine drinking your own…'"

I now discover nothing rhymes with "urine."

"I tried it once," the old man says. "Peace Corps, India."

"Avery, please," the wife says, tight-lipped.

"Tasted like piss."

I cock my head. "Can I quote you on that?"

"If you'll excuse us," Merrick tells me.

I apologize and slink into the hall, close the door behind me and slump against the wall.

"Who was that?" the woman asks from inside the office.

"She lives upstairs," Merrick says. "She's a little…"

He doesn't finish the sentence, but they all laugh, so that must've been some gesture.

So, he's still mad.

An hour later I'm in my apartment staring at my notebook, waiting for a column to appear, when a knock sounds at the door. Respectful and firm. It's Merrick, knocking pointedly. I let him in and he makes a production of checking the room to see if I'm alone before speaking. This is good. This means he doesn't hate me.

"Want to get a cup of coffee?" he asks.

"Well, I'm right in the middle of this column…"

We both look at my blank page.

"Where do you want to go?" I ask.

"Bread and Water?"

Which is the site of our first date…and of "The Coffee Condom Catastrophe," during which I did a convincing imitation of a malfunctioning rubber machine. Long story, involving Planned Parenthood, a juvenile delinquent and a ratty Coach tote. I say, "No."

"I'm sure they've forgotten," he says. "It's been almost five months."

"That's not the kind thing of people forget, Merrick. Ever."

"Remember how that one condom landed in the latté the waitress was holding?"

"How about the Coffee Bean?" I ask, rising above.

Miu has padded over to sniff Merrick's shoes, and I tell her to get her leash. She looks at me incredulously, so I tell her again. She drools, and I get her leash and the three of us head over to State Street, Miu straining in front.

"I'm sorry," I say, as we wait for the signal on Chapala Street.

"For what?"

Does he want me to apologize for last night? "For your clients, bursting in with the whole urine thing. I hope I didn't piss them off."

He shakes his head at my pun. "They hardly noticed," he lies, sparing my feelings.

"Well, I'm still sorry," I say, tying Miu to a metal chair in front of the Coffee Bean.

"What got you on the subject, anyway?" Merrick asks, as we push inside.

I tell him all about Randy, and how one of the recent prime ministers of India was an avid pee-drinker and lived to 107. "Oh, and drinking your morning pee is the best," I tell him, then turn to the guy behind the counter. "Vanilla latté, please!"

He stares at me in horror.

"This is why you should go back to school," Merrick says.

"What, to get away from pee-drinkers and people asking if my breasts are tender? One large vanilla latté, please."

The guy blinks.

"And to keep you from worrying you have a beige soul."

"Aura," I say. "Mental tan."

"Two weeks you were worried about the color of your

soul," Merrick says, then turns to the guy. "Two large vanilla lattés!"

The counter guy snaps back into reality and rushes our order, probably to get us out of the shop. We sit outside with Miu, the day is gray and cool, the coffee warm and sweet. Merrick is stern and officious. Well, he's trying to be kind and caring, telling me why I should get my master's degree in counseling psychology, but I hate this conversation. "...then there's the long-term potential," he says. "Where do you see this *going?* You know how proud I am that you're making this work, but at some point you need to get a rea— a different career, a long-term career, and the earlier the better. Being a fake psy—an intuitive counselor is fine, if you have a degree. That's all I'm saying. Why not take everything you've already accomplished and blah blah blah." He sips his latte. "Blah blah blah and I don't even want to mention the possible legal consequences."

"Apparently you can get B vitamins from eating your own poop," I say.

"That's revolting."

"There's more! He told me—"

He reaches under the table and pinches my thigh, then kisses me before I can shriek. He tastes like vanilla and Merrick.

"I'm sorry," I whisper against his lips. For embarrassing him in front of clients, for staring at him like an idiot when he asked me to move in.

He kisses my ear and says, "Sorry enough to apply to school?"

I groan before pulling away, but maybe he's right. I'm still new to this whole "life and career" thing, and judging from my experience this morning, I haven't quite mastered the concept. Is school the answer? I don't know, but Merrick and Maya both think so. "Okay," I say. "I'll look into it."

Merrick kisses me again. "I'm sorry, too, for last night. I sprung that on you. I thought...I don't know. I love you."

Hmm, if this is his reaction to looking into a master's, maybe I'll get my Ph.D.

The good news is that Merrick's not mad at me. The bad news is my article for the *Permanent Press* is due in a few hours. Well, that and I apparently have to research psychology programs or something. Normally, I'd borrow Merrick's computer (for some reason Teri demands that my articles be typed), but he needs it this afternoon so I give him Miu's leash—she'll happily curl up in a corner of his office—and head for the *Permanent Press.*

The office used to be a bank. The publisher and editor's offices are where the loan officers used to work, production is behind the teller booths, the sales force and reporters sit at large metal desks in the middle of room and accounting is housed in the old vault.

"It always smells like popcorn in here," I tell Patricia, the receptionist, at the door.

"Yeah, you'd think it used to be a movie theatre." Patricia reminds me of the Loni Anderson character on *WKRP.* She's black, with blond hair, and nothing escapes her. "Is Teri expecting you?"

"My column's due. I need to borrow someone's computer, mine's on the blink." I've never admitted to anyone at the *Permanent Press* that I don't own a computer—way too unprofessional, plus I plan on buying one. I've got my eye on a seventeen-inch PowerBook. I'm only $2,700 short, but that's just nine columns. Thirty-six columns? Somewhere in there.

"Rick's on vacation," Patricia say. "Use his. Just stay out of Teri's sight. She's on the warpath. O'Malley got hired away by the *L.A. Times*."

O'Malley was the *Permanent Press's* star reporter, with weekly political rants that made the paper a must-have for most Santa Barbarans. Well, those and the movie listings. His articles were always one step above the rest, and I'm not surprised the *L.A. Times* picked him up—actually, since I started my column I've sorta wanted to *be* him, disdainful of politicos, with the inside dope about local goings-on and oodles of biting wit. I'd tried that approach, but you can't really get all investigative journalist when you're promoting runes and high colonics.

But with O'Malley gone, maybe I have a chance. They'll need a fresh, hard-hitting, Young Turk to take over—unless Young Turks are actually from Turkey. Must look into that. Anyway, it's only my subject matter that's keeping me from being a great reporter, and if I get O'Malley's column, I'll have a legitimate excuse not to apply to graduate school.

I head for Rick's desk and pass a group of guys huddled around a computer. Probably working on a breaking story. I smile as the oldest man in the group catches my eye, and the guy at the computer, a blonde sales-type, clicks the mouse and says, "Wait'll you see this. Blow your mind."

I place my notebook investigatorially on Rick's desk. I'm working on a big story, too. I just need a good headline: Your Health Is Number One?

The salesman says, "Kissed by that Santa Barbara sun, and no tan lines."

I turn on Rick's computer and the older guy clears his throat.

"Now *that* is local news," another of the men says, gawking at the screen. "They're all from around here?"

"Ixnay on the ornpay," the older guy says, and the other men finally notice me.

Before I'm done working out "ornpay," they've scattered. Ick. Men and their porn. I should buzz Teri's office and rat on them, but she'd just wonder where my column was, so I coolly ignore them and consider: Urine Good Hands? Your Golden Years?

The problem is, I don't care about alternative healing and spirituality. I don't want to write about crystals and magnets and affirmations. I want something bigger and tougher—O'Malley's departure is exactly the opportunity I need.

Sadly, I know nothing about local politics. So how about the national arena? I wonder if there will ever be a woman president. I know some people think Hillary Clinton has the best chance, but I say they're wrong. Our first female president will be a Republican, like Thatcher in England. Although she wasn't a Republican, of course, but a Whig. Or a Tory. Are there still Whigs? Doesn't matter. No one's going to ask what I know about international politics. Stick with U.S. politics, that's my strong point.

I launch the word processor, ready to embark on a new career. First sentence: **Have you ever wondered who are first woman president will be?**

Sometime later, Patricia swings by. "You still here?"

"What?" I tear my attention away from my article. "What time is it?"

Patricia glances at the enormous news clock posted over the front door, visible from every desk in the office. "Quarter 'til two."

Shit. I've been sitting here for two hours, and my article,

so far, reads: **Have you ever wondered who are first woman president will be?**

Patricia glances over my shoulder. "Oprah Winfrey," she says. "And it's o-u-r, not a-r-e."

"Oprah?"

"Tell me you wouldn't vote for her."

"Well, sure I'd vote for her."

"There you go."

I place the cursor behind the question mark and start to delete.

"Haven't gotten very far, have you?"

"Computer bombed, I lost everything. Had to start again. This was just—" I finish deleting the sentence "—a bad idea."

"Rick's been saying that thing's a dinosaur, he's been having trouble, too."

See? I *am* psychic. I tell her that's okay and point to my noggin. "It's all in here."

Patricia shakes her head sympathetically and I finally start to type **Have you ever wondered what it's like to drink your own urine?** I finish an hour after the deadline, sneak the printout into Teri's in-box, and slink away.

chapter

3

Maya owns a bar with her father, a few steps off State Street. Well, a few steps and a thousand miles: Shika is like a dead zone, you step off the animated street into a still life. I show up about five o'clock on a Thursday, having spent the previous few days sequestered with wedding magazines.

I find my landlord, Monty—whom I met in the bar, that's how he became my landlord—perched on his usual stool. Other than him and the bartender, Maya's lone employee, an eyebrow-pierced, twenty-two-year-old named Kid, the place is empty. I slide into the stool next to Monty's and examine him carefully. As far as I'm concerned, Monty is the best-dressed man in Santa Barbara. I even tried to get the *Permanent Press* to add the category to their annual Reader's

Favorites poll, just so I could vote for him. Today, however, he's wearing ill-fitting black chinos and a black-and-white-striped Polo.

"Monty," I say, kissing his cheek. "What's wrong?"

"I'm in mourning."

"Oh, I'm so sorry! What happened?" And why doesn't the deceased rate a suit?

"Interest rates have gone up a whole point in the last month. My margins are keeling over." He takes a consoling swig of his gin and tonic. "It's not funny, Elle. I'm dying out there."

Monty owns half of Santa Barbara, so I'm hardly worried for him, but I sober fast. "You're not going to raise my rent, are you?"

I flash him my neediest smile and he glances away—possibly embarrassed for me—and says no. "But I finally rented some other spaces in your building. A new business across from Merrick's, and a guy on the second floor for mixed residential/commercial."

I hide my disappointment. It's been fun, me and Merrick having the place all to ourselves, though I know that Neil—carpenter, Merrick's best friend, conspiracy theorist—just finished renovating, so I can't say it's a big surprise. Well, at least my rent will remain at charity-case levels. "Who are these people? What kind of business? What kind of guy?"

"What're you, worried about their credit reports?" Monty asks, because he ran one on me and still laughs sometimes when he remembers.

Before I can think of a cutting retort however, Maya strolls out of the back room. "Hey, Elle—not drinking?"

"I thought we were talking wedding plans over dinner, so I'll need a clear head." Plus, Kid hadn't offered me anything.

"That means *I'll* need a drink," she says, but she gets her purse.

I offer Monty my condolences and follow Maya out into the fading sunlight. Against the pale blue sky, the tops of the buildings along the street shine in the fleeting light, their lower halves cast in shadows.

"Gorgeous day," Maya says. "Finally."

It'd only been a week since we'd had a beautiful sunny day, but Santa Barbarans start getting antsy if the sun goes two days without shining.

"Merrick's working late," I say. "Let's go to his house, watch the sunset and order pizza."

"Sounds perfect."

"Order from the bar, so it'll be at Merrick's by the time we are."

"You're so organized," she says. Possibly mockingly.

"Wait'll you see my wedding plans. I mean *your* wedding plans."

"Yeah, I, um—I can't wait, that'll be great. What kind of pizza?"

I ignore her obvious lack of faith. "You decide. Oh, and bring a bottle of wine. I'll get dessert and meet you there."

"You think the streets are paved with liquor around here?"

"Paved with liquor? That's a terrible metaphor. I don't know even what it means."

"It means—"

"If the streets were paved with liquor, the cars would run on wine. Anyway, pick a nice bottle, not that swill you serve as the house."

"It's not swill," she says, opening the front door of Shika.

Ha! That'll teach her to be mean about my wedding plans. She's going to be so thrilled when she sees them. I head up to Merrick's house, stopping for Snickers bars, which I put in the freezer before setting my wedding book on the coffee table. The pizza guy comes right before Maya, and I pay him and lift the lid. "Mushroom, huh?"

"Well, I'm not going to order pepperoni," she says.

"Oh, please. Like you have to worry about your weight!" Maya is petite and adorable—a pocket Venus.

"It's not the calories, it's the gosh root."

"The what? I think I did a story on a guy who smokes that."

"The kashruth. The kosherness."

"Since when do you keep kosher?" I ask, leading her into the kitchen where I pull plates, wine glasses and napkins from the cabinets.

"I have my standards."

I furrow my brow at the bottle of cabernet she brought. "So do I."

"Oh, please," she says, opening drawers in search of a corkscrew. "Like I haven't seen you suck down boxed Gallo, peppermint schnapps and rum and Coke all in one night."

I groan. "I still have nightmares about peppermint Coke."

We eat on the back patio, catching the final glow of the sun sinking into the ocean beyond the Channel Islands. A phalanx of pelicans glides over the waves, and dogs run on the beach, occasionally barking and provoking a companionable *huff* from Miu, who's lying at my feet. The pizza is good but the cabernet is better.

"So Merrick's house," Maya says, nibbling her slice. "Do you have a key?"

I take a refined gulp of wine. "He wants me to move in."

She chokes on the cheese. *"Here?"*

"No, in his office, he's turned the back room into a boudoir for me."

She frowns. "I don't see how that's much better than your apartment."

"Of course here, you numbskull!" I'd once told her how I'd been like a mistress to my ex-fiancé Louis and she'd taken it to heart. "And what do you mean not *much* better?"

"He really loves you, doesn't he?"

I feel I'm tempting the evil gods of breakup, but I nod timidly. "I think he really does."

"So when do you move in?" She glances through the French doors at the living room. "He's not gonna want your Ikea stuff ruining the ambience."

"Well…I'm not sure I'm gonna do it."

"Move in?"

I nod again, even more timidly.

"Sweetie," she says. "Why not? I thought things were going great. Merrick obviously thinks so."

"They are. That's the problem. They're great exactly the way they are."

"He loves you, Elle—he won't let you screw this up."

"Maybe I'm afraid *he's* gonna screw up?"

"Uh-huh," she says, eyebrow arched. "How long have I known you?"

"Yeah, okay, well…what if I get all Louis the First on him, and ignore my life because I've leeched onto his?"

"If you go back to school, that won't happen."

"Do you two secretly meet when I'm not around to plan my life?"

"We don't have to, it's just common sense. You'd make a terrific therapist. Merrick's right, you've got to stop with the whole—" she gestures with her slice of pizza, either sketching a crystal ball or just indicating general worthlessness "—intuitive thing."

"Intuitive *counselor*," I say. "Which is just another way of saying, 'concerned friend.' I don't see why I need training for that."

"Because you charge?"

Oh.

"So are you gonna apply to schools?" she asks.

"I promised him I would."

"So," she says, "are you gonna apply to schools?"

I stick my tongue out at her as she takes a fourth slice of pizza. Where does she pack all the food in her teensy little body? We finish the pizza and I make tea to go with the now-frozen Snickers bars. The sky has turned black and we move to the comfort of the living room where I present Maya with my wedding book—a lavender three-ring notebook filled the full two inches with plans for the perfect wedding. The scene is positively biblical, like the Hand of God presenting Moses with the Ten Commandments, and I can almost hear the heavenly choir hitting a high note, but it's only the teakettle.

"Now obviously these are just ideas," I say, pouring the tea. "Nothing is set in stone."

Maya flips through the pages. The book is a scrapbook, with menu, ceremony and cake ideas all carefully pasted to creamy linen paper along with dried flowers and reviews of caterers and award-winning jewelry designers.

"Lobster?" Maya asks, pausing at Light Brunch.

"Hard to get in April, but I called a lobsterman in Maine who promised he can airlift me at least fifty."

"You called a lobsterman?"

"Really nice guy. I found him on the Internet. Did you know they have their own calendar?"

"What?"

"Lobstermen. Like a beefcake calendar."

"Okay," she says. "Lobster's not even kosher, Elle."

"Oh, right. Maybe I can find a salmonman."

Maya bites her lower lip and keeps flipping. There are sketches of wedding dresses, tablecloth and centerpiece designs with details of textures and colors. "See how I've even included cloth swatches to go with the dresses?"

"I noticed," she says, running her nail over the watered taffeta.

"It's not scratch and sniff, Maya."

She flips to the next section. "You think I should wear a veil?"

"It's a classic look. Plus, you want to look all flowy-princessy, and a veil disguises lack of hair." I eye her short tussle of curls and finger one of my foot-long ringlets. Maya's far cuter than I, but even she admits I have better hair.

She rolls her eyes, and flips past all the good stuff in the middle of the book—party favors, registration possibilities, bachelorette parties from steamy to staid—to the final pages. She stops at the second to last page. "Um, what's that?"

"The cake."

"The Statue of Liberty?"

"For a patriotic-themed wedding—I mean, in case there's another attack."

"Isn't that a little tasteless?"

"Not if it's got buttercream. Plus, the torch lights up."

Maya slams the book shut. "This is *your* book," she says. "This is your wedding, your Amazing Disappearing Wedding with Louis. What about me makes you think I want mono-grammed sterling napkin rings, Veuve Clicquot and a gospel choir?"

"They're good ideas," I insist.

"They're recycled."

"*Recycling* is a good idea. And there's no one else I'd share them with. I'm giving you all my best ideas—if I ever do get married I'll have to come up with a whole new plan of attack."

"This is not me. Or Brad. Did you think about us at all? We don't want an orchestra. We want a guy with a guitar."

I shudder. "I *am* thinking about you, Maya. I've been to 'guy with a guitar' weddings. Trust me, you don't want a guy with a guitar."

"But we do."

"Playing Sting? Not good, Maya."

"Then maybe you shouldn't come, because that's how it's going to be."

Things get worse from there. We spend twenty minutes arguing about music, meals, and how Dominic Pergosi liked her better than me in the eleventh grade—which he didn't, until she got all flirty with him, which was totally unfair because she's cuter than I am, and I needed a date to homecoming—until I finally scream, "Fine! Get married in *Goleta!*" and slam out the front door.

Hmm. I stand there a moment, panting. A dramatic exit, but not what you'd call strategically sound.

Maya opens the door. "I'm supposed to be the one storming out."

"You were never good at storming," I say. "You're too small. You squall."

"I'll call you," Maya says. "You crazy loon."

Merrick comes home an hour later, rumpled and sexy. He flashes a secret smile and says, "I have a surprise for you."

"Really?" I nudge Miu off the couch with my foot and she stretches and trots over to greet Merrick. I untangle myself from the couch and follow. "Ice cream?" Because the candy bar barely made a dent in my dessert compartment.

He scratches Miu with one hand, the other clutches something behind his back. "Better."

The mind boggles. Better than ice cream? Two kinds of ice cream? I reach behind him, but he twists out of range and kisses me. "Shoes?"

He laughs. "Guess again."

I trail kisses down his neck to his chest and unbutton his shirt. Slip the tip of my finger in his waistband. "Honey?"

He twines his free hand through my hair, slower to answer this time. "Um…not honey."

"Licorice?" I ask, unbuttoning his pants.

"Getting closer," he says, though I don't think he's talking about the surprise anymore.

That's when I grab what he's got hidden behind his back and squirt away. It's a manila envelope addressed to Merrick. "Mail?" I ask disappointed. "Mail is my surprise?"

He smiles confidently. "Check inside."

Maybe tickets to Paris! I've never been to Paris. Paris in January would be very romantic. I rip the envelope and find a navy-blue folder that says Laverna University, Admissions. No matter how I squint, this does not look like the name of a travel agency.

"Oh." This is not a surprise. This is a tragedy, disguised as a letdown, masquerading as a surprise.

"They have a master's program in psychology," Merrick says, clearly thrilled with himself. "Only eighteen months if you go full time and it's located downtown. You can walk to school from your apartment." Then, with a little grin, I add, "While you still live there."

"Oh, wow, yeah. Thanks. Eighteen months." I toss the folder onto the kitchen cabinet. "So no ice cream?"

Merrick pulls a pink sheet from the folder. "They're having an information meeting tomorrow night, I think you should go."

"Maybe. If I have time. I'll think about it."

"Elle, you gave me your word," he says.

"I'm sorry. It's just, I'm your girlfriend, not your twelve-year-old."

"Sometimes you act twelve."

"It's not an act."

Merrick sighs. "You aren't taking this seriously."

"I said I'd think about it. I just don't want to *talk* about it."

"You never take anything seriously."

Not true! I've spent six years searching for the perfect pair of cognac-brown mid-calf boots that cost less than $300. Sadly, the only things I'm serious about don't matter. I'm better at shopping than I am at a career and relationships. I'm pretty much better at anything than I am at those. Except maybe pool. I'm really bad at pool.

I grab the cabernet and glug from the bottle. "Okay, I'll go."

"You'll give it a try?"

"The old college try," I say.

"That's all I ask."

He holds out his arms and I step into them. Everything feels so right when we're like this. If I could only stop that niggling little thought: Merrick wants me to change. Why can't he be happy with me the way I am?

I spend the next day depressed that Maya hates my wedding plans and Merrick wants to improve me. And they're not the only ones disappointed in me. Late afternoon,

I stop by the offices of the *Permanent Press* to pitch my idea for a political column to my editor, Teri.

"Like O'Malley's," I say, "but from a woman's perspective."

"Well, you're a woman."

What is that supposed to mean? "Um, yeah. And more national than local. Sort of the grand sweep of events."

"What do you know about the grand sweep of events?"

I can't focus as I'm standing in her office with my back to the window, worrying that someone is looking at my butt, which I believe appears inordinately large through plate glass. So all I manage to say is, "Um, like the first woman president, what if she's also black?"

"Here's the name of a pet psychic." Teri hands me a card. "I don't wanna see another bathroom story. Have her read your dog and give me 800 words by Tuesday."

A free reading. "That's not a bad idea." Maybe she'll tell me about Miu's past.

"I know, I thought of it. From now on, run your ideas past me before writing them up."

"For approval?"

"Or otherwise."

So I go home. At least Teri didn't fire me, but now I need to officially seek her approval? It's not like I didn't already want her approval, unofficially—unofficially, I want everyone's approval.

The building I live in is a Victorian, with all the traditional curlicues and turrets of that era. For some reason it always makes me think of *Tales of the City*—how I pictured the house on Barbary Lane, which reminds me to worry about the new tenants. Maybe we'll all become friends. And since Monty doesn't live here, I can be the surrogate landlady, like Anna Madrigal.

The thought cheers me as I step into the foyer and find Merrick and Neil sitting on the stairs, drinking beer. The conversation stops as I come in, which happens so often I've almost overcome my paranoid reaction.

"Why are you guys still hanging out in the hall?" I ask. They did this when Neil was working on the place and Merrick would keep him company, but now Neil's done and Merrick has a perfectly pleasant office to sit in.

They look at me like they can't even understand the question. "Grab a beer," Merrick says.

"All I'm saying," Neil says, "is that Dr. Noe got fifty million to invest, and twelve million disappeared—"

"The Ohio Coingate Scandal," Merrick tells me.

"Plus this guy, Noe, he's a Bush Pioneer being investigated by the FBI for violating campaign finance laws in *Ohio*—" a dramatic pause. "—2003!"

I sit next to Merrick and take a sip of his beer. "So we should have a housewarming party for the new tenants."

"A housewarming party?"

"Which decided the whole 2004 election," Neil says. "The twelve million probably paid for voter suppression."

"It'll be fun," I tell Merrick, returning his beer. "We'll need pot though."

"A housewarming potluck," Merrick says. "Does this mean—"

"Not *potluck*. Pot. Dope. Ganja. We'll have joints as party favors."

"You know why they criminalized pot?" Neil says. "To protect the petrochemical industry. Look it up, in '37, *Popular Science* predicted hemp would be a billion-dollar industry."

Merrick holds his beer out of my reach. "Does this have anything to do with your *Tales of the City* fantasy?"

"Don't be ridiculous!" Forgotten I'd mentioned that.

Merrick slides Neil a glance. "Elle thinks she's Anna Madrigal."

"You wanna be a transsexual?" Neil asks.

"What I want is pot. C'mon, Merrick, where do we buy pot in this town?"

He slides another glance at Neil—this one more pointed.

"Neil," I say. "You're not holding out on me, are you?"

"The problem with marijuana," Neil says, "is it's illegal. Overcrowded jails, broken families, denying the ill well-needed medication. Have you seen the numbers on glaucoma treatment?"

"Here we go," Merrick says.

And Neil tells a long story about the anti-marijuana conspiracy, finishing with what I think is an anecdote about a pot dealer who was busted for drunk driving, but I'm not really sure.

"Is he still dealing?" I ask.

Neil looks around shiftily.

"There's nobody else here, Neil," Merrick says.

"So you'll get me some?" I ask.

"No can do," he says, nodding.

"So really…yes?"

"I'm not saying." He nods more, then asks if we want to catch dinner and a movie tonight. "Kara's at her knitting class."

Kara is Neil's wife—I've never met her, and kinda suspect Neil is keeping us apart, so I find her fascinating. "She knits?"

"She goes to class. Usually comes home crying, because someone made fun of her yarn, or her purls or whatever. Those knitters are brutal."

Merrick gives me the end of his beer and stands. "I gotta get back to work before you start talking about how the knitters are in league with the Trilateral Commission." Merrick's business has taken off in the last couple of months, and for the past few weeks he's been working late.

Unfortunately, despite my intuitive design sense, there's nothing I can do to help, so I ask Neil, "What movie?"

"That one with Matt Damon?"

"A romantic comedy? Neil, there's no way you're going to like a romantic comedy."

"I liked *Four Weddings and a Funeral*. I liked *Bourne Identity*. Why wouldn't I like this?"

"Because you hate everything."

"I just said I liked—"

"*Four Weddings* and *Bourne Identity*," I repeat, shaking my head. "All right, I'm willing."

Merrick clears his throat.

"You want us to wait for you?" I ask hopefully. "How much work do you have?"

"Don't you have a previous engagement?"

"Why, Mr. Merrick," I say, attempting a charming Southern accent, "ah do believe you're propositioning me."

"Laverna University."

I drop the Southern charm. "Oh. That. Yeah. I—tonight?"

Merrick nods and I turn to Neil, like a preteen whose mother said she has to practice piano instead of going to the new *Princess Diaries* movie. "I can't go."

"Back to school, Elle?"

"I guess, maybe. It's only an information meeting. We'll see, I don't know."

"If I went back, I'd study entomology," Neil says.

"Bees?" Merrick asks, because Neil's got a dozen beehives scattered around town—including a few at Merrick's house—and collects his own honey.

"Beetles," Neil says, heading for the door.

"Don't forget my joints," I call as he steps outside.

Neil winces and looks furtive, but nods before closing the door.

"He's so weird," I tell Merrick. "How'd he get to be your best friend?"

"He asks the same about you."

"I guess it's a conspiracy," I say.

chapter

4

I hate Laverna University. The chairs in the classroom where they're holding the meeting are arranged in a horseshoe, so there's no hiding in the back row, which is a lifelong habit. I console myself with third from the end—I'd considered second, but decided third was ultimately more anonymous.

I'm five minutes early, because Merrick offered a ride (read: demanded I get in the car). He offered to pick me up, too, but I told him I'd walk home after stopping at the library to do more research. "Liar," he'd said, before kissing me and driving away. Which made me quite happy. He may not be perfectly satisfied with me, but at least he knows me.

Lately, during quiet moments, I mentally compose my First Female President article. Unfortunately, I haven't progressed much beyond my teaser, Have you ever wondered who the first female U.S. president will be? After that, I've got I think she'll be a Republican. And that's it. O'Malley made this stuff look easy. Maybe I need to bold some words, he used bold alot. **Have you ever wondered who the first female U.S. president will be?** No, that looks stupid. Perhaps I can drag Oprah into this thing, somehow. Maybe I could meet her....

I'm daydreaming about being best friends with Oprah and boycotting Hermès (which I never could afford anyway) when a nice young woman passes out folders and calls us to attention.

"Welcome to Laverna," she says. "I'm the financial aid advisor. I'm going to give you a brief overview of the types of aid available to you and how to apply, because money is always everyone's first question!" The class—there are ten or twelve of us—obligingly laughs. "Then I'll leave you to Bob Klein, chairman of the psychology department, who'll go into further depth about the program."

She starts talking numbers, and my brain goes numb until one number penetrates.

$18,500.

Per year.

That's what is available in financial aid if I attend Laverna University. Let me break this down. It costs $2,750 per quarter, part time, so multiply that by four, which is, well, somewhere in the $11,000 range. I'll round down to $10,500 per year. That means I've got at least $8,000 left in living expenses. That's in the neighborhood of several hundred bucks a month, just for going to classes part time. Plus, I'll be educated.

The rest of the evening is a blur. I remember some stuffy guy standing before the chalkboard, explaining the core curriculum and the educational philosophy, but I'm trying to divide $8,000 into twelve months. If there were only ten months, applied mathematics would be much easier. At ten months, that's $800 a month, plus two months of nothing.

Granted, the financial aid is mostly loans. Well, *all* loans. But still, that's a lot of gravy—and there's only one thing to do with gravy.

There's a sort of haze of motion, then I'm floating through Paseo Nuevo, the outdoor mall downtown, standing at my favorite boutique. Basically $800 a month for going to school part time, this is the greatest scam ever. I wonder how long I can stay in school before I have to start actually working as a psychiatrist. Or psychologist, whichever.

Just think, only a few short months ago, I was this close to applying for a job as a stripper—well, until the bouncer told me I was too old and saggy—but now I'm basically a therapist. Perhaps I'll develop gravitas in addition to wisdom and insight. Gravitas would be neat, though I'm slightly underwhelmed at the idea of a real job. Guess all that's required is a little practice…so I decide to practice the only real therapy I know: retail.

Inside the boutique, called Element, I run my fingers along the racks, luxuriating in the cashmere and silk. I've never actually bought anything here, it's only my favorite store because they carry Paper Denim & Cloth, Theory and Trina Turk, all labels I can no longer afford now that I'm supporting myself. My gaze falls on a gorgeous black wool pantsuit, the jacket is nipped in and flirty, the pants drapey and low-waisted. The saleswoman, a *Sex and the City* Patricia Field type, convinces me to try the suit with an aubergine Victorian teddy. She has a throaty voice and says, "Confident on the outside, sexy underneath," with this sort of knowing air.

Even the dressing rooms are delicious here, with parchment-colored walls, honey-wood floors, and gilt-framed mirrors. And the suit is phenomenal, I'm the new and improved Professional Therapist Elle. I look at myself in the mirror, a stern Freudian on the outside—nobody can tell me Freud wouldn't have approved of a low-waisted black pantsuit—and feminine and nurturing within. I give a little swivel: I do feel kinda sexy. Maybe I should've been a stripper, this would make a great outfit. Bumping and grinding with Dr. Elle. Though, I suspect I would never master the pole.

Actually, with sinking stomach I realize the suit looks a little *too* good. My hips aren't enormous, and as much as I bend and twirl, my chubby sections remain sleek instead of bulging. I check the price of the suit. Whoa. Or, as O'Malley would write, **Whoa.** That's a few months of financial aid gravy, so the suit might be flattering just from expensive tailoring—otherwise known as *honest* flattery, but what if it's the dressing room? The subdued lighting, parchment walls and a skinny mirror?

Only one way to find out. I remove the suit and pose in the teddy. Very sexy, actually, an outfit from some 18th century Viennese bordello. I pout and flirt at my reflection for a moment, *Why, Count Arabiatta, you naughty man! Emeralds? Oh, what will the Contessa say?*

Then I catch sight of myself. It's *not* a skinny mirror. It's definitely the suit.

Return home an hour later, fumbling with bags as I open the front door. Merrick hears me and steps from his office, his hair mussed, his eyes tired.

"Big sale at the library?" he asks, eyeing my bags.

"I didn't buy the most beautiful suit," I tell him. After approximately nine hours in the dressing room, I just couldn't bring myself to spend two months' financial aid on a suit. This is major progress…even though I wasn't so successful at not buying layering tees at Abercrombie & Fitch, jeans at Lucky Brand Dungarees and Cole Haan platform sandals at Nordstrom.

He tells me he's proud of me, ignoring the bags cluttering up the hallway. "So?"

"So I actually went to the information meeting."

"I know, I dropped you off."

"I mean I went inside. I was gonna scurry away after you drove off, but I didn't. That's good, right? And the program looks like—" $18,500 a year! But I can't tell him that. I try to summon repressed memories of the meeting, because I know loans are the last thing Merrick wants to hear about. All I can recall is the dusty man babbling about foundations in therapy and process classes. "They have great foundations. And the process classes!"

"What does that mean?"

"Oh, professional jargon, you know." I recall one useful tidbit. "It's considered the ideal program by some state board examining agency, if you want to become a Marriage Family Child Counselor." Which I don't. "So it's perfect."

"You're actually going to apply?"

"Absolutely. And I deserve a reward."

He cocks his head. "How much does that suit cost?"

"Two months' financial, er, income." I press closer to him. "That's not the reward I was thinking of, though. Spend the night here."

"I can't," he says. "I've gotta get home and pack."

"Pack? For what?"

"New York. The co-op didn't approve the plans." For an apartment he designed for bicoastal clients from Montecito. "I've gotta go sort it out."

"How long will you be gone?"

He winces. "Two weeks."

"Two weeks!" My fiancé left for two weeks, and married another woman. "Why so long?"

"Since I'm going anyway, I've got other people to meet. I want to jumpstart the Lower project."

I have no idea what the Lower project is. The only thing I want him to Lower is his ambition. It's seriously cutting into my Merrick time. "This sucks."

"I'm sorry, Elle—they just called. I have to do this. They know everyone, and if I get a reputation now…"

I want to sulk, but if he's leaving tonight, there's no time. So I kiss him instead. "How about I spend the night at your place and help you pack?"

"I've gotta get up at three, I couldn't get a flight out of Santa Barbara. I'm taking the airbus to L.A."

"I could drive you."

He laughs. "Elle, you know how you are in the middle of the night woken for anything but food or sex."

When I was kid, my dad took me to the Wild Animal Park in San Diego. The highlight of the trip was the ape display, where a huge audience marveled over the massive patriarch as he beat at his chest and made threatening calls. Then he threw ape crap at the crowd. That's what I'm like when woken up in the middle of the night.

"So you're just…going?"

Merrick kisses me again. "I'll call you from New York."

In other words, he's going to go to New York and I'll never hear from him again.

★ ★ ★

I wake late the next morning, deeply morose. The old Louis found a better woman than me in *Iowa*. God knows how many gorgeous, intelligent, professional, ambitious, stylish, cool, funny, intriguing, vivacious and charming women Merrick will meet in *New York*. In an effort to battle depression, I roust myself and tell Miu to prepare for a long walk. As I'm searching for her leash—ten minutes of apartment combing, before checking the dishwasher, having forgotten it was filthy from beach walk—I come across a little list from last fall—

Apartment.
Car.
Job.
Man.

The paper is worn and wrinkled, but I can still see that I was certain about the material things: apartment and car (each have multiple cross-outs) and less so about job and man. In fact, I'm not even sure when I crossed out *Man* I meant Merrick. I had a brief fling with a grifter named Joshua. I think the last thing he said to me was, "I'll call you."

On the way downstairs, with Miu tugging the leash, I decide it's time for a new list. My walk will be zen-like contemplation of internal goals and aspirations. Miu will romp through the waves at the beach, while I meditate in the sand. Am wondering if I should run upstairs and change from my jeans into yoga pants, when I notice the door across from Merrick's is open and two male voices are streaming out.

"Where have you *really* been spending your Tuesday and Thursday nights?" one voice asks.

Lee Nichols

"At the gym, like I told you," the other one says.

"Six months, Johnny. Why aren't you any stronger?"

"I don't lift weights, I do step aerobics. I don't hear you complaining about my ass."

"I'm complaining about your little chicken arms."

Suspicious, Miu freezes, hackles raised, then pokes her head into the room, jowls quivering with outrage. Equally surprised, but less jowly, I follow with my own head. Two men heft an enormous table from one end of the room to the other. The smaller one struggles, and even from here I can see his butt, encased in dark-wash denim, is quite nice. My new housemates have started to arrive. I'm about to introduce myself, but the bigger one continues, "But I've got nothing but praise for your ass."

Omigod! I totally see what's going on here, and I grab Miu by the collar and tiptoe out the front door. My mind races as we take a meandering dog-friendly route to State Street, so Miu can do a little romping and take care of her dirty sinful business. The implications of my new housemates is—of course—enormous. A gay couple. A couple of gays. The gay couple downstairs. Johnny and his husband.

I pick up cappuccinos and croissants for three and skip back to the building eager to meet the new tenants. This is exactly what I need: new gay best friends. Not that I have old gay best friends, but that's my problem—doesn't every carefree girl, living in small-but-cosmopolitan town need a gay best friend? Look at *Will & Grace*. Mary Ann and Mouse from—dare I say it?—*Tales of the City*. Or any book written about a young, single woman in the last five years. A gay man is the perfect accessory for someone in my position. And now I have two.

I return to the building with my welcoming committee

smile and breakfast offerings, ready to forge what will un-
doubtedly be the most *fabulous* relationship in my life. I poke
my head into the doorway again, and see that things haven't
changed much in the half hour I've been gone. Boxes scattered everywhere, and the two men still moving the table.
It's a really big table. This time, however, I get a better look
at them, and the bigger one is olive-skinned and almost bald,
with what little hair he has left shaved close to his scalp. He's
on the pudgier side, and wearing a loose purple T-shirt and
khakis. His face is friendly and open, the laugh lines around
his mouth and eyes make him look about forty. The smaller
one is younger, early twenties maybe, and looks half-Asian.
He is skinny and taut in a tight navy T-shirt, with the number
2 decaled on the chest. Nice butt.

"Knock, knock," I say.

The two men don't hear me, too busy arguing over the
placement of the table.

"C'mon Weldon. We put it there and people will trip over
us." The smaller one—must be Johnny—drops his end of the
table and squeezes circulation back into his fingers.

"But the light's best here," Weldon says. "My grandmother
went blind sewing in bad light."

"Your grandmother thought a twenty-five watt bulb was
extravagant. I'm surprised she didn't work by candlelight."

"Candles were too expensive."

"She was right about that. The ones I got at Target were
five bucks, and I'm not even sure they're real wax."

"Those red ones?" Weldon wrinkles his nose. "They smell
like shit."

"No they don't. They smell like…something red. Straw-
berries or something."

"Red shit."

"Well, if you don't like—"

"Excuse me!" I say from the doorway. "Hi there!"

"We're closed," Weldon says, with an apologetic smile, and swings the door shut in my face.

I stare at the door and listen to them mumbling inside, then more scraping and moving of the table. Well, Neil finally got the door fixed. He'll be happy to hear how smoothly it closed. But what am I going to do with all this pastry and coffee? How come these things always happen to me?

I square my shoulders and knock again, and when Weldon opens the door I say, "Don't-close-the-door-I'm-not-a-customer-I-don't-even-know-what-you-do!"

He cocks his bald head, and calls back inside. "For you, Johnny—someone speaking in tongues."

I snort-laugh and continue, the slightest bit slower. "Oh, ha ha! No, I'm your new neighbor. Or you're *my* new neighbor. I live in the apartment upstairs. I brought you coffee and pastry." I show them the egg crate coffee holder and bag of croissants to prove I'm not delusional. "Like a welcome wagon. That's me. The Welcome Wagon. Without the wagon."

Johnny stands behind Weldon and examines me, and I suddenly worry my nose is running. Sometimes when I take a walk in the morning, the cool air gets me dripping. I delicately sniff and hope for the best. He says, "What on earth is *that?*"

Miu stands at my side, staring dolefully up at them. When I mentioned she's growing her fur back, well…she's still midway through the process. She looks like an experimental animal at a hair transplant factory.

"That's Miu Miu," I say, hopefully. Surely two gay men will gush over her designer name. "She's a boxer."

They look at me like I'm to blame. "She looks like a throw rug, poor thing."

"You mean a thrown-out rug," Weldon says.

"I didn't do it," I say. "I saved her. Well, not me, this crazy dog lady at the shelter. But I adopted her. Well, they wouldn't let me have any other dog. Not that I didn't want her, I love her, but—" I am babbling, because this is not going how I expected. In my fantasy I show up with coffee or joints, they greet me like a long-lost brother (don't ask me why not a sister, but in my mind's eye I am a brother), and we live a scene from *Friends*: Skinny beautiful people laughing over cappuccinos in a really big N.Y. loft apartment with a wall of windows "—but, um, I'm so happy the crazy dog lady saved her, because she's wonderful, but she's growing her fur back, but the crazy dog lady said—"

"I think she means your mother, Johnny."

"My mother just likes dogs, okay?"

Oh, God, no. "Not crazy!" I say. "I mean *crazy*, not crazy! Like—like wow, we had a *crazy* time! I mean—"

Weldon guffaws. "We're kidding."

"She's not my mother," Johnny says. "She's my sister."

We all laugh, and this is what I'm talking about—a little brotherly teasing. I step inside the room and immediately bump into the huge table, which is resting two feet from the door. The tray of nonfat caps springs from my hand, and lands on the table, and a cup topples from the egg crate, top popping off and coffee spilling in great waves onto the table.

"Oh, shit—sorry! Sorry." There's nothing else to stop the deluge, so I use my sweatshirt to mop the coffee before it starts waterfalling to the floor. I've got nothing but a bra underneath, so I'm forced to bend awkwardly and use the loose fabric around my stomach to soak it up. You'd be amazed at how much liquid spills from a medium-sized cappuccino. My sweatshirt is saturated, and I still haven't gotten all the coffee. I look helplessly at the men. "A rag, paper towels, *anything?*"

"Everything packed away—"

I look toward this huge bolt of fabric resting against one wall. "How about that?"

They howl in protest, "No! Stay away! It's gonna spill!"

So I do the only thing I can think of. I hop onto the edge of the table and soak the rest of the cap into the seat of my new jeans from Lucky. Their expressions change from disgust to revulsion, which is—to my surprise—a very different expression.

"And who did you say you were, again?" Weldon asks, when I finish wiggling on the table to soak up all the liquid.

"I'm Elle. Hi. From upstairs. You must be Weldon. And you're Johnny. It's, um, really good to meet you. Are you new to town? There's another new tenant moving in upstairs— Monty mentioned him—isn't Monty great? I love how he dresses, like a pool shark in *Guys and Dolls.* Do you like musicals? I *love* them." My relentless cheer is grating even on my own nerves. "Anyway, I thought maybe we could have a housewarming party—I promise I won't spill."

"We really have to finish moving in," Weldon says.

"Yeah," Johnny says, gesturing toward the door. "So…"

"Oh, sure," I come this close to saying, *I'll leave you two lovebirds alone,* I swear. "I've got to change anyway. I, um— well, at least there's still two cappuccinos left." I set the bag of pastry on the table. "And croissants."

"Thanks anyway," Johnny says.

"We're off caffeine and carbs," Weldon says.

"Oh, right." I grab the coffee and bag. "Me, too." I step

into the hall and turn to apologize once more, and the door again closes in my face.

"And your little dog, too!" I hear Johnny saying from inside.

Weldon says, "What're we gonna do with the table now?"

"Leave it there. Maybe it'll keep her from getting back in."

My new list—

1. Convince Merrick to like me for who I am, or alternatively.
117.2. Attend school.
3. Political column. Hillary v. Oprah?
4. Increase income. Why not sell organs?
5. Plan Maya's wedding.
6. Figure out how to convince Maya I should be in charge. Maybe cake should be of Esther, not Statue of Liberty. Not sure who Esther is, but Madonna likes her.
7. Look into Kabbalah.
8. Order red string bracelet and see how it goes.
2.9. Become best friends with gay guys downstairs. First step: act like one of the humans.
3.10. Use psychic powers to convince Merrick not to marry sleek New Yorker who wakes him each morning with blow job.
11. Miu needs new look. Pink collar?
12. Rework free *Psychic Newsletter.* Make it so people like it. Or, at least, read it.
1.13. Plan trip to Paris.
97.14. Call mom.
15. Order hip-hop dance video advertised on *Ellen* show. Looks like great way to stay in shape. Wish I were Alicia Keys.
16. Cornrow hair?

chapter

5

I spend the first week of Merrick's absence hard at work: walking Miu, taking clients' calls, trying to make Johnny and Weldon smile as I pass them in the hall, window-shopping, sticking to my decision *not* to interfere in Maya's wedding, and missing Merrick. Mostly, though, I'm firm in my resolve to act like one of the humans. Last time Merrick left town for any length of time, he returned to find me in the middle of a human hurricane involving strippers, grifters, bouncers, private investigators, ex-fiancés and a laundry ticket. This time, I've vowed he'll return to find everything exactly as he left.

Today is my interview with the pet psychic that Teri recommended. Pretty exciting actually, and with hardly any opportunity for me to create disaster. Ever since I adopted Miu from the shelter, I've had *Punisher* fantasies about her former owners—especially after I rolled up a magazine to kill a fly, and Miu went into a cowering frenzy, afraid I was going to swat her. So in addition to being exploited in a puppy mill and neglected, she was abused. I am a gentle and pacific person—who would not hesitate to hunt down and destroy Miu's former owners.

So, needless to say, I eagerly greet Crystal Smith, Pet Psychic, when she knocks at my door, and manage to swallow all *Ace Ventura* jokes. Not only because I'm eager for her to tell me if Miu likes her food, her dog bed, her thrice-daily walks—and most importantly if she loves me—but because I want an address for Miu's previous abusers. That may be too much to hope for, though, given Miu isn't very good at remembering numbers.

Crystal is a vivacious fifty-year-old with shoulder-length bleach-blond hair, pale skin highlighted by coral lipstick, and a skinny figure that looks overexercised. She's wearing a turquoise blouse, jeans and staggering amount of silver jewelry, bracelets line both her arms, and rings cover her fingers and ears.

She sits regally in an old Windsor-style chair I bought at a tag sale, and says, "I know who you are."

Given that I called her for the interview and invited her into my house, that's not so surprising. "Well! Yes. Good."

"I know all about the 'Missing Bitch.'"

"Oh, right." When I'd first started writing for the *Permanent Press,* the caption Psychic who found the missing bitch ran under my byline. "I have a few quest—"

"*All* about it," she intones.

She knows I'm a fraud. There was nothing psychic about

my discovering the whereabouts of that poor little golden retriever puppy—just luck and desperation. I wake up every morning with a knot in my stomach, worried someone is going to expose me as a fake. Then I tell myself it doesn't matter that I have no actual clairvoyant talent, what matters is that I'm helping people. And that's what makes my gut unclench each morning. But if Crystal Smith now says, "The jig is up," I'll shatter like a wine glass in a washing machine. Not that I ever accidentally put a wine glass in Merrick's washing machine.

"Well," I squeak, about to start stammering excuses, and explaining how what I do technically isn't illegal. "The thing is—"

"I was on the case long before you were."

"You were? Um, what case?"

"Sheila Ameson—" the puppy's owner "—hired me first. If you hadn't been involved, I would've found Holly-Go-Lightly—" the puppy "—much faster. Your psychic energy interfered with my search."

"Oh! Wow." She doesn't think I'm a charlatan. She's in competition with me—I find that oddly heartening.

"That was *my* case."

"Well, the important thing is, we found the puppy."

"Yeah," she says. "Sure."

Which seems rather blasé coming from an animal psychic. "I don't know if you've seen my column, but I want to ask you about—"

"How did you get that column?" Her tone makes it sound like I've slept my way to seventy-five dollars an article.

"The editor saw me on the news and called me."

"Teri?"

"You know Teri?" I ask.

"I've been telling her to run a New Age column for years."

"Well, I guess she finally heard you," I say, smiling.

"I wanted to write it. That's *my* column. She should've seen me on the news. That was my case."

"Um, maybe we should get started. I'd like to have you communicate with Miu for a start, then we'll get into other practical uses of your therapy."

"Miu? Who's Miu?"

"Um…my dog."

She glances around like she's forgotten there's an animal in the room. Her silver bracelets jangle on her wrist, and Miu cocks her head from her cashmere throw in the corner, like she thinks it's the jangle of a dog's collar.

"Oh, him. Yes, he and I have been communicating since I walked in the door."

"Her," I say, apologetically.

"He says you've been feeding him too much junk food and he feels neglected and unloved. Those grocery store brands are terrible. I sell a line of my own products." She pulls a homemade brochure from her purse. "Anything less than the best is abusive."

"Actually, I feed her that natural—"

"I sell leashes, too."

I take the brochure. "And what about Miu's past?"

Crystal shrugs. "Typical family dog. A mother, father, two kids. All loved him, made sure he had the right food—"

"Your food?" I ask.

"Possibly." She closes her eyes. "Let's see what else." Her voice deepens. "The pack…food in the mountains…a picnic. Air ripe with the sweet smell of fresh water and wildlife. I followed the scent of deer into the woods. Close. Closer…

Confusion! Where is the pack? Only the wind blowing through the trees."

C'mon, this is so cheesy. At least *I* try to actually help people. "How did she get to the shelter?"

"A road…a pack of teenagers. Please, take me back to the pack…the *only* ones that treated me right." Crystal lifts an eyelid to check if I caught that last part. "I stay with a person-puppy, but he goes away on Monday—"

"Monday?" I ask, impressed. "She knows her days of the week?"

Crystal ignores me. "Boy's mother…car—to scary shelter."

"What about the abuse?"

"Abuse?" Crystal comes out of her trance. "He wasn't abused."

"Look at her coat—she was totally bald from mange."

"No, no abuse."

I try to give her an out, as a professional courtesy. "Maybe someone else got her from the shelter before I did? Abused her then returned her? Because clearly she's been mistreated."

"Well, as I said before he *is* a bit disappointed in you."

"I haven't mistreat—"

"And his name isn't Miu," Crystal says. "It's Hank."

So she's a charlatan. And I was worried *she* was going to expose *me*. How am I going to make this article work? I'm actually ethical about my stories. When I believe a practitioner hasn't much to offer, I let the subjects speak for themselves—otherwise known as "hanging themselves"—but Crystal is an out-and-out fake. I mean, worse than *me*. She wasn't even trying. She didn't even ask about Miu to learn what I knew before embroidering her own fantasies.

I still have time to find someone else to interview, but this is Teri's idea—plus, this woman already resents me, and now she knows where I live. Still, I'd be furious if I'd actually paid money for this load of crap. *Hank* indeed.

I spend the next half hour jotting down Crystal's bullshit stories, then usher her to the door.

"Don't you want to say goodbye?" I ask.

"Goodbye," she says.

"I mean to the dog."

Crystal doesn't bother looking at Miu. "Hank and I already made our goodbyes."

I watch her descend the stairs, because I'm worried if I close my door she'll do something weird in the hallway, and hear Neil's voice from downstairs. I haven't seen him since Merrick left. Actually I haven't seen anyone since Merrick left—Maya and I are still wary since the wedding blowout—so I'm pretty sick of myself. I wait a minute until I hear the front door close behind the evil pet psychic, then trot downstairs, hoping I can interest Neil in that Matt Damon romantic comedy. Anything but my own company.

Halfway down, I find Neil, Johnny and Weldon in the hallway eating lunch—subs and extra-large sodas. On the stairs. What is it about men and sitting in hallways? You never see women hanging around in hallways.

"I admit I wondered," Johnny is saying. "She looks... hangdog."

"Very sad face," Weldon agrees.

They couldn't be talking about Miu, could they? The pet psychic was trash talking my dog in my own hallway.

"She's a boxer," Neil says, gallantly. "That's how they look. She's a totally happy dog. You can see her little stub tail stick straight up."

"I dunno," Johnny says. "Those sad brown eyes..."

"Hi!" I say. "Whose sad brown eyes?"

Neil swallows a bite of his sandwich. "Hey, Elle. Didn't see you there."

Johnny and Weldon both glance at their watches and leap to their feet. "Look at the time," Weldon says.

"All work and no play," Johnny says. "Thanks for lunch, Neil."

"Anytime," Neil says.

I glance at the remains of their meal. Meatball subs and Cokes. "I thought you were off carbohydrates and caffeine."

"Oh. Right," Weldon says. "That was—"

"So last week," Johnny finishes. They slip into their shop and shut the door.

Neil chuckles as he finishes the last bite of his sandwich.

"What?" I snap.

"You sure know how to clear a room."

"This isn't a room, it's a hallway. What are you doing here, anyway?"

"Came by to see everything was okay in the boys' shop."

"'The boys?'"

"Sure. We got to talking, I offered to run over to Tio's and get us some subs."

"And they agreed?"

"Totally nice guys. Monty knows how to pick 'em."

"*Nice?* They're like Attila the Hun and Genghis Khan rolled into one standoffish couple. What do they do anyway?"

"They're tailors," he says.

"Dressmakers?" I grab the railing to keep from swooning. "Fashion designers?"

"Nah, more like hems and fittings and stuff. Tailors."

I've basically got Johnny Dolce & Weldon Gabbana living downstairs from me, soon to be best friends. If only I can get them to talk to me. "Anyway," I say to Neil, trying to keep my bearings. "You want to see a movie tonight?"

"Oh." He fiddles with the wrappings of his sub. "I sort of have a date."

"Taking Kara out on the town, huh?" I almost ask if I can come along, to finally meet her.

"Actually, Weldon and Johnny asked if I wanted to go bowling. They're in a league."

A gay bowling league? They think Neil's *gay*. This explains why they like him and not me. I allow myself the slightest smile. "You think *everyone's* in league, Neil." I consider this the height of wit, but Neil doesn't laugh. "Well, that sounds like fun."

"Yeah, plus Kara's excited to meet them."

"*Kara's* going?"

"Sure, y'know. Couples bowling. They asked me to bring her."

I'm about to shriek when I hear my phone ring. My almost-shriek changes from one of despair to one of triumph. Merrick's been gone almost a week and we keep missing each other, so I tell Neil I'll catch him later and gallop upstairs.

It's not Merrick. It's a new client, a guy calling from L.A. who saw my ad in the classifieds. All the ads I've run have a pay-to-play dial-up number, so I don't have to worry about billing him. I just have to worry that I'm not being screwed by the dial-up company, so I keep meticulous records of all incoming phone calls on the back of the pizza menu that lives by the phone.

"What can I do for you?" I ask, scribbling the time and date.

He says his name is Fred, but I know he's lying because he hesitates before telling me. I pull my tarot cards from the tele-

...le drawer, sit on the floor and spread them in front of me. I still don't know how to use them correctly, despite all Adele's attempts to teach me, but I got used to staring at them while I was at Psychic Connexion, and they give me ideas. Them and the stack of women's magazines scattered next to the whiteish linen chair.

"Fred" is thirty-nine, lost his job during the Internet crash and has been unemployed since. His story is unique, because although his layoff coincided with the crash, he hadn't actually been employed by a tech company. He'd been an advertising exec in San Francisco. His salary had been reduced a few months after the major losses of tech revenue, but he survived. Until 9/11. The company had been subsisting on its airline accounts.

He'd moved back in with his mother in L.A. when he ran out of money, which took quite some time considering he'd saved, rather than blowing his wad on Land Rovers, an overblown Bay Area mortgage, and tacky furnishings from Z Gallerie.

I admire his foresight. I've always been the grasshopper, but it seems unfair that the ant should get screwed in the end. However: "Passing up that overblown Bay Area mortgage..."

"Don't say it," he says. Housing prices have quadrupled since then, so even overblown mortgages turned into gold mines. "And I coulda used a Land Rover, too. I have to borrow my mom's car every time I want to go out."

"You go out?" This surprises me, because a) he has no money, and b) he sounds like someone who just discovered his iguana was dead in its cage. Well, I guess b) is really that he sounds like a guy with an iguana, which would make the "dead in its cage" part, c).

"To get cigarettes and Coke, maybe a burrito," he explains.

"Ah." I ripple the tarot cards into the phone with great fluency. Mastering the sound effect took hours of practice with Merrick sighing on the other end of the receiver. "Well. Number one, the cards say you should quit smoking."

"I can't quit smoking," Fred says.

"Why not?"

"Then I'll have nothing to live for."

"We're going to work on that, Fred."

"My name's not really Fred," he mumbles.

"I know," I say. "You want to tell me your real name?"

"It's Jim—no Jack!"

"Jim Nojak—like Pat Sajak."

"Yeah," he says, brightening slightly. "Cool."

"Wheel of Fortune," I say. "Let's give this thing a spin, Jim Nojak. So you've looked for a job in San Francisco, yes? Then L.A. But nothing yet, right?"

"Obviously."

"There's more in the cards…" Most of my callers are women, but I get a good number of men, and they're often unemployed. Maybe it's California post-Internet boom, but this is nothing new to me. The unemployed women who call usually see things differently—they're realists (present company excepted, of course) who know the "New Economy" is dead, get lower paying jobs and move on.

But men still wait for the "magic" to return. It's the opposite of dating, where women cling to the few good times of an increasingly crappy relationship. With jobs, it's men who can't let go. They sit at home staring at the phone, waiting for Google to call, and invent crazy theories, like one guy who told me the Internet crash was Hollywood's fault, because they refused to deliver movies for free on the Internet.

"Free movies?" I'd asked.

"Exactly," he'd said.

"But, um, how would they make money?"

"That's not the point. That wasn't how things worked in the New Economy. There was a bigger picture."

I'd told him what I tell Jim Nojak now—"You're looking for a job that doesn't pay much less than your last one, right?"

"Well, I don't want to go backward…"

"So your salary requirements are from 2000, when Enron was the hottest business around?"

"I guess."

"It's over, Nojak. You can't expect another job like you had in San Francisco—that was a freak Act of God. Some job paying ninety percent what you got comes along, there are a hundred other guys in line in front of you."

"So what do I do?"

"You settle."

"Settle?"

"Settle. This is the key to happiness. Settling, plus task orientation, but we'll get to that. What skills do you have?" I always feel sick asking, because I personally hate when people ask me—like Merrick did on our first real date. But that was because I didn't have any skills. Most of the actual humans do.

"Well, I know a lot about advertising."

"This is your task. Apply to every job in the sales and advertising section of the newspaper. Get a job-hunting book and follow all the advice. Are there *any* jobs you might get?"

"Well, there's this one in the paper, a community college looking for someone to teach an introductory course in advertising."

"What happened when you applied?"

"I didn't. It only pays five hundred a month."

"And?"

"C'mon, that's like a ninety-five percent cut in pay. Just not enough money."

"For what? Coke and cigarettes? That's a lot of burritos. How are you paying for them now? Your mom giving you an allowance?"

Silence on the phone, and I wait for the click and the dial tone. Doesn't happen, which means he's listening.

"Try for this teaching job. Pay for your little addictions, a few beers, flowers for your mother. There's still plenty of time to look for a real job, and you'll be ahead of the other ninety-nine guys because you're employed. You're not desperate. You're not needy. You already have a job. You're a teacher, an expert in your field."

"That almost makes sense."

"I'm good with other people's problems," I tell him. "The cards say this is the way to go. Now I've got one more question. If you were gay, would you—"

"I'm not gay."

"That's okay, some of my best friends are straight. But if you *were* gay, who would you want to be friends with—a young vivacious woman who brings you cappuccino or a schlumpy carpenter who brings you conspiracy theories?"

"Um…is this a trick question? Maybe the carpenter's a woman, too? Or maybe the woman is gay, um, or the cappuccino is, I dunno, has poisoned foam? This is one of those word puzzles, right?"

"It's some kind of puzzle," I tell him.

chapter

6

I spend Tuesday morning on a computer at the *Permanent Press,* writing a scathing article about the evil pet psychic, which is honestly my best work. Then delete the whole thing and write something Teri might accept, in which instead of skewering Crystal Smith, myself, I let her do all the work. I make a big deal over Miu Miu, the prettiest, girliest boxer ever to chew a slipper, then follow with Crystal's statements about "Hank." That's how O'Malley would've handled the thing, except he would've used plenty of bold and italics.

Spend another hour combing through the Yellow Pages trying to find someone remotely appropriate to interview for next week. Teri wants my "proposal" by Friday, but when I stop by her office to drop off my article, she hasn't any suggestions.

"Maybe another acupuncturist?" I say. "The one with the cute new office on Chapala?"

"It's too early for repeats, Elle," she says, without looking up from my column. "Find someone else. And *this?* No way. Stay positive, breezy—you think now O'Malley's gone, you can step into his shoes?"

"Well, if I bold some of the words…"

She shoots me a withering look.

Great. After the last two fiascos, I'm getting sick of the whole deal, and tempted to chuck it. I never wanted to be a writer—pasty-faced antisocial freaks. I'm about to suggest to Teri she hire someone else—anyone other than Crystal—then I remember she's paying me three hundred bucks a month. I need that money.

So I tone down the column, and after Terri gives me a grudging okay I head for the library. Laverna offered $18,500 a year in loans, and that's pretty tempting, but my middle name is Comparison Shopping. Maybe some other school offers $22,000 a year—who knows how much someone will pay for the privilege of educating me?

The Santa Barbara Public Library is one of those sad contemporary buildings that shot up from the 1950s to the early eighties. Merrick says this isn't true, and gets all worked up about the principles of design, but what does he know? The building is ugly. Though, I'll admit, practical. Centrally located, with plenty of books—which, you might argue, is the important thing.

I push my way through the turnstile entrance into the main room, grateful that my research won't require a trip downstairs. Always smells like someone's hidden a body down there. Fortunately, the stench fades inside the main room—or I get acclimated, but I prefer to think the former—and I stand happily in line at the reference desk. I love reference librarians. They help you with *anything*, and rarely laugh derisively. They're like poorly dressed saints.

One of them points me in the right direction, and I'm soon ensconced in a institutional chair sorting through college catalogs. There are three M.A. programs in psychology offered in Santa Barbara. I eliminate one immediately as too Jungian for my taste—I don't approve of soft Js. Plus, the financial aid situation is not good. I'm quite taken with UC Santa Barbara's program, though—despite being in Goleta—especially after I learn I've missed the deadline to apply for fall registration. That means the earliest I could start is September of next year—a year and eight months to come up with something better. "It's not my fault, Merrick. I can't fight the deadlines."

I check the admissions requirements for UCSB. Application (easy), B.A. degree (existent), letters of reference (manageable with wheedling), and G.R.E. (impossible).

The Laverna catalog mocks me from the shelf. Yes, reference letters and a B.A. are required, but no G.R.E. And here's what the catalog says about deadlines: "We at Laverna believe it's never too late to apply. Classes start every three months and you can be accepted right up to the first day of class." Maybe Laverna is a degree mill—that'd be kinda handy.

I return home and spend twenty minutes lolling on floor, wrestling with Miu. Better than meditation. She likes playing chase inside, but that way leads to disaster, so now we wrestle and box. When I first got her she was too weak and depressed to box, but now she's basically Hilary Swank, putting one paw in the air and hunching her shoulder and jabbing.

Okay. I gave my word, there's no way around this. I fill out the Laverna application. True, I use a purple pen obtained from color therapist during column interview, but if they deny me based on ink color, they're small-minded. Plus, I never told Merrick I'd use blue or black ink. Shit, what if I get in? What if I *don't* get in?

I lick the envelope, filled with a sense of foreboding as the sky fills with dark clouds and lightning spears the bat-infested belltower. Then I put the envelope in the mail and eat a box of Little Schoolboys cookies.

I call Merrick to tell him what I've done—seven o' clock in New York, and he isn't in his hotel room. He should be eating Indian takeout and watching *Seinfeld* reruns. Everyone knows that's what your boyfriend should do in New York. Why isn't he in his room at seven o'clock?

Because he's at Nobu asking a New York It Girl to marry him.

Why am I not an It Girl? In high school I was a Zit Girl. If I went to the gym, I'd be a Fit Girl. If my column works, maybe I'll be a Lit Girl. And if I ever found Miu's previous owners, I'd be a Hit Girl. But an It Girl? Impossible.

I look at Miu. I say, "Sit, girl."

She does.

I love her. I kiss her right on the jowl, which is repulsive-delicious, then take her for a long walk on the beach. Sunset exquisite, Miu adorable. Mood not improved.

Stop for meatball sub at Tio's on way home. Check movie listings in *Permanent Press* while eating sandwich in bed. Romantic Matt Damon movie started ten minutes ago. Turn on TV hoping to find *Seinfeld,* but am stuck with *Will &*

Grace rerun. Why does Will like Grace? Would Jack like me? I watch closely, but gleam no tips about getting the Gay Tailors to like me. I have good hair and a hyperactive bumbling personality, and still get the cold shoulder. Maybe if I lost twenty pounds...

I bite into my sub.

Maya calls on Thursday afternoon, finally breaking radio silence. We're both happy but awkward and have a strange, stilted conversation.

"How are you?" she asks.

"Fine. You?"

"Fine."

The silence is intense as, by effort of will, I don't ask about the wedding planning. Finally, I say, "So, um... what's up?"

"Brad wants you to come to his conversion."

"Conversion? Did he finish programming something?"

She sighs. "He's converting to Judaism, Elle."

"Brad's converting to Judaism?" I'm stunned. How can I not have known this? "But he's perfect already."

"Now he'll be even more perfect."

"You can't improve on perfect," I say.

"I don't know what you're complaining about. Merrick's perfect, too."

"Oh, he's anything but perfect." Perfect men remain in their hotel rooms, and don't go reveling in sushi and It Girls. "But converting? Isn't this sort of sudden? Don't you have to study the *tallis* for years or something?"

"I think you mean the Torah. And not for a reform conversion, you don't. We've been going to conversion classes once a week for six months."

"You've been planning on getting married for six months?"

"Um, sort of. We've been talking about it, that's all. We wanted to see how everything went. I didn't want to tell you while you were feeling bad about your own failed wedding."

"Oh. That would've sucked, you getting engaged right after Louis left me. Thanks for not telling me."

"You're welcome."

"But you could've at least told me he was converting."

"We didn't know if he'd really want to, after all the classes. We didn't even tell my dad until last week."

"What did he say?"

"*Mazel Tov*, then he cried. Said my mother would have been so happy."

Her mother died of breast cancer two years ago. "She would've. Brad's wonderful—you really deserve each other."

"So you're coming to the conversion?"

"Of course I'm coming! A Stella McCartney sample sale wouldn't keep me away."

"Yeah, sure."

"It's true! You know I don't fit into sample sizes."

Maya laughs. I think she's as relieved as I that we're not fighting.

"So what should I bring?" I ask. "Is there food?"

"Yeah, but don't bring anything. We're just happy to see you."

That makes me suspicious. "Really?"

"Yes, really. And Elle?"

"Mmm?"

"Sorry I was mean about your wedding plans. Bridal nerves, I guess."

"Good, because I found a salmonman! But he needs—"

"The ceremony's at five," she says, and gives me directions to the synagogue.

★ ★ ★

Seven seconds after I hang up, Merrick calls.

"What on earth is Nobu?" he asks. So he got my message.

"Do you think Scarlett Johansson is pretty?" I ask.

"Is she at Nobu?"

"Did you see her there?"

"Um… Could we have a normal conversation where you tell me how you've been and ask about work?"

"I'm good. How's work?"

"I'm still *at* work, that's how it is. You wouldn't believe how seriously these people take their co-ops. This board is like the House Un-American Activities Committee."

"Can't you stand up there and say, 'At long last, sirs, have you no shame?'"

"Elle—a quote from the McCarthy hearings? I'm…well, I guess I'm impressed."

"Hey, I went to college. And I may go to graduate school. I applied to Laverna."

"You didn't!"

"I did!"

He gushes approval, and I glow—until there's a scuffling on his end of the line. He says, "What?" More scuffling. "Right." Muffled talking, then Merrick says, "Sorry, Elle, I gotta go. Joe McCarthy has some questions. I'll call you later tonight." And he hangs up, but not before I hear a girlish voice saying, "Louis, come back to…"

To *the conference room?* To *the table?* To *meet the boss?* Please, oh please, let it be anything but *bed*.

I banish all anxiety about the girlish voice into the outer darkness. Merrick is the least underhanded person in the world—if he were leaving me, I'd be the first to know.

Right?

Right.

I chew my fingernail. Right?

Definitely. Yes. Banish that anxiety. Okay banished.

Instead, I should bask in his approval for applying to a master's program. I try to bask, and with his glowing praise still ringing in my ears, basking should be easy, but instead I feel a cold pit in my stomach. Not even about the girlish voice, but about Laverna. What if I get in? I don't *want* to go back to school. I don't *want* to be a real therapist. I *like* being an intuitive counselor, a friendly voice with pretty-good-if-obvious advice. If I become a real therapist, then I can't tell clients with real problems to call…well, a real therapist. That's what I do now, and I oughtta be getting a kickback for all my referrals. But honestly, you have to be a little psychologically off-kilter to want to deal with all those real problems. I'm way too healthy for that.

Still, Maya and Merrick both agree that I should get my degree, and they're all mature and tidy, so maybe they're right. I open the cabinets thoughtfully. Discover I'm out of ramen and rice, the staples of a newly self-employed businesswoman, so I open the fridge for some culinary meditation. There's half a head of lettuce and a can of tuna and jar of black olives. Consider whipping up niçoise-type salad, but have no idea what kind of dressing to use, and know it will ultimately taste like some lettuce and tuna with olives. I eat the olives. If I had mayo I'd make tuna salad. I eat the lettuce. And just as I'm eyeing the tuna thinking Merrick is due to call back any second, the phone rings.

But it is not Merrick, it's Valentine, one of my regular clients—one who refuses to make an appointment, and calls whenever she feels the need. Not that I'm complaining, she alone has paid my rent many months. She's a Montecito matron of indeterminable age with a lust for canary-colored clothing and hair the shade of cherry cola.

"Elle, I need a reading."

"I'm kinda waiting for a call, Valentine."

"Well, this is a crisis. I need a crisis reading."

"What's wrong?"

"It's Rowdy." Her Pomeranian. This is not unusual. She's always calling about Rowdy. I hope Crystal Smith, the pet psychic, never finds out or she'll firebomb my building. "He's coughing."

"Coughing? Did you—" I stop speaking because I hear Valentine moving the phone down to the dog. There's silence, with Valentine cooing in the background.

"He *just* stopped when I put the phone to his mouth," she says, "but he's coughing terribly. Do you think it's leukemia?"

"He's not choking is he?" That's the another thing that amazes me, the number of people who call psychics during an emergency. Can't tell you the number of times I've had to explain 911.

"Choking, my goodness." Valentine says, sounding like she's settling into a settee for a long chat. "Whatever would he be choking on?"

So we have a lengthy discussion about everything our dogs have choked on—a cupcake wrapper, a stuffed squirrel, ballet slippers—or regurgitated—a whole Vienna sausage, still in pristine condition. "You could've squirted mustard on that thing and served it for dinner," I say. Two hours fly by, then the cards tell Valentine: "Take Rowdy to the vet."

"Oh, he stopped coughing an hour ago!" she says cheerily. "Talk to you later!"

God bless her and Rowdy for keeping me financially

afloat. But I've missed Merrick's call. I check voice mail, and no message. Odd. Three hours of rerun TV later and it's time for bed.

Have finally admitted that Merrick isn't going to call, I'm still no further along with article idea, afraid of attending Laverna and I'm officially starving.

Next morning, there's a knock on the door—UPS, with a package. One of my definitions of success is a life in which UPS and FedEx are constantly delivering packages: shoes, jewelry, beautiful little bagatelles and Very Important Documents. And food. Like, for example, a breakfast cheesecake.

This package is too small for a cheesecake—it's tiny and there's no return address. For a moment I wonder if Crystal Smith sent me dog poop in the mail, but that's too juvenile even for her, right? So I rip off the paper and find a royal-blue velvet ring box.

A ring.

Ever since I hurled my engagement solitaire at my ex-fiancé, I've been sorta off rings. Oh, God. What if Merrick sent this? A marriage proposal? Would he think that was romantic, a surprise ring sent by anonymous post? Was he afraid if he asked in person, I'd just stare in silent idiocy, like I had when he talked about moving in together?

I bite my lower lip and pop the lid, pretending not to notice the box didn't come from Tiffany. Or Cartier. Is Fifth Avenue so difficult to find in New York? Then I pull myself together: I should enjoy moments like this instead of being such an ungrateful harpy.

Nestled inside the box is a chunk of turquoise big as peach pit and set in an ornate Indian-type silver ring. Very Georgia O'Keeffe. How am going to tell Merrick—

Lee Nichols

A shape looms in the door, a man between twenty and forty years and 250 and 300 pounds, baby-blue eyes and a childlike face. He blinks at me. "You opened it."

"Ye-es," I say.

"Why'd you open it?" he asks.

"Was I supposed to wait until Christmas?" I haven't even had the chance to try the ring on yet, or imagine wearing it for the rest of my natural life. Or figure out why Merrick chose *this.* Or, for that matter, how I'm going to answer him.

"Christmas?" the man says. "It's February."

"That's why I didn't wait," I tell him. "I'm impatient that way."

He looks confused, and I can't say I blame him. "Do you want to buy it?" he asks. "I'll give you a good price."

"Buy it?" Maybe this is some elaborate sales scheme, like my ex-sorta-boyfriend Joshua the grifter would've dreamed up.

"Yeah," he says. "I'm Ray Flood."

"Uh-huh," I say, waiting politely for the rest of his sales pitch, because I know what it's like to try to scrounge for business.

He looks even more confused, then points at the package. "Ray Flood."

And there, on the crumpled wrapping paper, sure enough, is his name. And address—which is the same as mine with a different apartment number. I've opened someone else's mail.

"You're Ray Flood," I say.

"I'm Ray Flood," he repeats, like an English teacher with the remedial class.

"The UPS guy must've thought it was for me. I've ordered a few things, now and then. So, you're moving in downstairs?"

He nods begrudgingly.

Merrick and the Gay Tailors are on the first floor, I'm on

the third, and now Ray will be on the second. I was hoping for a woman, for obvious reasons. "What're your thoughts about hanging out in the hallway?"

"Um." Ray nods toward the ring. "So, you want it or not?"

I slip the turquoise onto my finger. It's pretty in a bright and chunky way—which reminds me of me, so I say, "How much?"

"A hundred."

I'm feeling flush from Valentine's phone call, but I'm still saving for the drapey woolen pantsuit at Element. "No, thanks. You sell a lot of jewelry?" I hand him back the ring. "Your apartment is mixed use, isn't it?"

He blushes and mumbles something I can't quite hear.

"Right, sounds good," I say.

He looks at me like I've said the wrong thing.

"Anyway, I'm thinking of a having a housewarming party for the new tenants—I'll slip an invitation under your door."

He mumbles again and turns, gracefully for a fat man, and heads downstairs.

So no ring from Merrick, and no ring from Merrick, and the neighbors all hate me. I'm definitely gonna throw that party. Once Neil delivers the pot. At least everyone would enjoy seeing me stoned.

I go shopping. Turns out I owe the bank $183, but that's before Valentine's money, and I have a few checks scattered around, from long-term clients who pay by mail—plus a three dollar telephone company rebate check, which is the most exciting thing I've gotten in the mail in a month.

At least I have a legitimate gift expense in the form of Brad's conversion. I wonder if the gift has to be something Jewish—there aren't really guidelines for shopping for a conversion. Maya has a collection of antique menorahs from her mother, so maybe Brad should have one of his own. Besides, what other good Jewish gifts are there? A Philip Roth book? Maya has this whole list she learned from her mother, of good Jews and bad Jews, and I'm afraid to buy a bad Jew gift. I think Roth *was* a bad Jew, but redeemed himself. She also has a list of unlikely anti-Semites: Joseph Campbell, Roald Dahl, FDR. You'd be surprised.

Anyway, I check all my favorite home stores and find only one sad ceramic menorah, marked half-price. Yech. I consider a Chagall poster from the Santa Barbara Art Museum store, but run into the good Jew/bad Jew problem again. Frankly, if the conversion process is half as hard as this stuff, I'm amazed that even Perfect Brad could pass. I bet for the exam they ask him trick questions about Steven Spielberg.

I give up at the museum shop and mosey around the block to the New Age store, which carries religious items. Maybe I'll find a crystal menorah. I've never actually been inside, as it reminds me too much of my mother, who owns a similar business in Sedona, but I've loitered in the entrance reading flyers for massage therapy and healers, seeking inspiration for a column. Been meaning to post my own flyer, but I don't have one yet.

The inside is surprisingly well designed, with soothing sky-blue walls and shelves filled with inspirational tomes, greeting cards and miniature Buddhas. Dream catchers and wind chimes hang from the ceiling, and sitar music tinkles softly in the background. I feel uncomfortable. Partly because of the mother factor, partly because I'm fake psychic and partly because all the earnest-seeking makes me feel shallow. And, of course, there's the tacky factor.

I ask the clerk about menorahs, and she tells me I'm in luck. There are three. One is glossy metal and kinda seventies utilitarian, like what Jews on *Star Trek* would have, which is appealing because Brad is a computer geek, and they all like sci-fi, right? But Maya would kill me. The second is the same sad ceramic one I already saw. And the third is a stunning silver menorah I know they'd love. Actually Brad would probably prefer the new version of *Halo,* but I'm not gonna be the only person at the conversion ceremony with a gift rated *V* for Violence. Not to mention, I don't have a hundred-and-twenty bucks to spend. I'm thinking of calling Merrick in New York to ask if he'll split the cost 20/80, but what if the girlish voice answers? I don't want to play the jpart of the nagging, money-grubbing, soon-to-be-ex-girlfriend, with uncorroborated presumptions of joint gift-giving.

So I mutter and waffle and slink away. On my way out the door I pass the bulletin board and one of the fliers catches my eye. I grab it and stuff it in my pocket. Hey, I've got an idea, I should give Brad a gift certificate for my own services. Sure. Or I could buy him that drapey black pantsuit at Element. He'd like that.

Two days later, I still haven't bought a gift. Or written a column. Or befriended the Gay Tailors. I'm on my way to meet Adele and Darwin for coffee—well, herbal tea for Adele—when I realize Miu's nowhere to be found. I often let her hang around the hallway, like a real man, but when I lean over the stair railing and call for her, there's no answering jingle of dog tags. Could be moping around Merrick's office, she likes to sleep on his front mat when he's got the door open.

I whistle, and there's still no answer, so I trot downstairs to look for her. It's not like her to ignore my whistles. I hope the Gay Tailors didn't turn her over to the Humane Society after being brainwashed by Crystal Smith. She's nowhere in the house, so I take a deep breath and knock on Johnny and Weldon's door.

No answer.

What if she's locked in there? Maybe she wandered inside and they didn't see her. I call her name through the door. Silence. Ugh. She's so neurotic it's possible she's inside staring expectantly at the door waiting for me to open it. She'd never bark—that would be unseemly. She's has very definite ideas about proper dog etiquette.

"Miu?" I call. "Miu? Miu Miu?"

I listen for her to shake her dog tags in answer, but there's nothing. I head back upstairs, feeling panic rise. Did I leave her somewhere? Take her on a walk and get so involved in the chaotic swirl of my own neuroses that I forgot she was with me? As I'm trying to convince myself that even *I* am not that self-absorbed, I hear a murmuring behind Ray Flood's door…and the telltale jingle of Miu Miu.

"Miu?" I call out hesitantly. Why would the new guy have my dog in his apartment? Maybe I imagined the jingling.

Ray's door opens a crack and Miu slips out, licking her chops. The door closes. She presses her body against my legs.

"What were doing in there?" I ask. "What have you been eating?"

She drools.

I should knock and demand to know what he's been feeding my dog, but decide against. So far, he's only expressed mild disinterest in me, I don't want him forming active distaste like the Gay Tailors. It's gonna really suck when Merrick dumps me and they all unite against me.

I take Miu along for coffee, to monitor the possible-poisoning situation, and we get seats outside.

"Does that look like frothing to you?" I ask Darwin and Adele, wiping Miu's jowl with my napkin. "I think she's frothing."

"She always froths," Darwin says. He's wearing a Hawaiian shirt and beige shorts, and though he's a Santa Barbara native manages to look like a tourist.

"You think that's her normal drool?"

"A mother knows," Adele says, worrying the amethyst bead necklace around her neck, resplendent in a tie-dyed peasant dress. "Trust your instincts."

My instincts tell me to buy Chanel makeup, live off credit cards and forcibly forge a lifelong friendship with a couple of gay men who couldn't be less interested.

Darwin looks at his latté. "I could actually use a little more froth myself."

I nod toward Miu. "Help yourself."

"What about Woody Allen videos?" Adele asks. "For your friend's conversion."

I'd brought up the subject, kinda hoping one of them was Jewish and would know the perfect gift. "Maybe."

Maybe not. Maya hates Woody Allen. He was on the "bad Jew" list even before the whole stepdaughter thing. Not sure why, but Maya's mother had her reasons.

"I like *Crimes and Misdemeanors*," Darwin says.

"*Annie Hall,*" says Adele.

Crimes and Misdemeanors is about infidelity, not exactly what the happily engaged couple wants to see—even though the mistress is shot in the end. And *Annie Hall* is like Woody Allen doing a Woody Allen impression.

I take a bite of coffee cake and have an epiphany. "What about food?"

"Babette's Feast!" Adele says, like she's just rung the buzzer on a game show.

"Eat Drink Man Woman!" Darwin says in the same tone.

I sigh. What I really need is friends who are *less* weird. "I mean, I could make food. Bring some traditional Jewish delicacies to the ceremony."

"Can you cook?" Adele asks.

"I can boil. I'm a good boiler."

"Boiled Jewish delicacies," Darwin says, with a shudder, then, "Whoa! Miu's throwing up. Maybe she *was* poisoned."

But Miu's just puking yellow bile—her regular once-a-month puke. "Not a problem," I murmur. "A mother knows." At least it's not in her usual place, all over the living room carpet.

An hour later I'm home with a freshly walked Miu, who's peppy and bright, like there's nothing more invigorating than a good poisoning. We slink past Weldon and Johnny's shop, the door is open and they're charming a blond, middle-aged woman. I can tell Miu wants to say hello, but is unsure of her welcome. Nothing's sadder than realizing your child is afraid she'll be shunned by others. Johnny catches my eye and I smile and wave, but he pretends he doesn't see me. Miu looks embarrassed for me as we trudge upstairs past Ray Flood's place. My resolution not to annoy is overwhelmed by curiosity. What does he do in there? And I don't think he hates me, yet. If I can lure him to my side before Merrick leaves me, we'll be even in the building. Two for and two against, because a couple only counts as one—or at least is matched by Miu.

I knock, and Ray opens the door.

"Hi."

"Hello?"

"It's me. Elle. From upstairs." I point, in case he doesn't know which direction that is. "We met a couple days ago?"

He ducks his head and doesn't answer.

"Um, the UPS guy accidentally delivered your ring to me? Upstairs?"

A hint of a nod.

"Anyway, I wanted to officially welcome you to the building." And ask what you've been feeding my dog. "And, uh, what else do you sell? Other than jewelry, I mean."

"A little of everything," he says.

I strain my head to see around him into his apartment. "How about used cars?"

Instead of smiling, he closes the door more tightly against his body. For a man of his size I'm impressed with how snug he can get it. "No, I…I sell on eBay," he mumbles, and glances away shyly.

Ah! He doesn't hate me, he's just shy! If anyone can deal with shyness, it's Elle Medina. "eBay!" I gush. "I *love* eBay! Maybe you can help me, I'm looking for a gift for my friend, for a conversion ceremony. Reform Jewish."

"Judaica," he says, then steps back and softly shuts the door.

Am I supposed to wait? Is he checking something for me? Or is he standing just inside the door, making sure I don't break in? I wait five minutes, quietly cooing to Miu, then retreat upstairs to my den.

God, I miss Merrick.

I fill out my *new* application for school, for the program that wasn't listed in the library course catalogs, but on a flyer at the New Age store. At least this one doesn't require fabrications and exaggerations—or at least, not any that I'm not used to by now. Not sure Merrick's gonna approve of choice, but at least it's school. I'll get training and be all certified and official. Anyway, he's about to dump me, so who cares what he thinks?

Okay, I know he's not gonna dump me—at least not like this, long-distance, after two weeks in N.Y. cavorting with It Girls. But I need some excuse for dropping this application in the mail, and that girlish voice when we spoke is the only thing that pops to mind. So I lick and stamp the envelope, and prepare to greet my future.

chapter
7

What kind of food do you make for a Jewish conversion? Couldn't find a Jewish dish in any of Merrick's cookbooks, other than stuffed cabbage and various kinds of kugel, so I used a stuffed jalapeño recipe. Brad loves spicy food and these are kinda like stuffed cabbage. Plus, I elegantly displayed the jalapeños on a white platter with blue bachelor buttons, so I have a blue-and-white Jewish theme. Well, plus green, if you include the peppers. An environmentally sensitive Jewish theme.

The synagogue is nestled in the foothills of what I consider early Goleta, but because it's just over the border from Santa Barbara it's still safe. Late Friday afternoon, and another gray day. Starting to feel like Oregon around here. I hope it doesn't rain—Maya said something about a pool. I almost said, *Oh, for the baptism,* but bit my tongue.

I check the plate of jalapeños nestled in the passenger seat. You know how long it takes to stuff four dozen jalapeños, if you're culinarily challenged? I've been slaving over this dish for three full days, including the time wasted on kugel experimentation. (Resulting in proof that kugel is not, strictly speaking, food.) We're talking a minimum of fifteen hours of shopping, chopping, mixing, baking, basting, crying, and finally, triumph. But Maya's my best friend, and Brad's been…well, perfect to me. They deserve something special and I'm glad I didn't just get the ugly ceramic menorah. I really worked on these jalapeños: they're a labor of love.

Sadly, I've been so busy cooking I neglected to have breakfast or lunch today, and I'm starving, so I eye the plate hungrily. Maybe just one? No, they're perfectly symmetrical. If I have one I'll have to have two, and if I have two I'll have six, and pretty soon I'm back to offering a gift certificate to my own services, written on a parking ticket.

The synagogue is not dissimilar to the library in architectural splendor, built in the seventies, all beige stucco and brown trim. I doubt even Merrick would have something good to say about it. I called him last night to see if he wanted me to wish Brad *"Mazel Tov,"* as we say, but still got no answer. Probably having dinner with Scarlett Johansson.

I drive around the parking lot, looking for a door that might lead to the kitchen. I'm gonna be modest about this—instead of waltzing in the front and making a big production, I'll just slip the jalapeños in with the rest of the food. I know it's not a great gift—like plane tickets to Paris, say—but it's heartfelt, and they'll know how much they mean to me, making me go all pre-prison Martha Stewart.

I find a promising entrance and head inside. I've only been in a synagogue a few times with Maya, but they're just as scary as churches. Someone might pop through a door speaking in tongues, or Hebrew or whatever, at any moment, and God only knows what kind of rituals are going on. It's a little like meeting a therapist at a dinner party—you hesitate to say anything, for fear of being diagnosed and possibly institutionalized. What if the rabbi sees me and can tell what a bad person I am? What if he gives a sermon about being a fake? Jews are supposed to be good at guilt—this could get ugly.

But I locate the kitchen without exposing my soul to anyone. The counters are stainless steel, the walls dingy off-white, and dishes of wrapped cold cuts, casseroles and some fruit plates fill the counter tops. Institutional fare—they're gonna be thrilled with my more humane contribution. Plus, everything looks bland, so my jalapeños are gonna add a little spice to this conversion. In fact, though my presentation is stunning, I decide I should use the jalapeños as accent pieces, garnish for the other dishes, which range in color from beige to brown. I place a few among the cold cuts, the veggies and dip, and what I now recognize as kugel—glad I didn't bring one of those. Everything looks perked up with peppers and I am overflowing with righteous humility. I can't wait to tell Maya.

My plan is to hover near the food table to soak up the admiration, then off-handedly whip out the recipe, which I've printed on a few index cards in my purse. Make no mistake, these things are *gooood*. They're *Like Water for Chocolate* good.

I turn to go and a tiny woman with flaming red hair is standing two feet from me.

"Vat is this?" she says, coming even closer.

"Oh, I'm a friend of Brad's, and I—"

She sees my lovely pepper garnishes, and her face turns as red as her hair. "No food!" she yells. "No food!"

"They're jalapeños stuffed with—"

"Bad!" She waves her hands and scolds me in some language that sounds almost like Spanish. "Outside food! Very bad person!"

"I'm sorry," I say. "I'm sorry, do you—"

"You get out! You ruin kitchen—you ruin everything."

She shoos me out the door, and slams it behind me.

The lobby is empty but for Maya who's staring at a photograph on the wall.

"Look," she says, after I kiss her hello. "There's me with my confirmation class." Maya stands front and center in a group of eight sixteen-year-olds, smiling broadly.

"I remember that. You tried to convince your mother you should celebrate by piercing your belly button."

"Never should've asked her permission," Maya says.

"There's still time," I say. "Hey, we could both do it before your wedding."

Her eyes glint. "Yeah?"

"Why not?"

"Aren't belly buttons passé? Maybe we should do eyebrows."

"Or make Brad happy, do your clit."

"Elle," she says. "We're in shul."

"Sorry. You know I'm not used to this sort of place. Shouldn't there be more people here by now?"

"Yeah, Brad's brother, for one."

"Brad has a brother?"

"He's kinda the black sheep, you'll like him."

Well, with a brother like PB, of course he's the black

sheep. Even a light gray sheep would appear inky by comparison. "He's the only one coming? There isn't a service?"

"That's later, there'll be all kinds of people. First Brad has his *mikva*."

"Oh sure, his *mikva*."

"A ritual bath, only we don't have one in the shul, so we go to someone's house around the corner and use their pool."

"The pool? Like…a pool?"

"Yep."

"That's so southern California. I bet the New York Jews scoff."

She laughs.

"Why am I here now," I ask, "if the service isn't 'til later?"

"The rabbi said Brad should invite the people he feels closest to for the *mikva*, so he wanted you and his brother."

I think I might cry. "Me?"

She smiles. "Apparently you've rubbed off on him."

"What about his parents?" I ask. "They're not coming?"

"You couldn't pry them out of Vegas for anything less than a cruise ship."

A door opens down one of the hallways, and I pace the room, afraid the kitchen lady's going to appear. I stop at the photo Maya was inspecting. "Hey, is that Danny Blum? From high school?"

"Look how cute he was," Maya says. "Why didn't we like him?"

"He called me Elle-belly."

She nods. "Right."

"Wonder what he's doing now," I say.

"He's an orthodontist."

"Why is everyone always something? A vet, a psychologist, a paleontologist."

"Who's a paleontologist?"

"You know what I mean," I say. "Everyone's something but me."

"And me," Maya says.

"You're a bar owner," I say. "Like that's not the coolest job ever. What would you say if someone asked you what I was doing?"

"I'd tell them you're a consultant."

I brighten.

"Yeah, all my really good lies come from you," she says.

It's true. I was always the one who lied us out of trouble after I muddled us into it. "Where's Brad?" I say.

"Talking to the rabbi," she says. "Merrick's still in New York?"

"Yeah. Actually, he's not coming back at all, since he hooked up with some Mischa Barton look-alike. Her name's Sascha Burton."

"Not a Scarlett Johansson look-alike named Harlot O'Hanson?"

"That's a great porn name, Harlot O'Hanson. If I get into porn, that's the name I'm taking. Do you think I'm too old for porn?"

"Would you stop? We're in shul."

"What, no more clits and porn? If I were Harlot, I'd definitely pierce my clit. And my nipples, because—"

And the rabbi clears his throat behind me.

At least, I think he's the rabbi, because he's standing with Brad, both of them wearing dark pants, dress shirts, ties and yarmulkes. The rabbi looks about thirty, which is way too young for a rabbi if you ask me. I recognize his brown suede lace-ups from the Cole Haan catalog, and his mocha shirt really brings out his eyes. His hair is dark and curly, which I guess is par for the course, and as Brad introduces us the strangest thing happens: the rabbi smiles, takes my hand and checks me out.

I'm talking the full ogle, here, lingering on all the goodies. He says he's glad to meet me and has a few phone calls to make before we head off to the pool. He heads back down the hall and Maya says, "Stop staring, Elle."

"He totally checked me out!" I turn to Brad. "Your rabbi wants to get with me."

"Chillax, Missy Elle," Maya says.

"He's a rabbi," I say. "Should rabbis be ogling?"

"Why not?" Brad asks. "He's single."

"He's a rabbi!"

"They're not priests," Maya says.

"Yeah, but…" He's pretty good-looking, too, and that's got to be a solid job. "Hey, could you imagine me as a rabbi's wife?"

For some reason, they laugh.

"His mother wouldn't let him close to you," Maya says.

"His mother?"

"Little thing with red hair," Maya says. "She's a riot. She speaks Ladino, which is like Spanish Yiddish. She takes care of the—"

"Kitchen," I finish.

"Yeah, how'd you know?"

"Um…" Why was the rabbi's mother yelling at me? It's not like I stuffed bacon in the jalapeños. "I'm psychic," I say.

"So you're happy?" I ask Brad, now that I've got him alone. "I mean converting."

"I'm surprised how right it feels. Pretty strange at first, but it was important to Maya, so we kept coming to classes and somehow it clicked. Not that I'm going to be the best Jew, but it feels like I've filled a void, something I didn't know I was missing."

"Wow." I'm blown away by his sincerity, and a little jealous, too. "That's really really great. *Mikva tov!*"

He smiles. "Something like that. But thanks. I hear you've got big changes happening, too. Congratulations."

"Oh, um…" My column? The housewarming party? I am, in fact, stagnating in every conceivable way. "What?"

"Maya said you're applying to graduate school."

"Oh, that, yeah." Not exactly going to fill a void. "Listen, Brad, since we're being open here, what would you say if I applied to—"

"Hey, man." A young guy hails us from across the room. "Sorry I'm late."

"My brother," Brad says, half-apologetically.

His brother is a younger, raunchier version of Perfect Brad. Tall and lanky with dark hair—a Jake Gyllenhaal type. "I'm operating on JST."

"JST?"

"Jewish Standard Time. C'mon, Brad, I spent the last two weeks online, memorizing Jewish jokes—it's like a whole new vista of laughs."

"Yeah," Brad says, with a perfect lack of enthusiasm. "How's the bike?"

"Only broke down once." He smiles at me, then turns to Brad. "You gonna introduce us?"

Brad does, and his brother says, "*This* is Elle. Wow." He takes my hand. "I'm a real fan."

"You broke down?" Brad says. "I thought Mom and Dad gave you money to fix it."

"Well, they gave me money…"

"And…" Brad prompts.

His brother gets a glint in his eye, and I half expect him to answer, "Women, wine and song." Instead he glances at me like we share a secret, and I find myself charmed. He is a tad wicked, Brad's brother.

He is Wicked Tad.

Twenty minutes and a short walk later, we step into the garden behind a nice single-level house. There's me, Brad, Maya, Wicked Tad and the Lusty Rabbi. The pool is set deeply into a large yard filled with native plants, oblong and contemporary with tiny pearl square tiles lining the bottom. I admit to an incomplete religious education, but nothing about this really screams "Jewish ceremonial bath" to me. Still, the water is turquoise and inviting, and I wish I'd thought to wear my swimsuit under my clothes.

Brad stands in the shallow end wearing navy swim trunks. First time I've seen Brad without his clothes, he strips pretty nice. Figures.

There is something odd about standing in your Armani suit watching another person floating in the shallow end of pool waiting for a blessing and dunking. I stand on one side with Brad's brother under a palm tree, what I guess we figure is the appropriate distance for non-Jews, and Maya stands with the rabbi. We all watch Brad, who looks surprisingly unselfconscious.

"This is weird," Wicked Tad tells me.

The Lusty Rabbi starts explaining something to Brad and I whisper, "What?" I'm afraid of getting in trouble with Maya for talking.

"This," Tad whispers back. "Do you ever feel like you're in a movie?"

In fact, I often feel like the star of an Oxygen Movie of

the Week, but this doesn't seem the time to explain, so I murmur something noncommittal.

"This is like some low-budget indie film. 'Fade in on a swimming pool...'"

I smile. "What would the title be? *Conversion and Controversy,* sorta like *Pride and Prejudice.*"

"Sure, if Jane Austen wrote stories about southern California Jews," Wicked Tad says. "How about *The Conversion?* A thriller."

"The Mikva Code."

"An action pic," he says. *"The Jewniversal Soldier."*

I giggle, and Maya clears her throat. "Whenever you two are ready, we can begin."

The whole thing takes about fifteen minutes. There are a few head dippings, then several prayers in Hebrew, which Brad appears to recite quite fluently. The rabbi says they're done, and we all yell *Mazel Tov,* and I find myself unaccountably moved.

The service is held an hour later, in the little outdoor amphitheater behind the synagogue, opening onto a stand of trees and a wild hillside. There are about sixty people, and the four of us sit halfway back. I thought the service would be All Brad All The Time, but his conversion is officially over, and this is just the normal Friday night service.

I gotta say, they do a few things right. Being outside is nice—if you're in Santa Barbara, take advantage of more than the swimming pools. And most of the service is in Hebrew, so you can't understand what they're saying, which in my book is a big religious plus. On the other hand, if you don't know what you're doing it's hard to fake, so Wicked Tad and I don't exactly blend.

The whole thing starts with one kid, about six years old and cute as a snap. He eyes us for a while, and as I don't always mix well with precocious young boys, I ignore him. Wicked Tad, however, makes googly eyes.

That's all the little scamp needs. He rockets from his seat and points at Tad, who snaps his fingers playfully in his prayer book. The scamp giggles, which attracts his little sister, two other children, and well…me. The whole thing is adorable—perhaps a bit inappropriate considering the setting, but I get a little high watching inappropriate behavior that has nothing to do with me.

I keep checking Maya for her reaction. She seems not to notice anything, but her tongue is pressed against her cheek, always a bad sign. Well, that and reaching across my lap to grab Wicked Tad's prayer book out his hands.

"And now," the rabbi says, after the final song. "you're all invited to a reception, refreshments in honor of Brad, on the occasion of his *beit din*. I understand there's *tzimmes* and *borekas* and honey cake."

Thank God. I'm starving. And those stuffed jalapeños are calling my name. Everyone stands and wishes each other well using some phrase which isn't—to my dismay—*mazel tov*. But I mumble along with a smile and then the whole congregation files inside the synagogue for the refreshments. They're in for a surprise. I'm gonna knock their skullcaps off.

Which I kinda do. We step into a room with a bunch of tables in the center and Wicked Tad turns to Maya. "Where's the food? You promised food."

The tables hold only plastic cups, a few loaves of woven bread and pitchers of red wine. There are sixty hungry Jews milling around, and for no good reason at all I get a sinking feeling in my stomach. But, no way this has anything to do with my jalapeños.

"I thought your dad arranged a caterer," Brad tells Maya.

"He did. Where's Mrs. Alevy?" She looks around the room and spots the little redheaded old lady. "Mrs. Alevy!"

I attempt to slip away—too slow.

Mrs. Alevy sees me and yells, "Her! She ruin the kitchen! Unkosher! Unkosher! Crazy woman spread *tref* over everything."

The room quiets as all eyes turn to me.

chapter

8

You know how, in horror movies, the heroine runs to her car but can't get the key in the lock? Her hands shake as the killer approaches, she drops the keys, fumbles with the door handle?

Well, I'm *this* close to making a clean getaway when a dark shape looms beside me. "Don't mind my mother," the Lusty Rabbi says.

"I'm so sorry I brought *tref*," I babble. "I didn't even know what *tref* is."

He waves his hand airily. "My mother's a little overly enthusiastic. I don't keep kosher, myself."

He doesn't keep kosher? He's an ogling rabbi who doesn't keep kosher? He probably plays lead guitar in a thrash band, too. "Sure," Maya would say, "he's a rabbi not a monk. Thrash music is a mitzvah."

I continue mumbling apologies, and he says, "I haven't seen you here before, have I?"

I shake my head and feel like a bad Jew for not coming to services, even though, well…y'know.

"Now that you've found the place," he says, with a kind smile. "I hope to see you more often."

"Even after the *tref?*"

"*Especially* after the *tref.*"

Oh, my God! He's a bad boy rabbi! I can't help myself: I toss my hair the tiniest bit and smile.

"So, Elle for Eleanor?" he says. "What's your last name?"

What am I *doing?* I have the best boyfriend in the world—plus, I'd be embarrassed to convert. I don't like appearing in a swimsuit while others are dressed. So I say, with emphasis, to make clear that I'm not Jewish, "Medina. Elle Medina."

"Medina's a good Sephardic name."

I'm not sure what that means, exactly, so I say, "Thanks?"

"Do you like sushi?" he asks.

What do I say to that? It's a yes or no question, so if I tell him I have a boyfriend it's like I'm an egomaniac who thinks all men want me, but if I say yes, that's like "How's next Thursday?"

Fortunately, before I can answer, Wicked Tad materializes from the darkness and puts his arm around me. "Hey, babe—let's bounce."

"Oh!" I say, realizing I'm being rescued. "Well, Rabbi, lovely meeting you but I have to…bounce."

Wicked Tad shakes hands with the rabbi, praising the sermon that I'm absolutely sure he didn't hear, and we slip into my car.

I pull from the lot. "What about your motorcycle?"

"I sold the bike last year. Can I crash with you?"

"What?"

"At your place." He shoots me a grin. "I'm thinking Brad and Maya are gonna want a night alone."

"Consummate the conversion?"

"Hey, it's a mitzvah," he says.

I'm thinking too hard to ask what that means. I'm like a man magnet today, with the Lusty Rabbi and Wicked Tad. I barely know the guy, but he *is* Perfect Brad's brother, and after ruining the reception, the least I can do is give them some time alone. After all, they let me crash on their couch for weeks, so this only seems fair. Plus, Merrick will never find out. Sure he won't.

"You didn't *sleep* sleep with him, did you?" Maya asks over the phone the next morning.

I'm so relieved she's still talking to me, after ruining Brad's conversion, I can't even bring myself to tease her. "Of course not!"

"It's just the way you snuck off together. And when he didn't show up last night…"

"First off, he's like twelve—"

"He's twenty-two."

"In dog years," I say, scratching Miu on the chest. She's lying on the floor next to me in my bedroom, while Wicked Tad sleeps on the living room floor. I don't even have a couch for him to sleep on, but he didn't care. He even came with his own sleeping bag.

"Dog years? That doesn't make any sense," Maya says.

"No, but my dog makes the years go faster," I say in doggy voice to Miu. She bats me with her paw. "Besides, Merrick hasn't dumped me. *Yet.* Say what you will about me, I'm faithful."

"Then I won't even tell you about the rabbi."

"The Lusty Rabbi?"

"What?"

"*What* what? He has a total crush on me! He's a bad boy rabbi, I don't know how you ever settled for Brad with the Lusty Rabbi around."

"I saw you two flirting at the pool," she says.

"I barely looked at him at the pool. He has a nice voice, though. Does he play in a band?"

There's a moment of silence. "You're getting weirder. Anyway, the two of you were totally flirting."

"Me and the rabbi?" I ask.

"You and Brad's brother."

"Oh! Wicked Tad. Yeah, well—"

"Wicked Tad?"

"Yeah, because—"

She covers the mouthpiece, talking to Brad, and I hear them laughing.

"So what about the rabbi?" I ask, because I'm not sure what's so funny.

"He asked for your number."

"Get out! Really? Can you imagine marrying a member of the clergy? It'd be like living something out of Mitford. Except Jewish. Is there a Jewish Mitford?" But she doesn't know what Mitford is, so I explain, "It's like this perfect little churchy community, inspiring stories about the minister and all the good people and wacky scrapes they get in. Like Lake Wobegon for Christians."

"Lake Wobegon is Lake Wobegon for Christians. You read these?"

"Don't sound so surprised. I read."

"Back of the book cover?"

"Yeah. So he asked for my number? Even after the whole…thing?"

"You mean that you un-koshered the whole synagogue kitchen, ruined Shabbos, and his Mom has to wait until Sunday to—I'm not kidding—boil the silverware, scour every surface, and—she was telling everyone after you left—bury the plates and bowls for seven years before they're kosher again?"

How do I say this nicely? "You are a subtle and complex people."

"Yeah, she's whacked."

I hear Brad in the background, and Maya tells me, "Brad says I'm anti-Semitic, but he just likes saying that now."

"I'm sorry about the kitchen," I say. "I didn't know what to get Brad as a gift and I wanted to do something special, but stuffed cabbage looked sort of gross, and I thought—"

"It doesn't matter, Elle. We forgive you. If Brad hadn't wanted a memorable day, he wouldn't have invited you."

I pretend that's a compliment. "You didn't give the Lusty Rabbi my number, did you?"

"Of course not. If he can't be bothered calling information, he doesn't deserve to stalk you. Just, um, watch your step with…Wicked Tad."

"Don't worry, he's out of here by noon."

Three days later, I return home to find Wicked Tad still in his sleeping bag, at two in the afternoon, talking on the phone. He points at the phone and rolls over to face the wall. For privacy. Oh, yeah, he's staying here for a while. I know what it's like, having to beg for a couch to sleep on, and given it was his brother's couch I haven't been able to make myself kick him out. Not that I have a couch, but you know what I mean.

"So she was cheating on him?" he asks into the phone. "After all that? Uh-huh…uh-huh…"

I breeze into to the kitchen, pretending I can't hear him even though I'm dying to know who's cheating on whom, and put away the groceries. The kitchen is open to the living room, so it's not like I can avoid eavesdropping.

"Wait," he says. "The husband's cheating on her with her *mom?*"

Miu boxes the air at my feet, hoping I've remembered to buy her rawhides. I haven't, so I slice her a piece of cheddar. Oh, she's abused all right.

"So it started as a threesome, then the husband and the mom starting meeting separately? Right. No, that's totally uncalled for. Hmm?" He glances over his shoulder toward me. "Yeah, she just came in. Sure, I'll tell her. What? No, if his father wants a piece of the action, he can't—" He pauses, listening. "Yeah, exactly."

I finish putting away the groceries, wondering who on earth he's talking to—he's not even on his cell, but on my phone. Tad finally says goodbye, then tells me, "Your mother says hey."

"That was my mother?"

He nods. "She says hey."

"No she doesn't. My mother never says 'hey.'"

He laughs, like I'm joking, and crawls from his sleeping bag wearing nothing but his purple boxers. He doesn't strip as well as Perfect Brad, a little rangier, like a dissipated rock star. I guess some women would find him sexier, but I like a little paunch. Merrick's got a delicious hint of a beer belly—

at the thought of Merrick, I wonder what I'm doing with a half-naked guy strutting through my living room.

"Did I see grocery bags?" Tad wanders into the kitchen and opens the fridge.

"Let me get this straight. My mom calls, and I'm not here, so you start chatting. But then I come in and you don't hand the phone over to me?"

"She didn't want to talk to you," He says, leaning into the fridge, one arm draped over the door. "We were involved."

"Would you put some clothes on?"

He shuts the refrigerator door and gives me a look that makes me feel extremely uptight and priggish. An old maid at twenty-six.

"Did she say why she called?" I blurt, before he can tell me I'm a prude.

"She was wondering how your new job is going. I told her you weren't actually a wedding coordinator, and she said that's okay, the busboy job is still open."

"She said that?"

"Yeah, there's a restaurant next to her shop, they're—"

"I know! She's been trying to get me that job for a year."

"No luck, huh?" he says sympathetically.

"I don't want that job!" I howl. "I'm a professional counselor and columnist and—and I'm coordinating Maya and Brad's wedding, so I am too a coordinator! Put your clothes on, stop lazing around, clean your room!"

He moons me.

The phone rings, and I dive across the room and snatch it from the cradle before he can. "What?" I say into the phone. "What do you want? Hello? Hello?"

"So," Merrick says. "Are you staying out of trouble?"

"Of course!" I say, brightly. "Do you miss me?"

Merrick laughs. "God, yes!"

Tad, defeated in the rush to the phone, gyrates half-naked, and I grab the broom from behind the fridge and start swatting him into the bathroom. "Bad dog!" I yell. "Go! Go!"

"What is she *doing?*" Merrick asks.

I decide against admitting I'm living with Wicked Tad and his purple boxers. He'll be gone when Merrick returns anyway, and I'll wine, dine and screw him senseless before admitting I was living with another man for a couple of days, as a favor for Maya. "Chewing," I say. "Do you *really* miss me?"

"I really miss you."

"Me, too. I've been spending more time at your place, too." Because Tad's always at mine—and Merrick has better everything, anyway.

"And?"

If I tell him I'll move in, maybe he won't hook up with a girl in New York. That'd be a lie, though, I'm not ready. And I try not to lie to Merrick, unless absolutely necessary. "And it's still standing. I haven't even spilled a glass of water. It's like I'm not even me."

"You better be you. It's you I miss."

I get all weepy and gushy, now that Tad is safely in the bathroom, and we say those embarrassing things couples do. I love those embarrassing things. I sit on the floor in the kitchen next to Miu, as happy as I've been since Merrick left. Yes, I realize this is a bad sign as far as the whole "develop my own identity without reverting to a needy smothering Saran Wrap clingbot" thing goes, but I don't care.

"I have a surprise for you," he says.

"You bought me a present?"

"Kinda. You'll see."

"This better not be another course catalog."

He laughs. "It's not."

"Is this something, when I unwrap it, I'll find a gorgeous little *thing* inside?"

"Not so little," he says. "I think you're gonna like this one. Just as long as you're staying out of trouble."

"We-ell. I did kinda ruin Brad's conversion." I tell the story, and he seems amazed by my ability to turn the most innocuous event into a disaster…but amused, too. "When are you coming home?" I ask. "Have you bought the ticket yet?"

"I'll be back soon," he says. "What are you doing tonight?"

"Meeting Maya and Brad at Shika to listen to them pretend they have any idea how to plan a wedding."

"It's killing you, isn't it?"

"Planning a wedding is one of the few things I'm actually *good* at. It's like if they were designing an outhouse and didn't ask you for advice."

"Because I design outhouses?"

"Outbuildings! I mean outbuildings. You know what I mean. So what's your surprise."

"All in good time."

"Okay, just tell me if it's a blond, Prada-wearing attorney you met at a party where she was playing concert piano, which led to dinners at Balthazar, weekends in Paris and ultimately marriage?"

He laughs. "No."

"Thank God."

"She wears Givenchy," he says.

I tell him how funny I find that, and we have another smoochy five minutes before hanging up. I need a cigarette when we're finished. He's so not dumping me!

★ ★ ★

I dress for a night of ale guzzling, in stretch jeans and a belly-camouflaging black blouse. Consider asking Tad if he wants to come along, but I've seen more than enough of him today. Besides, he really gets on Maya's nerves. Or PB's nerves. Or both.

When I arrive at Shika, Maya's telling Kid how to make a B-52. This is her attempt to increase business, with trendy L.A. club drinks. The place is absolutely empty tonight, even Monty has stayed away. Problem is, it's not the liquor keeping people out of Shika, it's the decor. Red vinyl booths and dingy beige walls, the place would be retro if it weren't just crusty.

I sit at the bar and Maya slides me a martini glass of B-52. "What's in it?" I ask.

"Coffee, Irish crème and orange liqueurs."

I pull a face, and she giggles.

"Sounds like something you'd make." She makes a note in her little book. "I should add a cherry, and call it The Elle."

"What does a cherry have to do with me?"

"A little fruity."

"She's witty," I tell Kid, then ask her, "Is there a Perfect Brad? It would have to be served neat. Perfect all by itself. Where is he, anyway?"

"He stopped home to get his laptop, he wants to show you something online."

I frown at my cocktail, trying to imagine what he could possibly want to show me. Probably the rules of keeping a kosher kitchen.

"Stop staring and drink it," Kid says.

"What's in the Kid?" I ask. "Sarsaparilla?" His mother named him after Billy the Kid. I sip. "It's kind of sweet."

"Like you," Maya says.

I sip again, and there's a warm tingling in my toes. "Whoa. Strong." I knock back a gulp. "Got any cherries?"

"Did you eat today?" Maya asks.

"Not since this morning. I was saving myself for bar snacks."

"Then pace yourself. I don't want you kissing strange men."

"Hey, that hasn't happened in years." I don't want to talk about this, so am doubly pleased when Brad pushes through the front door, laptop case slung over one shoulder. "Brad!"

There's a flurry of greeting and kissing and another B-52 appears before me as if by magic. Maybe Kid doesn't hate me after all. Brad sits beside me and boots up his laptop. "You're gonna like this," he says.

"Have you seen it?" I ask Maya, who shakes her head. "Is it like the Dancing Baby or the Numa Numa Kid?"

"Kinda," Brad says, clicking on a Web site.

The screen is bright and garish, and bannered across the top is: Santa Barbara Grrrrls. Below the text are candid shots of drunk girls falling out of their dresses at local bars à la Paris Hilton and Tara Reid. There are options listed down the side, Drunk Girls, Upskirt Shots, Voyeur Cam and a bunch of others. In one corner of the screen, a mini-video plays a stripteasing woman.

"Your fiancé is showing me porn," I tell Maya. "*Santa Barbara Grrrrls,* with four *R*s."

"Maybe three *R*s was taken," she says, checking the screen.

"The guys at work are big fans of the site," Brad tells us.

"Yeah?" I say, looking at the stripteaser in the corner. "You think they're really girls from Santa Barbara?"

Brad says, "Pretty sure."

Kid says, "Oh, yeah."

And I recognize the Victorian-type bustier the stripteaser is removing. I squint closer at the screen. "Oh, my God."

"Hey," Brad says. "At least you're the *grrrrl* of the day."

chapter

9

"What are you *doing?*" Maya asks, eyeing the screen.

I want to tell Brad to turn it off, but have already developed a sick fascination with my own performance. And I've finally placed the outfit and location. I'm in the dressing room at my favorite boutique downtown, with the parchment-colored walls and skinny mirror. Except as I strip off the suit and start my burlesque routine, I recall it was the suit that took ten pounds off my figure, not the mirror.

"Um…" I say. "Playing Victorian psychiatrist."

Kid says, "Looks like I need therapy."

"What makes you think Victorian psychiatrists give stripteases?" Maya asks.

I emit a sick sort of moan as I watch myself pout at the

mirror, then bend over and press my cleavage together with my arms.

Brad pats me consolingly on the shoulder and I say, "It's not that bad, right? I'm mean at least I'm not naked, right?"

Brad refuses to meet my eyes. "Sure, it could be worse."

I turn back to the screen and see myself pirouette before sticking my butt out at the mirror, and gently prodding for cellulite.

Okay. Breathe deeply. This really *could* be worse. One, I could be totally naked instead of wearing a quasi-dominatrix bustier. Although being entirely naked would look more innocent, actually. Two, this is just some local skeevy Web site, nobody's gonna notice but the few horndog geeks who aren't downloading *real* porn. And three—Big Three—at least, thank God, Merrick's not here to see.

"I'd know that ass anywhere," Merrick says.

I spin on my stool, and there he is, wearing a pale gray button-down and charcoal sports jacket over jeans.

"Surprise," he says.

"What are *you* doing here? You're not due back for days."

"I missed you." Merrick doesn't say this to the real me, but the me pretending to be Nicole Kidman in *Moulin Rouge*. "Who wouldn't rush home for that?"

I slam down the screen on Brad's laptop. "Ha ha! Brad, you joker! Well! Well, well! Look, he fell for it! Oh, Merrick—you're so gullible!"

Everyone stares at me.

"No?" I say.

Maya shakes her head. Brad shakes his head. Kid becomes extremely busy mixing a drink.

"That," Merrick says, "is not staying out of trouble."

I hold my breath. I can't tell from his face which way this is gonna go. I'm pretty sure I hear Maya and Brad holding their breath, too. "Want a sip of my drink?" I ask him. "It's called the Elle."

"No, thanks," he says. "I've drunk enough Elle already."

Maya says she doesn't want to talk about the wedding tonight, and Brad is suddenly hard at work on a programming bug—so when Merrick asks to see the *Santa Barbara Grrrrls* Web site again, PB says he can't stop. Then he tells Maya to order pizza, they'll have dinner here. This is why he's so perfect.

So Merrick and I are left on our own, and are soon walking up State Street trying to decide on a restaurant. Merrick insists on making his surprise complete by taking me some place romantic. We decide on the restaurant at the new hotel on Carrillo Street. The space used to be a residential inn for the elderly, then for years a great gaping hole in the sidewalk, but now the swanky hotel has finally been built and the restaurant is elegant with Spanish tile floors and dark wood and rattan chairs.

We order the crab cakes and I pretend I'm not underdressed in blue jeans and Pumas. The waiter has never heard of The Elle—sadly out of touch with the latest and greatest—but promises I'll like the Bellini. Merrick orders a Manhattan.

"Okay," I say. "I know we've been together four months, but I still can't tell whether ordering a Manhattan means you're sending a message or enjoying a drink."

Merrick tilts his head. "What kind of message would I be sending?"

"Either you're reminding me how I cocked up your drink order, the first time we met, and have continued cocking things up on daily basis since then…"

He tilts his head the other direction.

"Or you're saying you're sorry you came home early and wish you were back in Manhattan."

"I'm glad I didn't get a Long Island Iced Tea."

"Merrick—"

"Or Jell-O shots."

I don't even want to know if that's a comment about my ass. Our drinks come and he sips his Manhattan, obnoxiously pleased with himself. "Look, I can explain—" I start.

He holds up his drink to stop me. "Let's talk like real people, first."

"Pretend to be like the humans, you mean?"

He nods.

"Okay." I sip my drink. "So, um, how was your trip? You didn't get blacklisted by the co-op board?"

"Turned out pretty well, actually. I think we're all set, but they're a little—"

"Anticommunist?"

"—mercurial. The board has strong opinions, which come and go like the wind." He jingles the ice in his drink. "You never know where you stand with them."

Now *that* is definitely a message—probably—but I'd rather talk about the co-op design, so I ask a few questions and he tells me about the job. Then I order another drink and ask about everyone he met, in a subtle and offhanded fashion, mentally separating them into male and female, and attractive-sounding and otherwise.

He tells me about them, then says, "And I didn't kiss any of them."

"Of course you didn't!" I feel myself unclench. "Don't be silly."

"Did you really apply to school?"

I'm so pleased he's here instead of off on his honeymoon with another woman, I forget and say, "Yeah, two of them."

"Two? Laverna and…?"

"Another one, just a school. I found a flier at a—" The New Age store "—bookstore. Plus, I met the Gay Tailors and the eBay man. I haven't had my housewarming party yet, because Neil is totally the worst drug dealer in the world."

"He's not a drug dealer, he only buys pot twice a year or something."

"Well, he has terrible customer service." I gesture for the waiter to bring me a third Bellini. I'm gonna make a film comment to show how worldly I am, but remember in nick of time that the director's name is Fellini. And I haven't seen any of his films. "Don't you want to hear about the Gay Tailors?"

"And the eBay man," he says.

So I tell him everything, which is wonderfully liberating. Sure, I'm keeping the whole weird grad school thing quiet, but other than that he knows all my dirty secrets and loves me anyway. By the time we order dessert, it's like he never left. We're the shiny happy couple I always hate, finishing each other's sentences, laughing and teasing, hardly able to keep our hands off each other. God it's nice to be that couple for once.

Then Merrick asks, "So how much did they pay you?"

Does he mean my clients? "Hundred bucks an hour, like I always get."

"You mean you charge the same as for pretending—for being an intuitive counselor?"

"Huh? Well, Valentine gives me a hundred-twenty—you know this."

"No, I mean your *other* job."

I get this sick feeling, like he's found out a terrible secret. Then I realize I don't have a terrible secret. "As a wedding coordinator? I'm doing that for free—except I'm not, because Maya thinks *she* can handle everything, which she can't, but—"

"For the Web site."

"The Web site?"

"I know you're not making a lot of money, Elle, and if this is really what you want to do, that's fine. But you don't have to pose for exploitative Web sites to make ends meet—I'm happy to loan you some money."

I stare in amazement.

"Or not a loan," he backtracks. "A grant."

"Merrick, I didn't pose for any Web site."

"Honey, I saw the video. Not the whole thing, but enough to recognize the tasty parts."

"Are you saying I have a huge ass that jiggles like Jell-O?"

"I'm saying you have a lovely ass that I'd prefer to keep for private consumption."

Lovely is good. Not as good as *skinny,* but good.

"So, how much do you need?" he asks.

I resist the lure of free money. "They didn't pay me, that's what I'm telling you."

"You did it for free? Now I'm confused." There's a glint in his eye. "And, I admit, slightly turned on."

I flush and fumble with my dessert spoon, but this has gone far enough. "It was a hidden camera."

"What?" He is outraged.

"Yeah." Now I think about it, I'm a little ticked-off myself. "Yeah, what the hell? I was trying on clothes in that boutique I like, you know, Element, and that's it. That's all. I didn't get a cent. That really pisses me off."

"A hidden camera? That has to be illegal."

"I got nothing! What do you think the regular rate is? I've been exposed to every deviant male with a computer and cable connection—which is basically every last one of you—" I shudder. "That libertarian who works with Brad has seen me prance around in my undies. Libertarians have seen me naked, Merrick! And what do I get?"

He starts to answer.

"A boyfriend who thinks I'm working for *Santa Barbara Grrrrls!*" I interrupt. "Please, if I'm selling naked pictures of myself, I'd pick a site classier than that. At least one that used a few less *R*s."

"What about the eye?"

"What eye? A private eye?" I used to work for a private eye. "Spenser? Get him on the case?"

"The *I* in *girrrrls*. It's missing an *I*."

"What are you talking about, the *I*? Who cares about the *I*? You're drunk. Who do I call? The FBI? The National Guard? The CIA? This is international—deviant Pakistani geeks are looking at my butt."

"So you didn't—"

I feel myself pale. "Omigod."

"What?"

"What if they put me in the big-bottom section? Is there a big-bottom section?"

Merrick talks me down and says, "I still don't understand how they got your picture. You think the boutique was involved?"

I am appalled. "Not *my* boutique."

"Elle, just because they sell Calvin Klein doesn't mean they're not guilty."

"Marni, not Calvin. And it does, too."

"We're going over there to straighten this out." He pulls out his cellphone. "I'll phone to see if they're open."

"They're open," I say.

"How do you know?"

"It's Thursday night. They're open until nine."

"Well, but maybe the manager isn't there."

"She's there."

"How do you know?"

"I just do."

"What about Saks? Are they open?"

"No."

"That shoe place you like?"

"No."

"Banana Republic?"

"Yes."

"Will the manager be there?"

"Why do you want to talk to the manager of Banana Republic?"

"I don't. I'm just curious how much you know."

"The assistant manager's there. Carrie."

"You know her name?"

"It's a gift."

"Or a curse," he says. "Imagine if you used your powers for good."

"I do! Shopping. Commerce. The free market. Consumer confidence is *up!*"

Merrick laughs as he signs the check. "What did I do without you?"

"You were a very sad man," I remind him. "With bright red hair."

★ ★ ★

I stand and the restaurant blurs around me, then the doorway blurs around me, then State Street blurs around me. A few too many Elles and Bellinis. Merrick's arm, also around me, does not blur. Santa Barbara in the evening, with a happy little buzz: there is nothing better. We window-shop toward the mall, contentedly arguing over whether or not Element, my boutique, is involved with the Web site.

"They're going to be just as surprised as you were," I say.

He looks at me. "You weren't surprised?"

"I was. But, well...*me.*" This kind of thing happens to me. "You know."

"True."

"At least this wasn't my fault. That's sort of liberating, when you think about it. I should concentrate more on all the really humiliating things in the world that *aren't* my fault."

"There must be dozens," Merrick says.

I almost agree before realizing he's teasing.

We arrive at the store, Merrick looks at the front window—which holds an extremely innocent white blouse and light blue pencil skirt—and says, "Ah, the culprits."

"I'm telling you, Element has nothing to do with this." I put a restraining hand on his arm, although I'm secretly delighted by this display of protective manliness. "Just don't piss them off."

"Why?" he asks. "You're afraid they're going to ban you from the store?"

"Don't be ridiculous. It's just that nobody who appreciates cashmere like they do could possibly be in league with zit-faced post-adolescent video voyeurs."

"Shopping here is more important than finding out why there's a video of you stripping on the Internet?"

"Well…"

I eye the blouse and skirt in the window. Looks like Narciso Rodriguez, plus they have a much better selection of Juicy than Saks, but before I can explain, Merrick drags me inside to speak to the manager. Her name is Wren, but there is nothing bird-like about her heavily pregnant frame. She's round and sweet and appalled that I've been filmed almost-naked in her dressing room. "That's horrible!" she says.

Does she mean this from a marketing standpoint? What if her other customers realize that she caters to bloated cavorting manatees?

"I mean, not that you aren't lovely," she quickly adds. "Anyone would want to see you naked. But how could this have happened? Are you sure? It couldn't be some other dressing room?"

I point at the aubergine bustier and black wool suit. *J'accuse!*

Merrick raises an eyebrow at the lingerie. "Which dressing room?" he asks.

"The middle one."

"You sure?"

"Positive. I was the only one here—I like being in the middle."

"But this is impossible," the manager says, worrying at a sales slip. "We'd never allow such a thing…I mean, aside from being illegal and totally reprehensible, what possible reason—"

Merrick stalks to the dressing room, pulls back the heavy scarlet velvet curtain and scans the mirror and walls.

"—could we have for doing such a thing? We built this

business on customer satisfaction." She appeals to me. "*You* know. Our return policy? Our—"

"There!" Merrick points to a little plastic square screwed behind the dressing room curtain.

"What's that?" I ask.

"A camera mount."

"Oh, my God," Wren says. "What's that doing there?"

"You tell us," Merrick says.

"Oh. Oh, no. I don't—" She fans her face, and I'm suddenly afraid she's going to faint. Or worse, go into labor. "I never saw that before, I…"

"You'd better sit." I take her elbow. "Do you want some water?"

She lets me escort her to the chair behind the desk, murmuring apologies, and I have the sense that Merrick is glowering behind me for being such a softie. But honestly, she's like eight months pregnant. And this is a *great* store.

"I'll call mall security," she said faintly. "I can't tell you how sorry I am. It's on the Internet?"

"*Santa Barbara Grrrrls,*" I say. "Four *R*s, no *I*." Like I want her to check out the site, because she thinks I look lovely naked. "Not that, I mean—so you know where *not* to click."

She calls mall security and we wait around awkwardly. Well, no reason to just waste time, so I do a little browsing. My big butt would look even lovelier in Narciso Rodriguez. Still want that drapey suit, too. All the silence is kinda oppressive, so I ask the manager when she's due, and the color returns to her face and we start chatting, as Merrick glowers darkly toward the dressing rooms. He's checked all of them, but only that one had a camera mount…and he even found traces of sawdust caught in the curtain hem, like Sherlock Holmes. Wren says she had those cleaned just two months ago, so we've actually narrowed down the time frame. I was going to offer my psychic skills to solve the case, but another suit catches my eye, so in the interests of fair-mindedness, I have to try it on. Not that I need a suit, strictly speaking, I just believe in being prepared.

A bulky middle-aged man in a snappy uniform finally shows up, looking like he's ready to arrest me and Merrick. Wren explains the situation, and we spend fifteen minutes explaining to him that I, a customer, was caught in here, the store, wearing that, the bustier, in digital splendor, in the camera, which was broadcast on the Internet.

"Four *R*s?" he says, with slightly too much interest.

"The Web site doesn't matter," Merrick interjects. "Are you going to handle this, or should I call the *real* police?"

"Well, in a case like this the jurisdiction isn't what—"

"Don't be an idiot," Merrick snaps. "Jurisdiction. I'm calling the police."

"We don't need police," the security guard says. "Why'd we need police?"

"I don't know," Merrick says. "Because a crime has been committed?"

I am so getting banned.

"No crime," the security guard says. "Voyeur laws ain't much. Remember that guy taking pictures through the blinds? Nothin' to charge him with—not even trespassing, he stayed on the sidewalk."

"All right, thank-you," Wren tells the security guard, pretty imperially for a tiny, round person. He leaves, and her voice turns pleading, "Please, don't call the police. This is *so* bad for business, and I'll do anything I can to help. If they report this in the newspaper, the publicity will kill us."

"This is an invasion of privacy," Merrick says. "Even if there's no crime we should report this."

"I know! I know. I'll check every day for cameras." She turns to me. "And I'll make it up to you... Please, accept a gift on our behalf. Anything in the store."

"Anything?"

"Anything," she says.

I can see Merrick's mouth moving, but his words are lost in a shop-drunk fog.

chapter

10

"I can't believe you did that," Merrick says, in the car on the way home.

He's been silent up until now, while I've been antsy in my seat, crinkling the bag holding my new black wool suit with drapey pants and pretending I couldn't feel the waves of *mean* emanating from the driver's seat.

"Elle, this is serious. You have a responsibility—"

"The bad press would *kill* them, Merrick. And she's pregnant, how's she supposed to support her baby without a job? Don't I have a responsibility for her, too?"

"What you—"

"And they have such gorgeous, perfect things. Did you see the lapis necklace she was wearing? I should've asked her for that. Even pregnant she's hip."

"She could be part of this. She and that security guard, too."

"I don't think so," I say.

"If not them, then who?"

"If not today, then when?"

He stops at the light. "What?"

"Nothing. Reminded me of an old Tracy Chapman song."

Merrick makes a disgusted noise as he turns right, and I realize he's taking me home. To my home. Not to his. That can't be a good sign. I expect him to drop me on the curb and speed away, but he pulls into the lot and follows me inside. "I just can't believe she bought you off with a pair of pants," he says, as we head upstairs to my apartment.

"It's not just a pair of pants," I tell him.

"Well, now you can't sue. Elle, you've got a civic responsibility to make sure this doesn't happen again. Instead, you got pants."

"I got more than pants. Think of them as a settlement."

"A settlement?"

I tell him what they cost.

"Really?" He seems reconsider. "Wow. That's more than you would've gotten for actually posing."

"Yeah—plus I got the excuse to spend it on clothes instead of rent and food!"

"And school."

"Right. School."

At the top of the stairs, Merrick leans against the railing. "But don't you feel…exposed?"

I take his hand. "Of course—this is a total violation of my privacy. It's disgusting and…and appalling. But getting frantic about it isn't helping. I need to sit down and decide what to do, not be accused of reacting the wrong way, or having my boyfriend alienate the manager of my favorite store. You really think I have a civic duty?"

"Yeah, but your first duty is to yourself. You're right, you need to figure this out. I know you can take care of yourself. It's just you're so…"

"Incredible?"

"Outrageous. On the outside, so I sometimes forget how strong you are inside."

To prove my strength, I melt into his arms, and he kisses me. And kisses me, and kisses me. Then swoops me off my feet into his arms. I squeal and open the door, and not until Merrick carries me over the threshold do I remember—

"Hey, babe," Wicked Tad calls from across the apartment. "I saw you on the Internet."

Hard to describe Merrick's reaction.

"It's not what you think," I say.

"What could I possibly be thinking?"

"This is Brad's brother. He needed a place to crash for the night."

"*Brad's* brother? You mean your best friend's boyfriend, who you have a crush on?"

"I don't have a crush on him!" I turn to Tad. "I don't." Back to Merrick, "He's crashing on the sofa, that's all."

"You don't have a sofa," Merrick says, ignoring Miu who's frantically vying for his attention. "You barely have a chair."

"No, but…" I point to Tad's pile of stuff, including his laptop flipped open on his sleeping bag, the screen set to *Santa Barbara Grrrrls.* "That's his corner."

Wicked Tad slips from his sleeping bag, clad in a Bob Marley T-shirt and boxers. "Hey, man—I just needed a roof over my head. Brad and Maya, you know, after the conversion, they wanted some honey time."

"Honey time?" Merrick says, looking Tad in the eye. He's a man talking to a boy—Tad looks away, exactly like a surly teen. Merrick finally pats Miu then heads into my bedroom.

I tag along behind Merrick and close the door. "You know I stayed on Brad and Maya's couch. I couldn't turn Tad away."

"His name is Tad?"

"Wicked Tad," I say.

He doesn't smile, but I think he wants to. "Why is he in his boxers?"

"I don't know. He does that. Kids these days. They didn't grow up with bra commercials where the models wore blue leotards under their crisscross Playtex."

Merrick shakes his head. "Okay. What's he doing here?"

"He just graduated from college, he's looking for a job. Actually, I'm starting to think he dropped out. He's been talking to my mom—"

"How long is he staying?"

I make a face. "I don't know. I wish he'd go, but I can't kick him out. Anyway, he's out there, and we're in here…"

"No way am I staying, Elle."

"Why not? At dinner you were all hot for exhibitionism."

"Not in front of people!"

I laugh. "That's the whole point."

"What, and give Wicked Tad more ammunition?"

"Ammunition?" I think of Wicked Tad and his boxer shorts, lying in his sleeping bag, surfing *Santa Barbara Grrrls*. "You don't think he was…"

"Definitely."

"Oh, God. To *my* picture?"

"I wouldn't blame him."

I shudder. "Sometimes I think I imagine how oversexed men are."

"Take your wildest imaginations and multiply by five."

"Really? Because in my imagination—"

"Where's your suitcase? Until he goes, you're staying with me."

And abandon my home to a serial masturbator? Hmm, better than sharing with one. "Until he goes," I say.

Merrick's been gone almost two weeks, so we have a hard time getting past the doorway of his house, what with all the groping and nibbling and unsnapping. Miu heaves a disgusted sigh and trots past to her place on Merrick's sofa, and Merrick and I tumble and spin and float toward the stairs, shedding clothing, making soft noises in our throats.

We're breathless and half-naked when we arrive at his bedroom door, and I push him away. He pulls me close. I push him away. He pulls me close. I push him away and put my shopping bag between us.

He looks befuddled at the sudden reappearance of the bag. "Come here," he says.

"Only be a minute," I chirp, and slip into the bathroom.

Merrick grumbles something in a lust-fogged voice, but exactly sixty seconds later, more or less, when I reappear in his bedroom, the expression on his face is worth it. I didn't just get the pants suit. I got the Victorian bustier.

"I'm really only staying tonight," I say, a little after midnight, snuggling in Merrick's arms.

"Good," he says.

There's a long pause as I try to figure what that means. Then I say, "What do you mean, 'good'?"

"Maybe you're right. I'm not sure we should move in together after all."

"What do you mean, 'not sure we should move in together, after all'?"

"Um…" he says. "I'm uncertain if we should cohabit?"

I roll out of his arms to look at him. "You can't tell me I can't move in when I already don't want to move in."

"What?"

"You can't tell me I can't move in when I already don't want to."

"I'm not saying you can't."

"You're saying you're not sure."

"Well, if you don't feel ready…"

"Oh, I'm ready. I was born ready. You bet your bottom dollar I'm ready. You can take that to the bank. I'm as ready as…as…oh, I'm ready all right."

"Good."

"Ha!" I say. Tell me I'm not ready, I'll say if I'm ready or not.

Merrick turns out the light and spoons me.

The window is open a crack and the fresh salt air is cool on my face, the ocean waves a distant rumble. I hear Miu's nails clicking downstairs as she wanders to her bowl, then the loud untidy splashing of a boxer at the watering hole. There are patterns on the far wall from the moonlight, and Merrick's breathing slows and evens.

"What if I'm not ready," I say.

"You were born ready," he says through the fog of near-sleep.

I get out of bed and cross my arms to stay warm. "I don't want to become dependent."

"Come back to bed."

"No. Because if I come back to bed, then I'll want to stay tonight, and tomorrow night, and forever—"

"Good."

"—until you resent me for having no career or ambition or common sense."

A soft sigh from Merrick. "What makes you think that's going to happen?"

"Because that's what happened before." I make a pattern in the carpet with my big toe. "With the old Louis."

"Things are different now."

"Because you're not the old Louis?"

"Because you're not the old Elle."

I look up from my toe. "Really?"

"Well, you're still…"

"Outrageous?"

"Eccentric. But you've changed. You've matured."

It's true I don't live in a trolley anymore, and I have a steady boyfriend and a steady dog and an unsteady income. I don't even get so many calls from Carlos, my credit counselor. That's progress, right?

"You won't be dependent on me if you move in," he says. "You've got your own goals. Grad school, your political column."

"I'm still on the first sentence."

"But it's a goal." Merrick scratches Miu's head, which she's placed on the bed next to his hand. "Besides, Miu loves it here."

"But how am I gonna make best friends with the Gay Tailors when I'm living here?"

"Um, why do you think you'll be best friends, again?"

"Don't you *read,* Merrick? A single girl—sorta—living a fast-lane life in the city—sorta—needs a gay best friend. It's in all the books."

"So what exactly is the motivation for friendship?"

"They're like girlfriends who can move furniture for you. Or like man friends who don't try to get in your pants. And can move furniture for you."

"I mean for them."

"Oh! Oh, well. Gay men, um…" I draw a blank. "Well, for gay men, you know, a single straight woman friend is, um… Have you never even *heard* of *Will & Grace?*"

"And *Tales of the City*—I know, I know."

"We'll talk about fashion and culture and…stuff."

"Don't they have gay friends for that?"

"Okay," I say. "Fine. I'll stay until Tad's gone."

"That's not moving in, that's just staying until Tad's gone."

"We'll pretend it's permanent. We'll get most of my things this weekend. You know there's not much."

"What if he gets a job and moves out tomorrow?"

"Believe me, he's not getting a job. He'll stay as long as I'm paying rent." Which sort of makes me feel better. For once, I'm supporting someone else.

I lie in bed—my new bed—the next morning, long after Merrick has gone to work. He'd tried to convince me to go with him, so I could pick up my car, but I persuaded him to come home—my new home—for lunch instead, and then we'd go back together. In the meantime I wallow in luxury. The sheets—my new sheets—are Calvin Klein-ish, though I doubt Merrick would spend that much on sheets, in a sage-green, with an organic white comforter. Sometimes I fear Merrick has better taste than I do. This would mean that, despite the evidence of last night, he's gay.

Is it homophobic to think that? I'd call the Gay Tailors to ask, but they hate me. I'd like to think they're heterophobes, but they like Neil, and nobody's straighter than that—he walks around in a tool belt and L.L. Bean jeans, and I've actually seen him wearing a construction helmet, and not in a Village People kinda way.

I check the clock—my new clock. Okay, I'll stop with the "my new" thing, but I wonder what the rules are. If you move in with someone, how much of the stuff is yours? With marriage, you get fifty percent so I figure I've got a strong minority stake in the bed and coffeemaker and the showerhead. I wish Merrick had left my thirty percent of the laptop home, so I could determine precisely how fat my ass really looked in the bustier, but he took a hundred percent of it to work. No doubt he's checking for me.

I promised to have lunch ready at noon, and haven't even showered yet. Decide hair can go a day without washing, so leave in braids and quickly rinse grime from body. Feel extra dirty, having been subjected to Internet smut—even though I was the smut—so I soap up twice. I'm downstairs in no less than thirty-two minutes, leaving me exactly twenty-four to fix Merrick something scrumptious.

Corn tortillas, a few tomatoes and some cheddar so I decide to make quesadillas and fresh salsa, despite uncomfortable similarity to buñuelos. As I wait for the tortillas to brown, I notice this week's *Permanent Press* on the counter—Merrick must've picked it up at the airport. He reads my column every week. But the cover is unexpected: the Wedding Issue. Wonderful. Now Maya will have all sorts of her own ideas about her wedding.

Miu trots into the kitchen, a long string of drool trailing from one of her jowls, because she smells the cheese. I flip the quesadillas and slice more cheddar for the next batch. I toss Miu a piece and rifle through the paper looking for my column on the pet psychic.

I pause to evaluate a few photos of wedding dresses, and finally stumble onto my column next to an ad for Café Lustre, the strip club I never worked at. Jenna, a dancer there who dared me to apply, is defying gravity as well as ever and now headlining her own show. I'm her hero for getting the old bouncer arrested, especially because she's dating the new bouncer, a soft-spoken Jamaican the size of a brick house. Or I guess this is Santa Barbara, so he's the size of a terracotta bungalow.

I scan my article, pleased at the tone: I appear to be boosting Crystal Smith while undercutting her. A pity she's a fraud, as I'd really like to know about Miu's previous owners—my *Punisher* fantasies again. But I guess the truth is, I've never been good at revenge.

Though this never stops me from trying.

The Vile Voyeurs invaded my privacy, and they're gonna pay. I told Merrick I wanted to approach the *Santa Barbara Grrrrls* thing after some serious consideration, and I've seriously considered: I want revenge.

I grab a pen from the drawer where Merrick keeps them organized by color and start a new list:

1. Find out who owns *Santa Barbara Grrrrls.*
2.
3.
4.
5. Make them pay.

chapter

11

Start on my revenge scheme early the next day.

"Yotam," I say, when Brad opens the door to their apartment. That's his new Hebrew name, sort of like Madonna and Esther. Pretty cool and gangsta: *Yo, Tom.*

"Hey, Elle." He's wet-haired and clean shaven, wearing his usual outfit of loose jeans and T-shirt. Remarkably un-geeky for a geek. "What's up?"

"I brought some peace pastry," I say, holding up a pink box. "From the bakery in Goleta. Land of the big boxes and tract houses."

"It's the good land," PB says.

"Why?" I ask. "What's so good about it?"

He shrugs.

"Yeah," I say. "No one ever has an answer."

I follow him into the kitchen and set about making coffee while he unties the string on the pastry box and helps himself to a cruller. "Why peace pastry?" he asks.

"Because of the whole kosher catastrophe."

"What?"

"Y'know, ruining the food at your conversion."

"That? That was nothing. With you and my brother in the same room, I figure we got off easy. You sick of him yet?"

"I'm staying at Merrick's."

"Kiss your security deposit goodbye."

"Oh, he's not that bad." I take a doughnut. "Um, there's something I wanted to ask you about the Internet."

"I have work today. Can't you get Merrick to show you how it works?"

"I know how the Internet works, Brad!"

He grins.

"I just don't know…well, *how* it works."

"Elle—"

"I need to find out who's responsible for *Santa Barbara Grrrrls.*"

"Oh, is that all? Gimme a second to run a WHOIS search."

We go into the living room where Brad keeps his computer. He clacks at the keyboard then says, "Hmm."

"What do you mean *Hmm?*"

"The domain name is registered to Pom Teeping, at 69 Naked Way."

"Naked Way?"

"Yeah, 93102 zip code. Right downtown."

"I've never heard of Naked Way," I say.

"That's because there is no—"

"I know there's no Naked Way—"

"Here, wait…" He clicketys.

I grab a pen to write down the name on what I realize is this week's *Permanent Press*—the one with the woman in the wedding dress on the cover.

"No," Brad says. "Sorry, I've got nothing."

"That's okay," I say, wandering back into the kitchen with the paper. Upon closer inspection I discover it has been leafed through repeatedly. Many corners are dog-eared. There is nothing subtle about my look of horror as Maya bounces in, fresh and perky and gorgeous as usual in a pink T-shirt and jeans.

She laughs at me. "There are some great ideas in there." Her eyes hit the pastry box and she helps herself to a chocolate-frosted. "Everything you need to know about having a wedding."

"Okay," I begin, and don't know how to proceed.

"Dresses and cakes and photographers, it's all there."

"Listen," I try, and then stop.

"Menus," she says. "Invitations…"

"Mail-order bride!" I blurt.

"What?"

"Would you order a bride—a groom—from a catalog? Would you buy a house without doing a walk-through? No. But you think you can order a wedding like it's from a fast-food menu—'I'd like the chunky meal number three, please. Extra sauce.' You can't design a wedding out of a stupid free newspaper. You can't just choose one from the list of photographers and one from the list of stationery stores. You have to talk with them, you have to investigate, you have to compare. You know what a nightmare a bad photographer can be? And you saw *Seinfeld*—George's fiancée *died* from bad invites. This is life or death stuff, this is the rest of your lives together. Perfect Maya and Perfect Brad, you need the Perfect Wedding. Anything less would be a catastrophe, a tragedy—a god-awful shame."

I pause for breath, and Brad and Maya look at each other.

"Okay," Brad says. "I'm late for work. Sorry I couldn't help with the porn thing, Elle."

After he goes Maya shoots me a worried look. I guess because of my wedding rant. "But the only thing that matters," I say, "is that you and Brad are happy. I know you're missing your mom, and you two woulda done this together, and I'm sorry I tried to force my wedding plans on you. I still say this is an incredibly important day in your life, but it's *your* life. I can't stand in for your mother, but I *can* be the sister you never had. And I can even be the supportive caring one, instead of the pushy narcissistic one. That's your other sister. She's gone now and I hope she took her big ass with her. But this sister helps with *your* wedding, even if it involves music by Sting."

Maya smiles and we hug and I say, "Let's go wedding dress shopping."

"Yes!"

"Can you take the day off? I was thinking Beverly Hills for Saks and Les Habitudes. Then we can hit Melrose for—"

"I was thinking Petticoat Junction," Maya says.

Is she kidding? Can't tell. "Oh! Where you got your prom dress!"

"It's a bridal boutique, now."

"Uh-huh." This is only a reconnaissance mission, there's still plenty of time to drag her to Beverly Hills. "I bet they have something—" I swallow "—great."

So Petticoat Junction. When Maya bought her dress for our high school prom, the store was located half a mile farther down State Street in the bar district. Cocktail and prom dresses graced the upstairs, while the downstairs—in what had obviously been a storage basement—were the naughty bits. Lace teddies, pasties and thongs that Maya and I once giggled at but now wear every day, as part of the creeping pornification of America.

Today Petticoat Junction is Santa Barbara's premiere wedding dress destination, despite the name. Sadly, no pasties, just miles and miles of white, in silk, lace and linen. Maya and I arrive at the overly air-conditioned store just as they're opening their doors.

"It's freezing in here," I say.

"Maybe they have to keep the dresses refrigerated," Maya says.

"What? That makes no sense."

She's about to explain but is interrupted by a saleswoman. We don't have an appointment, but because we're early on a weekday, she agrees to fit Maya. She's a champagne-haired woman in her early fifties on a tight schedule. She gives us exactly twenty-two minutes to scan the racks and come up with Maya's five favorites.

Maya heads for the circular rack marked Sale.

"No," I cry. "It's your *wedding*."

"Exactly." She flips through dresses. "That's why I'm starting here. I love a sale."

I glance to the champagne-haired woman for help. She grimaces at me, but smiles when Maya turns her way. "Some of those are very nice—and such good deals."

I roll my eyes—but even my rolling eyes can spot quality from fifteen feet away. I head for the rack against the far wall. "How about this one?" I pull out an ivory Givenchy sheath with an empire waist, the bodice embroidered with tiny clear beads and a strap crossing one shoulder and ending in a beaded knot. "Very Nicole Kidman."

Maya crinkles her nose. "Too contemporary."

"Nicole is classic. Timeless."

"Which sister…?" she asks.

"The good one," I groan, and replace the sheath. This isn't as fun as wedding dress shopping is supposed to be. For one thing, it's not me trying on the dresses. For another, it's Maya. She takes less than her allotted twenty-two minutes to pick her five faves. Well, four from the sale rack and my one pick, a $3,500 Vera Wang she agrees to try on to humor me.

The saleswoman escorts us to the dressing room, where before allowing Maya to undress, I conduct a thorough inspection, running my fingertips across every surface, feeling for inconsistencies, a concealed camera or recording device. The door is shuttered, I check each slat, then drop to the floor to probe the carpet.

"The saleswoman's gonna think you're a freak," she says.

I don't say, "*I'm* not the one with four sale-rack wedding dresses." Instead, I say, "Better she think I'm a freak than you get caught on *Santa Barbara Brrrrdes.*"

"Santa Barbara Birds?"

"Brides. Four Rs, no I."

She looks at me, then calls over my head—because I haven't finished with the floor—to the saleswoman, "We're ready."

As Maya tries on the first gown, I plop down on the stool in the corner and surreptitiously feel under the seat for a camera.

"Stop it!" Maya says, having poked her head through the top of the dress.

I cross my hands in my lap and look interested in her first

selection, a cream satin slip dress with spaghetti straps and a diagonal bodice. Does the good sister tell the truth or offer encouraging lies? I try the truth—"Too simple."

Maya sticks her tongue out at herself in the mirror. "Yeah. I always like this style on other women, but on me it's a nightgown."

She wriggles out of the dress and hands it to me to re-hang (normally, I'd balk, but it gives me an opportunity to bug-check the hangers). She steps into the next cream puff of a dress, one of those floofy cotton candy dresses you see in bridal magazines and wonder who'd ever wear that to her wedding.

I look at Maya. Maya looks at me. "Next."

Next is not what I would have picked. Partly, because it's by Jessica McClintock who immortalized Gunny Sax dresses in the seventies—the preferred style of Laura Ingalls and sister on *Little House on the Prairie*—and partly because it's two pieces. That's not exactly a dress, there's a reason nobody talks about buying a wedding skirt. The top is tank-style and buttons down the front with large triangular rhinestones, and the skirt is a variation on an eighteenth-century court dress, yards of dupioni silk gathered into several poofy tiers that cascade down from the waist.

Maya glances at me.

"I wouldn't have picked rhinestones…"

"But…"

"But that," I say, "is adorable."

She giggles and spins. "Fits perfectly, too!"

"What size is it?" I ask, and immediately bite my tongue. I don't want to know how tiny Maya is.

"A six," the saleswoman says.

A fucking six!?

"Guess how much it is," Maya says, smugly. And not even about her dress size. She takes the six for granted. They oughtta revoke her six. If I were a six, I'd show some respect, I'd kneel on my skinny knees and put my slender elegant hands together and thank the good Lord every night for the sheer lack of me.

"Elle?" she says.

"What? Oh! Sales rack…three hundred fifty?"

"Ninety-nine."

"What?"

"Marked down from $279."

I try to muster some enthusiasm. "Wow."

The saleswoman holds up the fourth gown, trying to hurry Maya along.

"I picked that?" Maya asks.

She nods. "But I can tell you right now you're not going to like it."

"Then let's not bother. Especially when I love this one." She twirls again, watching herself in the mirror.

"At least try the Vera Wang," I say.

"Why?"

"Because you'll look gorgeous. And because *everyone* should wear Vera Wang for their wedding. Everyone."

She shrugs cheerfully. "If you insist."

The saleswoman reverently removes the dress from the hanger. The gown is white and strapless with lace on the bodice, and a full skirt. A matching wide grosgrain ribbon ties around the waist. Simple, elegant, stunning—amazing.

Oh, I'm good. "You look like Renée Zellweger," I say.

"Only because everything she wears is strapless."

"It works for her. Remember what she wore *before* she hooked up with Carolina Herrera?"

"Not so good," saleswoman says.

"You know who designs Renée Zellweger's dresses?" Maya asks.

I'm stunned. Honestly flabbergasted. I don't even know what to say. Does she not know the President's name? Is she one of those people, you interview them on the street and they think England is the capital of Europe?

Maya examines herself in the mirror, then turns to me. "You're going to hate me."

"No, I won't," I say. "I'm sure I'll get my chance to wear Vera Wang, too."

"But I like the other one better."

I shake my head with a warm, indulgent smile. "That's not possible."

"I do, though."

"You're just saying that because of the price."

Maya lifts one shoulder, looks back in the mirror, bites her lip. "It's beautiful." She lifts the skirts in an I'm-late-for-the-wedding-and-better-run-to-the-altar fashion. A look you can't pull off any other time in your life. "But this isn't the kind of wedding I'm having." She drops the skirts. "This is city wedding, churchy wedding. I'm having neither of those things." She squints at me. "You know what I mean?"

Unfortunately, I know exactly what she means. "But you're not getting married at the all-for-a-dollar store either."

Maya laughs. "Let me try the other one again."

She does, and says, "This is the one. I'm getting this."

"A ninety-nine dollar dress? You're going to wear a ninety-nine dollar dress to your wedding? Your prom dress cost more."

"Which was a waste. I only wore it once."

I turn to the saleswoman. "Can we have a moment?"

She checks her watch. "I've got an appointment anyway." She carefully re-hangs the Vera Wang and places it under protective plastic. "Let me know what you decide."

I close the door behind her. "Okay, let's think about this rationally. You deserve better than a ninety-nine dollar dress for your wedding."

"It's not the price," Maya says. "Well, maybe a little. The Vera Wang is gorgeous, but I'm not spending $3,000 on dress. We can't afford that."

"That's only like a dollar a day for a year!"

"For ten years."

"A dollar a day! That's not even half a latté."

She gets a mulish light in her eyes. "It's just a dress."

Forgive her, Vera, she knows not what she says. But like any good general, I know when to retreat…to marshal my forces for the counterattack. "You're right. That's expensive, that's crazy. I'm sorry, You know how I get. But that doesn't mean you have to buy this one, either. We can keep looking. You've only tried four dresses. Everyone tries more than four dresses. I tried fifty-three."

Maya raises an eyebrow.

"I know, that's me. Still, there's gotta be a happy medium between four and fifty-three."

"What did you end up with?"

"I'm not saying you *have* to get a Vera Wang." Though anyone who doesn't is insane. "Because it's not my wedding, it's your wedding. And if you don't want to invite Vera, you don't have to. But be sure you get what's right for you. We don't even have a venue yet, or a menu or a theme."

"Well…"

"As a favor for me," I say. "This whole *Santa Barbara Grrrrls* humiliation has ruined me for retail. I have a phobia about dressing rooms now. You have to help me overcome my fears. Through repeated exposure."

"I'm not sure retail-phobia would be a bad thing for you," she says. "But all right, four dresses does seem too few."

She slips back into her jeans and T-shirt, and looks as good as she did in the dresses. "How about Yosemite?" I say. "You can get married in jeans."

She smiles, knowing how I feel about how she looks in jeans. "But what would you wear?"

"Khakis," I say, because we both know I don't look good in jeans.

"You bought the Victorian psychiatrist bustier?"

"I got it for free." As she puts on her sneakers I tell her the whole story.

When I finish she says, "You should write about that in your column."

"What? How to get free stuff? I'm not sure if—"

"I mean write about the humiliation, the disgrace, the shame, the mortification—"

"Okay, Ms. Thesaurus, I get the point."

"Your editor would publish that. It's got all the elements of great journalism—sex, lies and videotape."

"Those aren't the elements of great journalism. That's just a movie."

"A good one though."

"True."

There is a soft knock on the dressing room door and the saleswoman is standing there. "Thanks for your help," I say, "but we're going to wait on the dress."

"I couldn't help but overhear," she says. "You were video-taped for *Santa Barbara Grrrls?*"

I frown at Maya. "I knew someone was listening."

"My daughter…she was filmed, too. At a bar, she was drunk, but that's no excuse for what happened to her."

"Oh. Well. Um."

"I thought maybe—if you might want to talk to her, she's so embarrassed. Maybe if she meets another victim that might help her get over it."

"Well, sure, if you think it might help, of course, I'll talk to her."

"Thank you," the saleswoman says, and hands me a 3x5 card.

> Name: *Gabrielle Campbell*
> Phone: *555-1458* Wedding Date: *1/12*
> Personal Style: *casual traditional fairy tale trendy*
> Favorite Dresses: *Fell out of black stretch sheath.*
> *Also flashed underpants.*

"Um, this happened when she was getting married?" I ask, glancing at the card.

"No, that's the date she was filmed."

"Oh. Right." Nice of her to underline her sense of style. I might not have known otherwise.

chapter 12

Tuesday morning, and my column due at two o'clock. I received approval from Teri for a profile of a feng shui decorator, but neglected to tell the feng shui decorator, who selfishly went to Taiwan for the week. Dredge brain and classified ads for other possible candidate and come up with nothing.

Merrick's at some meeting, so I have free range of his office and laptop. I check online for ideas, and am not sure if I should be pleased or disgusted that he has my page on *Santa Barbara Grrrrls* bookmarked. Watch myself pirouette roughly 376 times, trying to decide if, to the casual viewer, my cellulite could be mistaken for a shadow, or even some dangling strap of the bustier. Would like a second opinion, and think this might really break the ice with the Gay Tailors. After some deliberation, however, I decide this is unwise: without even a smidge of prurient interest in my body, they might offer a truly objective opinion.

I finally summon enough willpower to sign off, and open Word and stare at the cursor. What I'm gonna try, here, is a sort of overview of New Age businesses, a chatty breezy informative overview. And funny—Dave Barry-esque. How would he start? Um… Maybe Merrick has cookies in his cabinet. No, he has no sweet tooth. He might have a banana. A banana sounds good. He could have a banana. A banana is within the realm of the possible. I could be eating a banana right now. I check his kitchenette. No banana, but there is a tub of yogurt.

I eat the yogurt.

Okay. Instead of 800 words, I'll tackle an easier task: I'll write my resignation. I can't take the pressure anymore—there's a deadline *every* week—and writing is agonizing, trying to get all the words in the right order. Not to mention the hours I spend contacting and interviewing weirdos. I mean, at least I *know* I'm a fake.

Dear Teri:
This hasn't been my week. Not only did my feng shui practitioner travel—with no notice whatsoever—to Taiwan, but I was videotaped naked in a dressing room at a boutique downtown. A pack of Vile Voyeurs hid a video camera behind the dressing-room curtain in a shop (which will remain nameless) and this is only one of their tricks for catching women unaware. They haunt the bars downtown, they place cameras under sidewalk grates and in pubic bathrooms, they—

An hour later, I have three pages about the Vile Voyeurs—
and my humiliation and invaded privacy—and haven't mentioned my resignation once. I scroll back to the beginning.
Hmm. I delete all mention of feng shui, and rework the
pages, attempting to balance the seriousness of the invasion
of privacy with the offhand wit—and many bold words—
of a professional columnist.

I insert a final comma and close the document. I'll take
the laptop with me to the *Permanent Press* office and print
the article there. I doubt Teri will publish this, but at least
I'll have the distinction of being fired, instead of quitting.
Quitting makes me feel like a quitter, but being fired is just
the natural end of the career life cycle.

I head upstairs to change, as I arrived from Merrick's in
magenta velour sweats, having not packed quite enough
clean clothes. I knock on the door, which is odd, as this is
my apartment—but I'm afraid to find Wicked Tad doing
something unspeakable in the middle of the living room. He
doesn't answer, so I check that he's locked it—he has—and
use my key to get in.

The place is a shambles, with Mountain Dew cans, pizza
boxes and M&M wrappers everywhere. I toss the largest bits
of debris into the trash can, ignoring what appears to be a
Coke stain on the beige Berber, and check my watch. Half
an hour to deadline and I haven't put on fresh clothes. I slip
into my bedroom and discover Wicked Tad in my bed,
sprawled on my comforter in deep sleep, surrounded by a
rich compost of potato chip bags and candy wrappers.

I lean close to his ear. "TAD WICKED!"

Tad shrieks and scrambles at the covers and shoots off the
other end of the bed onto the floor, where he lands with a
satisfying thump. In a moment, his head pops over the mattress.

"You're in my bed," I say.

"Elle," he mumbles, closing his eyes to block out the light, or maybe the sight of me in magenta. "What time…?"

"Almost afternoon," I say. "You're sleeping in my bed?"

Tad stands, yawning and revealing his omni-present boxers. Today they are blue with the word Britney embroidered in red across the front. "Hey, least I was alone…"

"Okay. Yuck."

He scratches the Brit, then the ney, then appears about to remove the boxers altogether. "Need a shower."

"You, wait! And keep your clothes on!"

I fumble in my closet and flee to the bathroom, where I change and add a little lipstick, a deep burgundy called Diva that I bought for the name despite not liking the color. The phone rings as I'm putting the finishing touches on my harried-reporter-on-a-deadline look. Afraid that Wicked Tad will answer, I burst from the bathroom and grab the phone.

A man says, "May I speak with Elle Medina?"

It's a measure of my personal progress that I don't feel nauseated: not too long ago, the only men calling were credit card companies demanding payment. And although Carlos calls with the occasional stern warning, he doesn't scare me anymore because we're friends.

These days, people asking for Elle Medina are usually clients: the phone is a source of money, instead of only debt. So I automatically say, even before asking if he'd like to subscribe to my annual newsletter, "This is Elle. I sense you're having a problem? You need help. Is there…a woman involved?"

Unless he's a motherless gay man living in a secluded monastery, there's always a woman involved. But all I get is silence.

"Odd," I say. "I'm sensing a woman. No? Hmm…" I settle into my chair and flip the pages of *Allure* magazine, to sound like cards. "Yes, I think there is a woman, but also…work?"

"No."

Hoo boy, one of the strong silent types. Without contextual clues I'm pretty much lost, so I stall for time, asking him to pick a number between one and seventy-eight—the number of tarot cards in a deck, I think.

"You have me confused," he says.

"Ah!" I say. "Confusion. Yes, we can work on that. Favorite number, please?"

"Um, twenty-three."

I start flipping through *Allure* to page twenty-three. "Ah, a powerful number…"

"But I'm not calling for a, um, what did you say? Reading?"

"Not really a 'reading,'" I say soothingly, because some men are afraid of the word. "We'll just discuss the—"

"I'm the admissions director at Laverna University."

And I remember: I forwarded my business line to my cell while I'm at Merrick's. Readings by appointment only. Very exclusive. If only Tad hadn't rattled me, I'd have remembered. "The admissions director, excellent. I thought you were a…friend."

"I see," he says in an officious tone. "I'm calling for your admissions interview. Is this a good time?"

"Um, definitely. Yes." The column deadline is five minutes away. "Sure."

"My first question, this isn't on my list but I'm always interested…" He says this as if asking a question that's not on the list will really humanize him. "How did you get interested in psychology?"

"Oh, well, I wouldn't say I'm *interested,* exactly—"

"Then why did you apply?"

$18,500 in loans per year. "I'm more…riveted."

And we're off. An excruciating hour later, he winds down by explaining the requirements of the course work and certification process. I'm struck, not only by the years of grinding course work followed by the years of unpaid indenture laboring in the fields of the psyche, but by the fundamental tedium of the job itself. You've got to listen to all kinds of horrible stories, and you can't just say, "Try this. Then try this. That didn't work? Try this." No, it's all Serious Important Work. And I'd probably have to wear pantyhose.

After we hang up, I dig the course catalog from under a pile of newspapers and leaf through the class descriptions. Then I yawn. Shouldn't you be excited to go back to school?

Maybe I'm just not psychologist material. I'm simply not good at Serious Important. I'm a fake psychic—that's Silly Unimportant. If I study to become a real psychic, is that a step in the right direction? At least then I'd have credentials, though somehow I don't think this would sway Merrick. I dig through the newspapers again and find the catalog from the other school I've applied to: the Virginia Hanes Psychic Healing Program. Not really a catalog, more a pamphlet promising enhancement of psychic ability and a facility with subtle energies such as chakras and auras. Even more mind-numbing than the class work at Laverna, and I haven't even admitted to anyone that I applied, how would I admit I was actually attending? At least, during the 3,000 hours—I'm not kidding—of traineeship to become a Marriage Family Therapist, I'd legitimately be helping people. Like alcoholics, drug addicts, and wife-beaters. I imagine myself coming home from my first hour of traineeship with a crystal meth addict, and thinking: One hour down, only 2,999 to go.

I drop the psychic training pamphlet and—finally—find my pack of tarot cards. I open to the Wheel of Fortune card, so on a whim I find my book and turn to the page.

The Wheel of Fortune challenges you to meet change with composure and grace. Learn to anticipate change by noting the wave-like patterns of circumstances and the cyclical nature of past events. In other words, "Go with the Flow." However, understand that there is often an unpredictable element. A wild card.

A composed and graceful wild card. Well, I've mastered the "wild card" part, at least. I check the time, grab my things and head out the door. This wild card is going to note the wave-like patterns of circumstances all the way to the *Permanent Press* office, and turn in her article on an unapproved subject an hour late. How's that for "Going with the Flow?"

chapter

13

Time expands into a silent desert of desiccated, um… Days pass in a sluggish march of hopeless, er… Anyway, a week of nothing much happens.

Nobody calls, not even Valentine, so I'm losing money every day, because I'm running ads that aren't producing. I was calling myself from Merrick's phone, to see if the 900 number was actually working, until I realized I was charging him $3/minute. Fortunately, I only called around fifteen or twenty times, and didn't stay on long, so he only owes me like a hundred bucks.

Also, I was so discombobulated at finding Wicked Tad in my bed, I grabbed armfuls of linens, and no clothing, so I'm pretty much living in my Juicy Couture sweatsuit. Extremely comfy, but so over. I think people are staring at me and wondering: *Why can't she buy a pair of 7 for all mankind jeans and move on?*

I do really want a pair of 7s.

Plus, I may no longer have a column in the *Permanent Press*—haven't heard a single peep from Teri about my Vile Voyeurs exposé, and haven't even tried to come up with another New Age business to profile. The whole industry is dying anyway, starting with fake phone psychics. And gas is almost three bucks a gallon. Why? There's oil right off the coast. I can see the rigs from Merrick's living room. Why does gas cost more in Santa Barbara than in the Midwest, when we have the stuff washing up on our beaches?

Anyway, point is, I'm going nowhere. Both literally and figuratively.

Maya's probably decided on paper plates for her wedding, the Gay Tailors didn't return my call, with a young and hip question about hemming, and even Neil's avoiding me, because I keep hounding him for dope. My new theory is that once I have this housewarming party, then everyone will be my friend. Despite all the evidence, I still believe that to know me is to love me. I have no money, no prospects, no desire to become further educated as a psychologist or a psychic. I've spent three entire days indulging in my "magazine fantasy," the one where I grace the cover of my own journal each month, like Oprah, with an army of airbrush artists to make me look as young and vibrant as she does at fifty-something. Which is sad, considering I'm only twenty-six. Even sadder is my lack of imagination when it comes to the content of the magazine: **Have you ever wondered who the first female president of the U.S. will be?** And the **Rice is an Economical Food** column.

What I really want is to work for someone else as a phone psychic, for twice the pay, and not worry about being self-employed and finding clients and having no health insurance. Or about that underlying nagging notion of being unethical.

Truth is, I'm tempted to give up. Move in with Merrick and let him support me. I step through the French doors that lead out to the Jerusalem stone patio, where the olive trees flutter and flirt with the cool breeze. I flop into the deck chair and eat peanut butter from the jar with a spoon. Living here would be so easy. I could just laze around all day—I mean, go to classes and volunteer at nonprofits—and make Merrick buy me a pair of 7 for all mankind jeans.

And start to hate myself again. Not fair to Merrick. Not fair to me.

So I give the almost-empty jar of peanut butter to Miu, and slip back inside and into the one decent outfit I've packed—a black wrap dress and leopard print flats. I twist my curls into a French knot, trowel on makeup and stand at the ready.

Ready for what? I thought dressing up would make me feel better, but it just makes me feel dressed up. I want to be attired to face the world, forge new contacts, meet my goals. Maybe I'm asking too much of an outfit.

Hmm. Guess I'll drop by Merrick's office. Let him see me dressed up.

Merrick glances up from his desk and offers a distracted smile. He left the house at some ungodly hour this morning—before six—and looks tired and drained.

"Hi, Angel," I say brightly, trying to cheer him, almost tripping on the mail piled on the floor inside the door. Looks like the postman slipped everything through a slot in the door, but there is no slot—which means Merrick dropped the mail there on his way in. "Um…are you okay?"

"Hmm? Oh—what?"

"The mail all over the floor. Should I feel your forehead for a fever?"

He smiles weakly, making notes on some drafting paper. The only light in the room comes from the lamp over his drafting table, highlighting his work.

I raise the blinds to save his eyes and help him see my outfit. Otherwise he might miss the leopard spots on my shoes. "What're you working on?"

He squints at the light. "Plans for the, um…" He gets back to work.

Sigh. I'm inclined to make a fuss, and demand his attention, but that's not the Elle I want to be, so I sit quietly in one of the wooden Chinese chairs. My silence and maturity immediately freak him out. He raises his head. "What's wrong? What happened? Is the house okay? Are you okay? It's not Miu, is it?"

Hmm. The house, then me, then Miu. But I guess he's looking at me, so he knows I haven't burned *myself* down. "We're all fine."

"Then what's up?" He checks the clock on the far wall: 12:43. "I'm due at the Wine Cask at one."

I stand into my best red-carpet pose. "I love the Wine Cask. Plus, you'll notice I'm dressed appropriately."

"You look beautiful," he says absently. "But I can't, I'm meeting clients."

"What if I promise not to say anything? You can tell them I'm mute."

He sorts through the papers on his desk, an uncharacteristic mess. "I promise we'll go another time."

I open my mouth, frozen in my red-carpet pose, and don't say anything: I'm mute.

He gets to the door before realizing I'm not saying anything. He laughs, tells me he loves me and disappears.

The moment the door closes, I abandon my red-carpet pose and revert to my usual slump. He says I look beautiful, but clearly not beautiful enough to be his trophy girlfriend at a lunch meeting. I mope around his office for a minute, but c'mon, the poor guy was working at six in the morning, cut him a break. So I grab hold of the scruff of my neck and shake vigorously, like a stern mother cat. Then, taking a few deep breaths, I surprise myself and start cleaning. I scour sink counters, empty fridge of old cheese, discard trash, create aesthetically pleasing piles on his desk, stack magazines, organize mail by size and dust furniture.

Finished in the office, I go outside and snag some early nasturtiums blossoming at the base of the mailboxes. Tuck them into a lowball glass with a little water and leave them on Merrick's desk. I check the room once more to see if I've missed anything, straighten one last chair, and plant a lipsticky kiss on a blank sticky note that I place in the center of Merrick's desk.

He's either gonna love this, or panic that I'm dying of some obscure tropical disease—or perhaps have been replaced by the Stepford Elle. Which I'm afraid he might prefer to the real thing.

I head upstairs to my apartment to finish packing some clothes, wondering if it's time to call PB and Maya and suggest that they…what? Forcibly remove Tad from the premises? I can't do that to Maya and Brad. They're so pleased that he's not crashing on their couch, and were so good when I *was* crashing there, I simply can't let them down.

I pass Ray Flood's door, on the way to my apartment and stop and consider. I really didn't act as a proper Welcome Committee for him—on the other hand, I think he'd prefer if I didn't. I think he'd prefer that I never speak to him again. As I'm deciding to honor his wishes, Miu scratches at his door.

Miu never scratches at a door. She shakes her head, thus jingling her collar, that's her way of notifying me that some sort of action is urgently requested. But this time, she scratches, and a moment later, Ray Flood opens the door.

I smile. "Ray!"

He looks down. " 'Lo."

"Um—any new jewelry recently?"

He shakes his head.

"Well!" I say. "Well, well, well!"

I'd intended to say something a bit less content-free, but Ray smiles at the floor, and rubs Miu's wrinkly head and tells her she's a good dog. She waggles her skinny rump and curls into "kidney bean" shape: she likes him. So I like him, too. You can *always* trust people your dogs likes—I learned that from TV. Ray scratches Miu, and I tell him her life story, which he doesn't appear to hear. He finishes scratching her and tells her goodbye and, without a word to me, disappears back into his apartment, closing the door with a quiet *click*.

Okay, not what you'd call a conversation, but still: progress.

Now all I need is to make similar progress with Wicked Tad. Upstairs, I pause outside my own front door, unsure of the right approach. I want to interrogate him about his job search, but don't want to appear fish-wifey. Want to ask if he's got a timeframe for leaving, yet don't want to make him feel unwelcome. He's practically family, like a brother-in-law twice removed. I'm still trying to decide what to say when

I hear voices through the door. Male voices, which is good news, as at least I can assume he's fully dressed.

Feeling like an idiot, I knock on my own apartment door.

"Yo, Ray, that you? Come in."

Ray? They're friends? "It's me," I say, opening the door. "Your landlady, ha ha." Oh boy.

Sprawled across the living room are Wicked Tad, Weldon and Johnny. Why are the Gay Tailors hanging around with Wicked Tad? They're *my* best friends. A straight man doesn't need gay best friends—and I know Tad's not gay, because I heard all his tales of romantic conquest. Sheesh. Not bad enough he's committing unspeakable acts in my apartment, now he steals my almost-best-friends, too?

"'S'up?" he says, not unfriendly.

Oh, twist the knife, Tad. This is like *Single White Female.* On the other hand, maybe now the Gay Tailors have been in my apartment, they'll find me more interesting…or at least not annoying. "Oh, just, y'know. How're you?" I beam at Johnny and Weldon. "How's business? How was the move? How's it hanging?"

Weldon doesn't say anything. Johnny doesn't say anything. Finally Tad says, "So I was showing off your Web site."

Oh, sweet Jesus.

"I think it's horrible," Johnny says, and I can't tell if he means my exploitation or my body.

Must change subject. "Yeah. Anyway, um…I've got this idea for a *New Yorker* cartoon. I heard *Bombay Wedding* was being made into a musical? And *Debbie Does Dallas* was made into a musical. And *The Wedding Singer,* you know, with Adam Sandler and Drew Barrymore, is being made into a musical…"

Three sets of eyes begin to glaze. I'm losing them.

"Picture this," I say. "A couple walking past a movie theater with a large marquee. One says to the other, 'Did you read the book?' and the other one says—this is the funny part—'Nah, I'm waiting for the musical.'"

Crickets.

"I'm waiting for the musical," I repeat. "Because—"

"Did you tell us that because we're gay?" Johnny asks.

"What?"

"You think we like musicals because we're gay," Weldon says.

"No—no—no." I say. "No, I told you because—because—because—"

"She thought it was funny," Tad says.

"It is!" I insist. "Did you read the book? I'm waiting for the musical!"

"Sounds like a *Ziggy*," Weldon says, and I think I'm in the clear.

Johnny snickers. "And she dances like one, too."

Whatever the hell that means.

chapter

14

> **My boyfriend was shocked to discover I'd been selling my body on the Internet. So was I.**

Teri liked the column. So much so that I got a full page, the above sentence as a teaser in bold—and they included a copy of my headshot, which I'd given for use on my first column, despite being told they never run a columnist's picture.

They also captured a shot of me off the Internet, pouting at the mirror. Which, in the days since the article ran, has resulted in six fan letters, three date requests and one marriage proposal.

I call Maya at the bar to brag about the wedding proposal. "So, Miss Smarty-Bar-Size-Six-Ninety-Nine-Dollar-Dress-Pants isn't the only one people want to marry!"

"Miss *who?*"

"Miss Size-Six-Smarty-Bar-Owner-Dress-Buying-Smarty-Pants!" I breathe. "For-Ninety-Nine-Dollars!"

She laughs. "How did he ask you?"

"Voice mail at work—and *very* romantic. He lives in Lompoc."

"What's his address?" she teases. "The Correctional Facility?"

I don't answer.

"No!" she says.

"Hey, he's salt of the earth. I'm thinking of visiting him on my publicity tour."

"Publicity tour?"

"I'm a star, Maya," I modestly confess. "They sold more copies of the paper this week than ever before."

"The paper is free."

"Yeah, *technically.*"

A slight pause as glasses tinkle on Maya's side of the line. "So what did Louis say?"

"Louis?" My ex-fiancé? "What does he care?"

"I mean Merrick. Just because you refuse to call him Louis doesn't mean nobody else can."

"He's...proud?"

"What does that mean?"

I blurt the truth. "I have no idea! He hasn't mentioned it! It's terrible, there I am, with my first non-New Age column causing an international incident, a storm of controversy, a—"

She laughs. "A page in the *Permanent Press.*"

"Okay, fine. But why hasn't he said anything? Maybe he didn't see."

"I thought he always read your column."

"He always usually does. But he's so busy right now. He comes home late, exhausted. The house is a shambles—it's so bad that *I'm* cleaning."

She gasps.

"Yeah. And I just…" I pause. "What if he regrets asking me to move in with him?"

More tinkling and conversation.

"Maya?"

"Sorry, big group came in. Gotta go." She hangs up.

Shit. She definitely thinks Merrick wishes I was long gone. The phone jingles, Maya calling back, having realized she cut me off at a sensitive moment.

"I'm fucked," I say into the receiver. "Aren't I?"

"Hey," says a halfway familiar male voice. "From what I've seen, if you're not, there is no justice in this world."

"Um…Rabbi?" Because I just said "I'm fucked" to a stranger, chances are it's clergy.

A deep resonant laugh. "This is Blake Conahy. SB's AM/FM DJ."

"Huh?"

"Santa Barbara's favorite morning show disc jockey."

"Oh! I thought I knew your voice." I've heard him on the radio a few times. "Omigod—I'm not on the air, am I?"

Another laugh. "The way you swear? Glad to say you're not. Listen, I—"

"Wait, you're the AM/FM DJ? You're on both?"

He sighs, like he's heard this before. "I'm on an FM channel, in the a.m. The morning. SB's a.m. FM DJ. Got it? Good. So—I read your piece in the *Permanent Press.*"

He's gonna ask me out. First a convict, now a DJ. I'm almost as popular as Jenna from Café Lustre. Who knew the road to dating gold was paved with naked pictures? Hmm. Actually, I guess *everyone* knows that.

"Sex," he says. "Technology, privacy. Did I mention sex?"

"Um…" Let him down easy. "Well, actually I live with my boyfriend, and—"

"Whoa, TMI, Elle," he says. "I saw you doing the dance of the seven veils, I don't need to hear a play-by-play."

"Um—"

"The reason I'm calling, is that I want you on our morning show."

"Oh! As a guest?"

"No, we need a receptionist."

I laugh, though I'm tempted to ask what they pay. "Well, I don't know…"

"It'll be fun. You'll share your insight."

My insight? True, I plan to write important think pieces— very public radio, very All Things Considered. Didn't David Sedaris start on radio with that gay elf story? I bet he'd be my best friend if he lived downstairs. "Well, if you think—"

"Great! We tried to squeeze you in tomorrow, while the article's still running, but we're booked through next Wednesday. That work for you?"

"Sure, but do I need to prepare or something?"

"Nah. You're used to the phone psychic work, this is no different. In fact, we'll open the lines for a few quickie psychic consultations."

Not exactly Terry Gross, but maybe I'll stir up some business. "Sounds fun."

"And then you can solve this mystery, like you did the 'Missing Bitch.'"

"Um—which mystery?"

"Who's behind *Santa Barbara Grrrrls?* Who are the Vile Voyeurs?"

"Oh, right—right—right. Right, right. Right."

"A lot of listeners are gonna be skeptical of your abilities, so we'll give you the opportunity to prove them wrong. Solve this mystery on air."

"Right," I say. "Right."

I have five days to solve the Vile Voyeurs mystery.

Only one man can save my sorry ass.

I hang up with the DJ and immediately dial Spenser, P.I. When I first moved back to Santa Barbara, Spenser hired me as a store detective—I pretended to be a shopper at Super 9, and kept my eyes peeled for shoplifters. I was quite good at the job, in many ways, but I admit I shouldn't have acted as a personal shopper to one shoplifter, or inadvertently helped a grifter scam thousands of dollars from the company. But every job has a learning curve, right? Still, couldn't really blame Spenser for firing me, so when I stumbled onto the puppy-stealing scam, I shared the credit.

"Elle Medina," Spenser says. "I saw you on the Internet."

Yuck. "How'd you hear about that? My article?"

I hear him flick his silver lighter and light a cigarette. "What article?"

I tell him about my column in the *Permanent Press.* "So you just sorta…"

"Yep," he says. "Found you surfing for porn. I like to buy local—wouldn't have recognized you, but there was something familiar about the way you moved. Reminded me of that videotape of you at Super 9 showing that shoplifter what to steal. Not everyone would make the connection—I mean, in *this* surveillance video you were naked—but to the trained eye of seasoned detective—"

"Well, I'm not *naked* naked." I say. "I'm wearing an extremely tasteful bustier."

He drags on his cigarette. "Not on the page I saw."

"Santa Barbara Grrrrls?"

"Four *R*s, no *I*," he confirms.

"And I'm *naked?*"

"On the members-only page."

I moan. *Naked* naked.

"Don't worry, you can't see anything good. Kind of a scam, though at least they don't charge. Let me ask you this—what do you get paid for something like that? More than I ever paid you, huh?"

"Nothing! I got nothing, okay?"

"You shoulda held out for minimum wage. C'mon, Elle."

"Would you shut up! This is why I'm calling." I explain my predicament to him, finishing with, "So I need to find who's responsible."

"The Internet's beyond me, you know that. You need a—what do they call those people? Begins with an *H*."

"Heinous? Hellhounds? Hyenas?"

"Hackers. That's what you need."

He's right. That's exactly what I need. I thank him, and he tells me he'll give me a shout if he ever needs a woman willing to go *all* the way undercover.

A hacker. Perfect Brad was no help—some perfection that is—so I try Carlos, at the credit collection agency. He has access to everything online. I know, that's how he tracked *me* down.

"Carlos, *mi hombre*," I say when he answers.

"Hola, senorita. ¿Cómo esta el libro de recetas que le envie?"

But I've exhausted my Spanish. *"¿Qué?"*

"How's the cookbook?" he asks. "Try any of the recipes?"

"Oh…*bueno.*" I fill him in on the burning buñuelos. "So now we live together."

When he finishes laughing, he says, "I don't know how you get into so much trouble. The buñuelos, the Internet."

"Oh, no," I groan. "Not you, too."

"Gotta keep tabs, Elle. I Googled you."

"Well, that means you owe me, Carlos. I need some help." I explain the situation.

"Does the site accept credit cards?"

"No. I don't understand how they make money. I mean, they've got advertisers, mostly porn sites, but is that enough? It's like the blog sites."

"What's like the blog sites?"

"They're free. There's like a million new blogs a week, and it's all free. How are they paying for servers and salaries and all that?"

"Okay—are we talking about blogs or porn?"

"Porn. *Santa Barbara Grrrrls.*"

"I'll check—but without any credit trail, don't hold your breath."

"Thanks. And um, can you get back to me soon?" I tell him about the upcoming radio gig. "So I need something to prove I'm psychic."

He mutters something about *loco,* but says he'll see what he can do. "And now," he says, "let's talk about your credit."

"*¿Qué? ¿Qué? Esta*—sorry—*muy, Elle no aquí.*"

"Elle, you've gotta stop using your credit cards. Your debt load is—"

"Oh no! Spaghetti! Gotta go!" I hang up, thanking him profusely over his stream of Spanish, and telling him to call back soon. But not too soon. Hmm. I made up that part about spaghetti, but now I've got a yen.

★ ★ ★

Merrick comes home from work early. Well, he comes home at 5:30, which isn't actually early but at least isn't late. There's still enough light to take a walk on the beach, so we go down the block to Thousand Steps, the stairs leading from the bluffs to the sand. There aren't really a thousand steps. I counted once, and while there are more than two-hundred-something, where I lost count, there are definitely less than a thousand.

We take our shoes off at the bottom of the steps, and the sand is warm on my feet, though the air is cool. A half-dozen people walk on the beach, and three surfers in wetsuits catch the last few swells before sunset.

Miu's allowed off leash here and she uses the freedom wisely. She canters horse-like down the beach, chasing birds through the shallow water, her paws leaving prints in the wet sand. The sight of her running at low tide, backlit by the sun, is one of the happiest things I've ever seen. She is grace perdogified.

Merrick and I set a more sedate pace behind her, wearing jeans and sweaters to protect us from the dropping temperature. We often walk silently together, just enjoying each other's company, and the beach and sand and sky. I like to imagine one of those scenes in a movie where they pan out from a person to a house to a town to a state to a country to the world. I'm just this tiny person on a beach. It's one of the few times I actually have perspective.

Tonight, however, the dilemma of the Vile Voyeurs looms. I hesitate to ruin the moment, because Merrick is overtired and overworked, but I'm afraid he'll collapse into bed when we get home, and be no good for anything.

So when we reach our turning-around point, and start

walking back towards the steps, I ask, "Did you read my column this week?"

He watches Miu gallop. "Mmm-hmm."

"And…"

"It's different from what you normally write."

"C'mon Merrick." I say, exasperated. "What did you think?"

"I think it's nice you didn't use my name."

Was neglecting to take me to the Wine Cask just the beginning? Soon he'll want no public association with me whatsoever. "They want me on the radio."

"Who does?"

"The…radio people." We walk a few steps, and when it becomes clear he's not going to ask, I say, "The morning guy. That morning show."

"About the dressing room?"

"I'm gonna use my psychic powers to hunt down the Vile Voyeurs. On the air."

"Uh-huh."

"It'll be good for business," I tell him.

"What business?" He stops walking. "I thought you were quitting that and going back to school."

Tears well in my eyes. "Well…if I figure out who's behind the Web site, maybe I'll get enough publicity that I won't have to go back to school."

He turns away and starts walking again.

I hurry after him. "I called Spenser and Carlos, but I don't think they're going to be much help. They want me on the radio next Wednesday, that's not much time. I need a lead."

Again, he doesn't answer.

"So," I say, "what do you think I should do?"

"You know what I think," Merrick says. "You should stop pretending you're psychic."

Well, what am I *supposed* to do? Pretending to be psychic is my only job skill. He knows that. He wants me to be a psychologist so I don't embarrass him, and he can take me to dinner with clients, and not cringe when someone asks what I do. I don't want to cringe, either. I don't want to pretend, either. But that's all I've got. That's all I'm good at.

"I'm sorry," he says. "I know you don't want to hear that. But it's true. And now you're going to take this Internet thing, this invasion of privacy, and connect that back with being a fake psychic? This is how you stir up more trouble for yourself."

There's no more room for the tears in my eyes, they begin to stream down my face. I turn away from Merrick so he won't see and call to Miu. I surreptitiously wipe my tears as I clip Miu's leash to her collar. I know Merrick notices but he doesn't say anything.

Maybe there aren't a thousand steps, but each one is steep and weathered. This is my life. Not a movie, more like a Greek tragedy. I am Sisyphus. I wish I had something as interesting as a stone to roll, but instead I'm stuck climbing an endless staircase, going nowhere. Call me Ellephus.

chapter

15

The next morning, I mentally run through my contacts, and in ten seconds am finished. But I do turn up someone possibly useful: Wicked Tad. He apparently has his degree in engineering, and is younger and approximately twelve-hundred times looser than PB, so more likely to be a willing hacker. Or as I'll present the situation to him: co-conspirator. I think that'll appeal to his sense of romance.

Only problem is, when I show up at my apartment, he's not there. The place is a shambles, with dirty clothes and Mountain Dew empties everywhere. Including my bed. I consider making a dent in the mess, but I'm due on the radio in less than a week—I need some vague clue about *Santa*

Barbara Grrrrls before then, to embroider into a convincing psychic reading. Plus, what am I, his mother?

No, I'm not even his girlfriend. I check he hasn't done any structural damage—the last thing I want is to get on Monty's bad side—and finally pack my clothes. Not sure why I'm bothering, now, given how Merrick feels about me. We had a silent night, then a silent morning. I'm keeping myself together by not really thinking about the fact that my boyfriend, who's supposed to love and cherish me and all of that, is deeply disappointed in the person I am. I blink back momentary tears, then drag my suitcase to the front door and leave.

I stand lost on the landing outside my front door. Now what? Back to Element, to press the pregnant manager for more information? My instincts tell me there's no way she's involved, and if I press too hard I might squeeze the baby out. On the other hand, my instincts tell me denim miniskirts never go out of style, so what do I know?

I'm going to have to bother Brad again, or maybe the libertarian geek at his job will know something: he saw me in a bustier, he owes me big-time. I start down the stairs, my suitcase clumping behind, lost in thought—and bump into Ray Flood, the eBay guy.

"Sorry!" I say. "Are you okay? I didn't see you."

"Sure," he mumbles, rubbing his knee. "I'm hard to spot."

Because he's big, this is funny, so I smile. "I was lost in my own world. I spend a lot of time there. Everything's free and there's a really good soundtrack."

He mumbles and moves toward his apartment, and I realize: he's Ray Flood *the eBay guy,* he must know something about computers.

"Wait!" I say. "Wait, don't go. I need help."

He nods in agreement.

"I mean—not like that. With the computer. You must know about computers, right? Do you have five minutes?"

"Kinda busy…"

"Me and Miu would *really* appreciate it. Look at her."

He pats her, and very nicely tells her he's got other things to do.

"But this is life or death! I mean, almost. Except for the death part. I promise I'll—I'll…" I think, but have nothing to offer. This is often my problem. "Well, I got nothing to promise. But I'd *really* appreciate it."

He tells Miu he'd love to help, but really couldn't.

So I explain how I've been exposed on the Internet. "…and they posted the video on a Web site."

"Yeah, I saw that."

"*You* saw it?" I ask. "Did *everyone* see that? How did you—"

"Guy upstairs."

Wicked Tad. "Please," I say. "I'm being interviewed on the radio, and I have no idea who's behind this, and the producer wants me to solve the mystery on the air and I don't even have a computer."

"Aren't you supposed to be psychic?"

"Yeah," I say. "But I'm not."

"You're not?"

"I couldn't psychic my way out of an L.A. weather report."

His eyes brighten slightly, and he says, "All right."

Those are the last words I hear for an hour. He shows me into his apartment, which is surprisingly different from mine. Somehow Merrick managed to transform a dark fussy Victorian parlor into a contemporary apartment without destroying the period details. The floors are the original oak, the walls a pale mushroom, and the ceilings and the strip of wall above decorative moldings are bright white. A long kitchen lines the far wall, kinda Shaker contemporary. Say what you will about Monty, for a slum lord he does okay.

Ray's taste, however, is questionable—perhaps a side effect of the trade, selling used items. Everything looks second hand except the computer at which Ray hunts and pecks with impressive speed.

"How much of this is for sale?" I ask, gesturing to the room.

Ray grunts.

"Everything?"

He nods.

Hmm. I like that idea. You'd never grow tired of things. I amuse myself by mentally arranging his items according to category, then by physically doing the same. He shows me how to use his digital camera and, with the expertise born of a lifetime examining store windows, I display the items in charming little tableaux.

"Found something," Ray finally mumbles.

"One sec." I'm absorbed in my new career as an eBay stylist. I unearthed a box of unsorted antique rhinestone shoe buckles and cleverly wove them with red silk ribbon into rhinestone wreathes. "Almost done." Hard to get the lay of the ribbon right, and the drape of white sheet background, but I finally take the photographs. "There! Now, what was that?"

"Got something."

"About the Vile Voyeurs? What'd you find?"

"No way to track them. Registered with a company that promises confidentiality."

I stand behind him, looking over his shoulder at the computer screen. It is filled with the page from *Santa Barbara Grrrrls.* I am front and center doing my burlesque routine, with a separate box for a closeup of my cleavage, with a caption that reads: Permanent Press On These.

"That's new," I say, sickened. "So nothing? I can't do anything to stop this?"

"Well…"

"What?"

"You could try the porn sites."

"What, I'm already stripping, I might as well get paid?"

He frowns. "I mean call the porn sites that advertise. See if they'll tell you who's behind the site."

I stare at him. "That's brilliant!"

He mumbles.

"*You're* brilliant. You're a genius. You're a brilliant genius."

He slips Miu another Atkins Advantage low-carb bar—that's what he gave her last time. Apparently she loves the Pralines 'N Crème.

I get the sense that he's done with socializing, so I invite him to my housewarming—whenever that might be—and leave him in peace. Things are looking up. At least now I'll have something to give the radio people, and soon revenge will be mine. Well, after I spend a few days calling porn vendors. That oughtta be fun.

There are four messages on Merrick's machine when I get home.

First message: "Elle, it's Dad. Your father. Your mother called. I was shocked…you know your mother and I haven't talked since…well, I'm trying to remember who was president. Possibly Reagan. She told me about the Web site. If a call from your mother shocked me, how do you think I reacted to my daughter stripping on the Internet? Eleanor, if you need money, you could've asked."

Right. Last time I asked for money, my mother suggested I live with her and work as a busboy, and my father itemized how much alimony he was paying each of his four ex-wives.

"She thinks you're mixing with the wrong crowd," he continues. "And I can't say that I think she's wrong. Call me. No, better not. You might get Mathilda and she's disgusted by your Internet antics. She wants nothing to do with you, finds the whole thing sordid and embarrassing…"

Mathilda? I thought he was married to…hmm, can't remember her name. Not Mathilda, though. And *he's* embarrassed? What about me?

"Well, I've called, I promised your mother I would. Stay out of trouble will you? I really don't want to speak with her again. I don't need reminding why we divorced."

I press the delete button on the machine. A beep, a scuffling sound like a phone set to speaker being picked up and then, "Elle Medina. You'll never guess who this is."

Joshua Franklin. Grifter ex-boyfriend.

"It's Joshua, babe. Joshua Franklin. Saw you on the Internet—and I gotta say, you're looking *hot* these days. What've you been doing, Pilates, weight training?"

Okay. I blush in agitated pleasure. I'm sorry, I know this is disloyal to Merrick, but Joshua is so gorgeous he physically weakens knees from across dimly lit rooms.

Then he continues, "I've got an idea…a business proposition. This thing's really blowing up." He leaves his number. "Call me."

I press delete again. He's gorgeous, but he's a cretin and a creep, and I can do better. Hell, I've already done better. Now I just need to *keep* better, even if "better" is currently acting like a jerk.

The next message begins with a murmur of crowd noise,

then Maya saying, "No, Kid, more bitters. Over by the, yeah. Right. Elle, are you there? Pick up. The key to a good *Cabaret* is two dashes of Angostura bitters. Not one, not three—two. Okay, I guess you're not there, Elle. What do you think? Am I right or am I right? Tasty, huh? I'm buying the dress. That's a *Cabaret*. The sale dress at Petticoat Junction. Call you later, Elle! Next gin drink, Kid—the *Delilah*. You better brush up before the pop quiz."

Click.

And the final message begins with an extended throat-clearing, like someone gargling spit. "This is the admissions director at Laverna University. We sent you an acceptance letter, which was returned due to an incorrect address. We're hoping you've found a more, er, permanent residence and will be pleased to attend starting in April."

Wrong address? Talk about self-sabotage. But they called me anyway. Hmm. So I've been accepted, I'm going to grad school. Yay?

I should've given them the wrong phone number, too.

"That's great," Merrick says, from behind me.

I shriek and spring eight feet skyward.

"Sorry," he says. " I guess you didn't hear me come in."

I'd left the front door open for Miu, who will only sleep on the front step if the door's open—otherwise she stands and stares forlornly at the closed door. She's kinda weird.

"You could have said something," I say.

"I did." Merrick kisses me, the most affectionate he's been in days. "Congratulations! Dr. Elle."

"Yeah," I say. "Isn't that great?"

If he hadn't been there, I'd have deleted the message to preserve my options. Now he'll pressure me to go and my ready-made "I didn't get accepted" excuse is utterly filleted.

"Any other messages?"

"Just Maya," I say. "What are you doing home?"

"I couldn't take the office anymore. Want to do something?"

Yes! I almost leap into his arms, happy we're getting along—but remember the radio show and the all porn vendors I need to call. "I can't. I've gotta work."

"I thought you were getting your calls here."

"I—I've got to work on Maya's wedding," I say. "That's why she called."

I hate lying, but don't want to hear another lecture from Merrick—he won't approve of my calling porn companies to track down the voyeur site, to embroider a story on the radio, to prove I'm psychic. He's funny that way.

"Oh," he says, disappointed. "I can't afford to take the time off anyway."

"Maybe we can have a romantic dinner?"

"I promised I'd meet Neil for pool. We'll probably grab Mexican."

"Oh," I say.

"I could cancel."

"We'd never hear the end of it from Neil. Just remind him he's my drug dealer."

"Right."

Merrick decides to work at home, so I leave to keep him from overhearing. I go to my apartment, and am relieved to find Wicked Tad absent. I re-stake some of my territory by cleaning the pizza boxes from my mostly white linen chair, and start on the list of porn vendors Ray Flood gave me. I call the first one:

"Hi! I noticed you advertise on *Santa Barbara Grrrls,* and I—"

Click.

Hmm. I call the second: "Hello—I'm calling from the *New Yorker.* We're doing an article on—"

Click. Jesus. Who doesn't want to be in the *New Yorker?* I call back: "Listen! I have a cartoon! There's this couple and they're walking past a movie—"

Click.

Okay. I call Porn Vendor 3: "I'm starting a porn site, called, um, Café Lustre, and I noticed you advertise on *Santa Barbara Grrrrls.* Is that a good place to advertise?"

I finally get a response. "You want to speak to our marketing manager."

The marketing manager tells me: "They're not bad. The click-throughs are low, but it's cheap, so we're making a few pennies."

"Great!" I say. "And, where do you send the checks?"

"The checks."

"I mean when you pay them. I want, um, contact information."

"Lady, if you don't have contact info, what the hell are you talking about?"

Click.

To Porn Vendor 4, I say: "May I speak with your marketing manager, please?"

I am very politely transferred. I say: "Hi! my name's Elle Medina and I am desperate, on one of the Web sites you advertise with, they have a videotape of me, stripping in a dressing room, I mean a regular shop dressing room, they put a hidden camera there, and I was trying on a suit, this black drapey pantsuit, which was really slimming, and a bustier, and they didn't have my permission, and I got no payment, and now I'm gonna be on the radio because I'm a psychic, kinda, and they want me to solve this mystery—who put the camera in my dressing room—*on the air,* and my boyfriend, who's an architect, thinks I should go to graduate school and become a psychotherapist, which is how I got in trouble in the first place, pretending to be a psychotherapist, I mean in the bustier, but I don't want to go to school I just want to be on the radio and wreak—is it *wreak?*—my revenge on the Vile Voyeurs and become maybe an investigative reporter." I breathe. "But I need your help, because you see, I don't actually know—"

Beeeeeeep.

Yeah, that was voice mail. I guess I exceeded the time limit. I left my phone number with the receptionist, though, and while I know they're not going to call back at least I feel slightly better for having unburdened myself.

I call PV5, the last on the list, having prepared an elaborate lie about starting my own porn Web site, and how I'm a big fan, and I'm trying to establish my marketing budget, and I get three words into my explanation and the woman says: "Twenty minutes ago, you said you were from the *New Yorker,*" and hangs up.

Porn Vendor 5 is the same as Porn Vendor 2. So that's the end of the list. I'm considering calling PV1 back, when Tad opens the door.

"What are you doing here?" he asks.

"Oh, um…" For some reason, I'm embarrassed. "This is my apartment."

"But I live here."

"You crash here."

"Sure, if you wanna be all…*y'know.* Could you call next time you come over?"

"Um." I want to put my foot down, but he's so much

younger and cooler than I am, I feel like Mr. Furley from *Three's Company.* "Okay."

"Actually, I'm glad you're here. I had a job interview today. I totally scored."

"That's great!" I say, thrilled he'll be moving out. "What kinda job?"

"Tech industry, like Brad has. Neat thing is, they know who you are."

"Who does?"

"The guys who own the company. Your name came up— from your column—and I said that I knew you. They're big fans, told me all about 'The Missing Bitch' and the new thing, what do you call them?"

"Vile Voyeurs. They're fans?"

"Total fans."

I have to ask, "Do they live in Lompoc?"

"What? No. Why would they live in Lompoc?"

"Just wondering."

"You're a little goofy, aren't you? Anyway, since you're here…they're, like, coming over in a few minutes."

"Here? The people who might hire you?" And end the Siege of Chez Elle?

"Yeah, we're going for beers." He smiles boyishly. "A little schmoozing to get myself the job. So could you hang around and be nice to them? They're huge fans—might help me seal the job."

"Of course," I say, magnanimously. "I have an obligation to my public."

"Cool. Great. Thanks. Oh, and I told them you're crashing with me. And, um…"

There's a knock on the door.

"You said I'm your girlfriend?"

He laughs. "Or course not. I said we're fuck buddies."

He opens the door and I close my mouth. These guys aren't just a couple skeezy geeks looking for the thrill of meeting the Grrrrl of the Day—they're Tad's ticket out of my apartment. The skeezy computer geeks step inside, and have the clean-cut good looks of Sears catalog models, only dressed better, in pale dress shirts, black pants and jewel-colored silk ties.

"Elle," Tad says. "This is Brian and Randy."

I say hello, though I miss which of them is which. They're fairly indistinguishable, except one is just slightly cleaner cut than the other.

"This is so cool," Clean-Cut says. "I can't believe we're meeting you. You rock!"

"You rule," Cleaner-Cut says.

"You rock and rule," Clean-Cut says.

"Well, I don't know about that…" I say.

"Plus you're even sexier in real life," says Cleaner-Cut. "You've got charisma, presence."

"Electricity," Clean-Cut says. "Heat. Buzz."

I resist the urge to fan myself.

"So, tell us everything," Clean-Cut continues. "Are you really psychic?"

"You're wasted at the *Permanent Press,*" Cleaner-Cut says.

"You should be an investigative journalist for the *News-Press.*"

"Fuck the *News-Press*—for the *L.A. Times.*"

"Fuck the *L.A. Times*—the *New York Times.*"

"Fuck the *New York Times*—network newsanchor, the new Diane Sawyer."

"But sexier."

This seems to satisfy them for a moment—they pause,

breathless, out of compliments. This is like being in the sixth grade and getting more Valentine cards than anyone else. I modestly murmur, "Oh, surely not the *New York Times*," as if the *L.A. Times* is a real possibility. "But, um, tell me about yourselves. A technology company? What exactly do you do?"

"Couldn't be more boring," Clean-Cut says.

"Yeah." Cleaner-Cut agrees. "We write scheduling software."

"Scheduling?" I ask "Like…?"

"Scheduling," they say in unison.

"Oh." I nod. "Right. That sounds…interesting."

"Yeah," Tad says. "Fascinating."

"You just want the job," Clean-Cut tells him, grinning. "Which is looking more and more likely."

"Anyway, we'd better go." Cleaner-Cut checks his watch. "Before we outstay our welcome."

"Plus we don't want to miss happy hour," Clean-Cut says, then looks at me. "Unless…you don't want to come along, do you?"

Actually, if they'll keep spewing praise, that'd be the happiest happy hour of my life. I'm about to accept, when I notice Wicked Tad subtly shaking his head. He wants the schmoozing time to get the job—that's fine, then I can have my apartment back. "I'd love to," I say. "But I've got some… investigating to do."

"Elle's on the trail of the Vile Voyeurs," Tad tells them.

"Any luck so far?" Clean-Cut asks.

"Well, not really…"

"Keep us posted," Cleaner-Cut says. "Can I use your bathroom?"

"Sure," Wicked Tad says, before I can answer, and kinda nudges me toward the door. "See you later, Elle."

★ ★ ★

Kicked out of my own apartment. That's pretty low. I don't want to rattle around Merrick's house while he's working, but I've struck out with the Porn Vendors and can't think of anything else to do. I could write another column, more in the "personal is political" vein, except I have no subject. Nothing's happened to me. So I go shopping.

Three hours and one Chanel lipgloss later, I drive by the pool hall where Merrick and Neil usually play. But I can't see them through the windows and feel like a high school girl driving past an ex-boyfriend's house, so I go home.

Not home really. Merrick's house. I put the key in the lock and click the latch and the door doesn't move. Locked. My first thought: *he changed the locks.* But the tumbler definitely moved, so the key works—I guess the door was already unlocked. Merrick, however, never forgets to lock the door. Odd. More evidence, I guess, that he's working too many hours.

I re-unlock the door, and step into the great room, which has stairs on the right leading up to the second floor and the kitchen on the left. The living room has a wall of windows facing the ocean, with doors leading to the patio and beyond that the cliffs. During the day the view is glorious, but at night, the endless blackness can be daunting. Tonight, however, lights flicker on the patio like little fairies fluttering.

Fireflies? I blink, confused, and move to the windows. Merrick's on the patio, using a lighter to start candles in white glass holders.

I open one of the French doors. "You're home," I say. I mean to say something more romantic and flowery, but that's what comes out.

"Kara wouldn't let Neil out to play."

I laugh. "I have a feeling I'd like her, if we ever meet."

"Mmm." His eyes glint. "That'd be like worlds colliding."

I keep laughing, though I don't know why. He's covered the teak table in white linen, and a bottle of California chardonnay stands in a ceramic wine cooler. "What's all this?"

"For you." He uncorks the wine and pours. "The success of your article. That was gutsy and important and I'm proud of you."

He hands me a glass and we toast. Maybe he's had a change of heart, maybe he *wants* me to be a cheesy fake psychic now.

"You're wondering if I had a change of heart," he says.

"I'm wondering if there's food involved in this little celebration."

"Pizza."

"Get out!"

He nods, overflowing with smugness. "Be here any minute."

As if on cue, the doorbell rings. "Like magic," I say.

"Watch me pull a pizza out of this hat," Merrick says.

We sit in the adirondack chairs closest to the cliff and eat slices out of the box. "How did you know I'd come home?" I ask.

"I just knew."

"Maybe you're the psychic."

He washes down a bit of pizza with some wine. "After you start grad school, neither of us has to be the psychic."

"Are you sure about Laverna? You don't think they're a degree mill? They accepted me pretty quickly. I mean, when I applied to college I had to wait months, and this was like three weeks. Plus, they want me to start in April instead of the fall."

"They might not be the most selective, but that doesn't

mean you won't get a good education. A lot of the training is hands-on, isn't it? That's probably where you'll learn the most."

"Yeah, I guess."

"I'm pushing you, aren't I?" he says.

I feed Miu my pizza crust. "A little."

"Just like I'm pushing you to move in with me. You know why I'm pushing you?"

Because he loves me.

"Because I love you."

"I know. I can't go home anyway." I tell him about Wicked Tad.

"Stay as long as you want," he says, happily.

"This is only a trial period."

"You need a trial period for school—I bet if you ask, they'll let you sit in on class, maybe it's not as bad as you think."

"Hmm, that's not a terrible idea," I say, sipping my wine. "Now we just have to get your life worked out."

"What's wrong with my life, aside from my girlfriend not wanting to move in with me?"

"Your office is in a complete shambles—I've been tidier in the house than you. This from the man who used to wipe the toothpaste cap clean every time he used it? *Something's* wrong with your life."

"Apparently crusty toothpaste caps."

"Merrick." Feels good to be on the other end of the name-calling for once.

"What can I say? You've had a mellowing influence on me."

"Mellowing is one thing. Slovening is quite another."

"First, there's no such thing as "slovening." And second, there's nothing wrong. I'm busy is all."

"You don't have to tell me." I look at him over the top of my glass. "But I'm gonna find out."

He smiles like he has a secret. I smile back like I've got two. We finish the pizza and the bottle of chardonnay. The night grows dark leaving moon-silvered waves, and Merrick chases me to bed.

chapter

16

The day before I'm due on the radio, I call the admissions director at Laverna and ask if I can sit in on a class before officially matriculating. He suggests Human Development, which meets that afternoon, and I reluctantly agree to show up—which must have confused him considering I asked to go. Question Number One: What do I wear to Human Development?

Must be professional yet sensitive. Authentic and wise and, of course, slimming—I decide upon the black jacket I'd bought a while back from the Barneys outlet in Camarillo, over a T-shirt and my non-7 jeans. Aspiring therapist/full-time student, on an $18,500 financial-aid budget.

Turns out I should've worn a cotton dental smock—it's like having teeth pulled. Except not as quick. Basically, they tie a string to the wrong tooth, the other end to a doorknob, and repeatedly slam the door over a period of three hours. Human Development, my fat ass. First, the teacher wears a lavender batik gypsy blouse, an offense against lavender, batik and Gypsies. And blouses. Second, she's not a teacher, she's a therapist, and conducts the class like a group therapy session. The chairs are arranged so that the group can sit in a tight therapy circle, and while a few students have notepads, most are armed with nothing but the internal workings of their own neuroses. There's no chair for me in the circle—I'm the last to arrive, of course—but a heavy-looking wood armchair sits in one corner.

"Join the group, Elle," Ms. Batik says.

I point to the chair, raising my eyebrows, and she nods. So I self-consciously move towards the chair as the group—I mean class—begins.

"Last week the reading touched on social psychological theories," Ms. Batik says. "We had a terrific discussion on interpersonal relations. The Kinsey movie was a great springboard for exploring our sexuality in terms of developmental stages."

Movie? Sounds good. I grab the back of the wooden chair and drag, but it doesn't budge. Hmm. I pull again, and get nowhere. Okay. I move to the other side of the chair and shove, and the thing is rooted like an ancient redwood. I take a deep breath, put my shoulder against the back of the chair, and heave.

"This week," Ms. Batik says. "We're focusing on Erik Erickson's eight stages of human development. Can someone name the stages for me?"

A hand goes up as I step back and consider the chair. The thing is like bolted to the floor. Wait a second…

"Yes?" Ms. Batik says.

"Uh," a girl says, "I'm not sure of the stages but Elle is still standing there."

All eyes turn to me—and the girl is totally wrong. I'm not standing, I'm on my hands and knees checking for bolts. I find them, too.

"Looking for gum?" someone asks, and the class laughs.

"The chair is bolted to the floor," I explain, standing.

"Yes," the teacher says sympathetically. "The chair is bolted to the floor."

Is she mimicking me, or mirroring me, or using some kind of psychological technique? I'm afraid she'll repeat anything I say, but fortunately have a brainstorm: I studied Erik Erickson in my Introduction to Psychology course, and always wondered, "Don't you think it's strange his mother named him Erik? I mean, with the last name Erickson? That's like if I was named Elle Ellesdaughter. Isn't that strange?"

"Why don't you come sit on the floor?" Ms. Batik says.

I suddenly remember that one of Erikson's stages is about shame and inferiority, because that's what I'll feel if I'm forced to sit on the floor in a circle of adults. "Um, I'm only here to observe, why don't I sit over here, quietly, and you can just continue, and I'll listen. Over here. Quietly."

"Would you rather not sit on the floor?" she asks.

"Honestly, I'm okay over here."

"Stage One," she says. "Trust versus Mistrust. It lasts through the first one or two years of life. Elle, come sit on the floor."

"Well, I'd really rather—"

"Elle!" she says, harshly.

"No," I say, sitting in the chair. *Hey hey, ho ho, Batik Woman has got to go.* I will not be moved. I'm an observer here, and she's bossing me. Why is she bossing me? "I won't."

"Stage Two," she says. "Autonomy versus Shame. Tantrums, stubbornness and negativism are the norm. Think, the Terrible Twos. Usually lasts no longer than to four years of age." She glances at me. "Usually."

"Hey!" I say.

She smiles at me. "Oh, I'm just teasing. Come, come. You can have my seat."

But she's still sitting in her seat. If I go over there, she'll make me sit on the floor. I say, "Um…"

"It's okay, Elle. First, stand."

I stand.

"Now come over here."

I don't want to. I stay near the safety of my bolted chair.

"Stage Three," she says. "Initiative versus Guilt. A healthy child learns to cooperate and play with others, a fearful child remains at the fringes of the group."

"Would you stop that!" I say. "I'm not here as a show and tell exhibit. I'm here to observe the class. Stop using me as some kind of worst-case scenario."

"I'm sorry, Elle. Those are the rules. We must be willing to reveal ourselves to the class. This isn't just academia, this is the process of therapy. Without vulnerability, we cannot proceed. Those are the rules."

"I'm just an observer, though. I'm not in the class yet."

"Those are the rules."

I mutter something about her stupid rules, and where she oughtta stick them.

"Ah!" she says with great pleasure. "Stage Four, Industry

versus Inferiority. At this stage, the well-adjusted child masters rules and self-discipline, while the shame-filled child experiences failure and inferiority."

A young woman says, "Well, when someone—" she glances at me "—doesn't progress normally through the stages, does this mean…"

Three hours extend into eternity, as my psyche is probed and prodded. There are exactly two heartening notes: one, they don't know about my burlesque performance on the Web, and two, Erickson apparently considers people young adults until the age of forty. I'm still young!

I take Miu to Hendry's Beach to walk it off.

So that was horrible. People looking for serious answers to serious problems. When I get called for advice, my callers are troubled, but if they have real issues I direct them to emergency lines, trained professionals—though I now suspect that even the professionals are clueless. I don't want to be the authority, to be responsible for someone's life. I can barely handle my own—and, frankly, those students in that class were all just as fucked up as I am. Though some may have progressed beyond Stage One.

What now? I throw a stick for Miu across the slough into the waves. She runs down the beach and waits for the tide to bring the stick to her. I follow at a more sedate pace, trying to avoid the warm, yucky slough water that I have to cross to walk Miu off-leash. Well, what am I gonna do? Being a serious therapist is obviously out. I have this radio interview tomorrow, though—if I really can expose the Vile Voyeurs, I'll be a serious journalist, à la Woodward and the other one. Plus, hell, my Internet appearance puts me halfway into Deep Throat territory already.

So all I need to do is solve the mystery of the Vile Voyeurs, preferably while I'm on the radio, despite the fact that I've gotten nowhere with traditional research. I need a flash of inspiration. This would be a good time to discover that I truly am psychic.

I walk farther along the beach with Miu, the waves approaching high tide, and free my mind, open my spirit to inspiration in an internal pool of silence and peace:

I really want a pair of 7 for all mankind jeans.

No, no—silence!

Can't believe Maya's a size six. If I were a size six, I'd take out a full-page ad in the *Permanent Press*. I'd only wear Dolce & Gabbana, and—

Shut up! Shut up! Ooooom. Ooooom.

I like strappy shoes. Hey! Shut up. Focus. Internal pools...

Ooooom. Ooooom. Oooo...ld MacDonald had a farm, E-I-E-I-O! And on his farm he had a cow—

Shit! Shit! Silence, Goddammit. Shut up! Deep breath. Silence. Peace. Here we go...

Waves beating. Sun shining. Dog barking. Must remember to buy dog food. Try new brand? What kind? Wysong? Solid Gold holistic? Solid Gold dancers. Dance Fever...

Oh, fuck. Maybe I'll just walk.

After an hour, the only insight I have is that I still don't understand why the Gay Tailors don't like me. Plus they're always talking sports and drinking beer—they might as well be straight, which is no good to me. And I'm definitely not feeling the whole investigative journalist thing. Who am I kidding? If anything I should aspire to be a newscaster on *E! News,* and a size four.

If I were a size four, I wouldn't have any problems.

So Miu and I clamber into my 1974 orange BMW beater

and I realize we stink too much to go home to Merrick's. Maybe he's a little untidy at the moment, but he's still anti-stench. I head to my apartment, hoping Tad will be absent, while daydreaming about appearing on MTV's *Pimp My Ride*. I want chrome hubcaps embossed with my initials, a tricked-out trunk that opens to reveal a skinny mirror, a red carpet that auto-unrolls from the driver's seat, and an air-brushed paint job and custom leather interior in shades of violet—my current favorite color. Last week it was smoky aquamarine.

I think Xzibit and I would be friends, too. He'd be *X* and I'd be *E,* and we'd have little pills to make others feel the joy of our personalities.

I turn into the parking lot of my building. There is a car in my space, so I park in Merrick's. He's probably at a meeting or the courthouse or something. Upstairs the apartment is empty, except for Tad's ubiquitous wreckage. I rinse Miu in the tub, then jump in for a quick shower myself. Good to be in my own shower again, though it's not as nice as Merrick's—doesn't have the elephant shower head or the soaking tub that overlooks the ocean—but it's mine. I luxuriate. I wash my hair and condition twice. I shave my legs, and I think of all the things I *should've* said at Laverna to the batik-wearing freak.

As I rinse Tad's shaving cream from my legs, I realize I'm not ready to move in with Merrick. I know it's lame, but I'm simply far too excited to be in my own shower. I'm not at the Ericksonian Stage in which I can move in with a man as good as Merrick. I need to deal with my Autonomy versus Dependence, first.

I step out of the shower, and start applying body butter, nervous but resolved. Merrick's my dream boyfriend—smart, sexy, sensitive—which means he'll understand I'm not ready yet. Right. I'm finishing the final slather of cream on my butt when the bathroom door opens. Merrick, having tracked me to my perfumed lair. I smile in anticipation—there's something sexy about being naked when he's fully clothed.

Except this is not Merrick. This is Wicked Tad.

"Whoa!" he says, gaping.

I squeal and clutch at a towel. "Get out!"

"Hey, the door was unlocked."

I wrap the towel around myself. "Somebody seems to have broken the lock. Jesus, what the fuck?"

"How was I supposed to know you were here?"

Miu stares in from the hallway. She doesn't like raised voices. "The dog didn't clue you in?"

"I thought you were downstairs. With your boyfriend."

I check the towel is secure and poke Tad in the chest. "Don't you say anything about this to Merrick."

"It's not like I was in there with you."

"Get your stuff and move out."

"What?"

"You heard me."

"Where am I gonna go?"

"Brad and Maya's."

That scares him. Living on Maya's couch is no picnic, especially if she doesn't like you. He begs and pleads, and I can't say no: not for his sake, but because Maya doesn't like him. I can't inflict him on her, not while she's planning her wedding.

So I content myself with issuing demands—cleaning the apartment, washing the sheets, wearing clothes—and slamming the door in his face. He's conspicuously absent when I come out. I call Miu off the chair, lock the front door, and head downstairs.

Halfway down, my name is called. By Ray the eBay guy, waving at me from his doorway. The shiest man on earth, trying to catch my attention.

"Hey Ray," I say, jogging back up a few steps. "You're cheerful."

He mumbles an answer and feeds Miu what appears to be a samosa.

"What did you say?" I ask.

"Got the owners of *Santa Barbara Grrrrls*."

"You did not!"

He nods, looking at the dog.

"You brilliant bastard." I kiss him on the cheek. "You *are* a genius. Do you realize what this means?"

He mumbles at length, apparently shocked at the kiss.

"I can go on the air and pretend I know what I'm doing."

"That's what I said."

"Oh. Well, and that's why I agreed. So, who?"

"Barbalicious."

"Barbalicious?"

"LLC," he says. "Local company."

"LLC?"

"Barbalicious Limited Liability Corporation."

"Well, who's that?" I ask.

"You wanna know? Hire a corporate attorney and wait six months."

"Why don't *you* find out for me?"

He looks at me. Looks at the dog. Mumbles that he's not a corporate attorney. Glances into his apartment, and disappears. I thank him brokenly through the door and float downstairs, where I find Merrick and the Gay Tailors sitting on the stairs.

Merrick occupies his usual stair, with Weldon beside him,

and Johnny lies at the bottom like he's hoping for a suntan. The three of them are talking about football. Or baseball. Whichever has the Bruins. When did *Merrick* become friends with them? They befriended Merrick, Neil and Kara, Tad, everyone but me. Have they no standards?

Don't answer that.

Anyway, I'm too cheerful to be ignored. I plop down on the step below Merrick's and tell them about Ray's discovery.

"How did he find out?" Merrick says.

I frown. "I forgot to ask. But now I've got something to say on the radio tomorrow."

"You're going to be on the radio?" Johnny asks.

I smile—this is the first non-snarky question he's ever asked me. "Blake Conahy called me. You know, SB's a.m. FM DJ. Wants me on his show tomorrow."

Johnny sits up straight. "Blake Conahy? He's adorable. You're really gonna be on?"

"Did you read my article in the *Permanent Press*? We're talking about that—plus, now I'm gonna use my psychic powers to unveil Barbalicious."

"With the information you just got from Ray?" Weldon asks.

"Exactly!" I say.

They laugh. I laugh, too, which means they're laughing with me. Yeah, I think they really are. This is a crack in the ice—so I immediately forge through with my pickax, finally realizing how I can get them to like me. "Have you two ever made a wedding dress?" I ask.

They glance at each other. Hopefully? Scornfully? Playfully? Gayfully?

"Because I have a crisis," I tell them. "My best friend is

threatening to buy a wedding dress from the Petticoat Junction sales rack."

"Eww," Johnny says.

"Petticoat Junction," Weldon says.

"Eww," Johnny says again.

"The sales rack," Weldon says.

"I know," I say. "I know."

"Elle," Merrick say. "I don't think Maya—"

"Hush," I say, nudging him towards his office. "Finish your work so we can go out later."

Merrick cocks his head. "Did you hear that?"

"What?" I ask.

"The distant rumble of a terrible idea."

"Shut up—go away—I love you."

When the door closes behind him, I turn back to Johnny and Weldon. "Okay. She refuses to go to L.A. She found a Vera Wang at Petticoat Junction, and *didn't buy it*." I expect the hiss of horrified indrawn breath, and am not disappointed. "Instead, she wants this dress on sale that isn't even a dress! It's two pieces, the top is basically a lace vest. This is what I'm thinking—how about a little Weldon and Johnny couture?"

"Oh, I don't know," Weldon says, in exactly the same tone I use when I spot a dessert cart.

"We really couldn't," Johnny says.

"You'd be doing me a huge personal favor…" Oops. "Doing *us* a real favor, Merrick and Neil especially."

"Well, we do have a few sketches…"

"What does your friend look like?" Johnny asks, sharp again. "Not like…" He doesn't quite gesture at me.

"She's blond and adorable."

"Is she all…lumpy?"

I sigh. "Size six."

Weldon swings open the door to their shop, and I step inside. I have breached their shields! We'll be trading friendly insults any minute now.

We sit at their huge sewing table and Johnny says, "What does she have in mind?"

I describe the Petticoat Junction dress. "Adorable but...extremely off-the-rack."

"What're they asking?"

"Ninety-nine."

"Ninety-nine what?"

"Dollars. Ninety-nine dollars. But of course—handmade, couture—yours will cost more."

"Way more," Weldon says.

"Way, way," Johnny says.

"How many 'ways' are talking?" I ask. "Maya's kinda short on the 'way.'"

All the warmth dissipates, as Johnny says, "Well, we're just tailors after all. Not designers. You wouldn't want to pay us more than we're worth."

"But wait, no!" I blurt. "This could be my wedding gift. I'd pay. For the dress. It's on me! As a gift. For my best friend. She's only getting married once. Most important day of her life."

"Ballpark?" Weldon asks Johnny.

Johnny mentions a number, pauses for breath, and keeps mentioning the number, which has approximately seventeen digits.

This is Maya's wedding. She deserves to be a perfect bride. I gulp and say, "Fine! Fine, fine, fine. You, um, take credit cards?"

Weldon nods and turns to Johnny. "Silk."

"Satin."

"Seamless."

"Sensuous."

Triumph! We will bond over the wedding dress, best friends even though I never taped joints to their door à la Anna Madrigal (Neil's fault for never bringing me pot).

Um, but how am I going to tell Maya?

Forget Maya, it's Carlos I should've worried about. He catches me at Merrick's the next morning as I'm trying to decide what to wear to my radio interview.

"What is this?" he asks, when I answer the phone. "A down payment on a house?"

"Don't be ridiculous," I say. "Do you have any idea the cost of Santa Barbara real estate?"

"So what is it, a car? Your BMW died and *Pimp My Ride* never call you back?"

Okay, so I visited the *PMR* Web site and discovered I'm too old. You have to be between eighteen and twenty-two to have your ride pimped: apparently MTV's never heard of Erik Erikson. "Um," I say, brightly.

"Elle, you're getting in over your head again."

"It's a gift, Carlos."

"For what?"

"Maya's wedding." I tell him about the dress.

"Why can't she wear the ninety-nine-dollar dress?"

I look to the heavens. "If you don't understand, I can't explain it."

"What?"

"You're romantically challenged, that's all I'm saying."

His voice rising, he says, "You can't afford it, that's all *I'm* saying."

I try to calm him. "Everything's under control, Carlos. I'm sure to make oodles of money once my radio interview airs, the phone'll ring off the hook. Clients will be knocking on my astral door."

"Someone's going to come knocking if you miss your payment. And they'll want your ass."

I tap the receiver with my finger nail. "Oh! I think it's my call-waiting."

"That's not call-waiting, that's you tapping on the phone. Listen—"

"Gotta go."

I hang up and quick dial Maya, so when Carlos calls back he'll get a busy signal. But wait—if it's busy, he'll know I don't have call-waiting. Shit. I'm about to hang up when Maya answers. And honestly, who am I kidding? Carlos knows I don't have call-waiting.

"What's up?" Maya asks.

"Um…" I dig deep and surface empty. Can't mention I'm avoiding Carlos because I spent a fortune on her couture dress. So I say, "I'm getting interviewed on the radio in an hour. Wanna come?"

She does—she even comes over to help me decide what to wear. "Black T-shirt and the prairie skirt."

"Prairie's not out?" I ask.

"Not if it flatters your figure."

Is she telling me I have a big ass? As if I didn't know. I feel self-conscious in my underwear, and step away from the mirror to look at Maya. She gazes back with perfect innocence, so I put on the skirt and T-shirt. I look good enough for radio.

"Right," Maya says. "Did you eat anything?"

"Piece of toast," I say.

"Good," she says. "Do you need a shot?"

"Of what?"

"Whiskey. Settle your nerves," she says. "You're not nervous?"

"Should I be? They'll ask questions, I'll answer them—this is what I do for a living, Maya. I even have a lead on the Vile Voyeurs. You just sit back and be amazed."

"What about the hundreds of people listening on their way to work?"

I wave my hand à la Marie Antoinette. "Let them listen."

We park outside the station, a square, beige building with small, dark windows. The inside is equally bland, with florescent lighting, institutional gray carpeting and matching walls and cubicles. I was expecting something sexier: glass offices, sleek black desks with a fine dusting of cocaine and swaggering DJs.

Maya—clearly enjoying masquerading as my handler—tells the receptionist I'm here.

A moment later, Blake Conahy, SB's a.m. FM DJ appears—short, dark hair, tan skin and a stocky but athletic body. "Elle? Blake. Welcome. And this is…?"

"This is Maya," I say. "My entourage."

They both smile politely, and he tells me, "It's great to meet you in person. I mean, after seeing you on the Web." He manages not to ogle me, which is nice. I've seen a few speculative looks since appearing in my near-altogether.

"Thanks for having me."

"Though maybe I shouldn't joke," Blake says. "Must've been a traumatic experience."

"Oh, well…" I'd been furious, humiliated, mortified and definitely exploited. But traumatized? Not really. I worry that I'm too shallow to get traumatized—only the really deep people are traumatized. "It's certainly not an experience I'd recommend."

We follow him down the hall and he tells me they're at commercial, and we'll be on when it ends. We step into the studio, and Blake sits at a computer with a touch-screen monitor, from where he apparently controls the whole show. I sit in my seat and wear headphones, and Maya perches nervously on the couch at the other end of the room.

Blake says, "Thirty seconds and you're on."

I adjust my headphones, concerned they're crimping my hair, and smile at Blake's sidekick—Sally? I've totally forgotten her name. She smiles back, and I glance at Maya and give her a thumbs-up. She offers a sickly grin—I don't know why she's so tense. For me, this is nothing. The equivalent of her opening beer bottles in public.

Blake says something to his sidekick. "Sarah, we'll—"

"Sarah," I say, loudly, attempting to lodge it in my mind. Everyone stares at me.

"Yes?" she says.

"Huge fan. Love your work."

"Really?" she smiles. "Everyone seems to favor Bl—"

"Here we go," Blake says. "Five, four, three…"

"Welcome back, Santa Barbara," Sarah says into the microphone, her voice suddenly deeper and more colorful. "In the studio with us this morning is Elle Medina. You may recall Elle from her role last fall in finding the 'Missing Bitch.'"

"Whoa, that's some nasty language," Blake says. "We're a family show, here."

Sarah laughs. "She's a local psychic and—"

"What kind of woman are we talking about?" Blake says. "And if she went missing, who'd try to find her?"

Sarah laughs. "We're talking about a missing *dog,* Blake. A puppy, in fact—"

"Lucky it wasn't a cat, or they'd say Elle found her missing pus—"

Maya and I startle at a sudden cat screech before realizing it's a sound effect, and Blake winks at me from his seat, where he just touched the computer screen.

Sarah laughs. "It's a dog, okay? Kidnapped, until—"

More sound effects, the refrain from the "Who Let the Dogs Out" song with the woofing *who, who, who,* chorus.

"Until Elle found the kidnapper with her psychic powers, and—"

"You don't really believe in that, do you?" Blake says, touching the screen. A cuckoo clock chimes, *cuckoo, cuckoo.* "So, Elle, I don't know about the psychic stuff, but I want to get into the reason you're here. Nothing to do with dogs, but a lot to do with females." Cue "wolf whistle." "All I can say is, everyone with a Web browser knows you're no dog."

I laugh. It's catching. "Thanks, Blake…I guess."

"There's no guessing about it," he says.

Sarah laughs. "Not if you check out the Web site, Santa Barbara Grrrrls dot com."

"Four *R*s," Blake says. "No *I*s. I mean, not 'no eyes.' Believe me, this isn't a site for our visually impaired listeners. Unless you have a braille monitor, then I heartily recommend you check this out and hell, give us a call!"

Sarah laughs. "So, Elle, we were talking about how you got started in this business."

We were?

"You were a phone psychic, right?" Sarah says.

Now I can pitch my services! "That's exactly right," I begin, and see the sign hanging over Blake—

On the Air

It's fire-engine red and built into a black box the size of a toaster oven. On the Air. My words are being broadcast into the ether, into the great beyond, they will travel at the speed of sound toward the sun, growing ever fainter as they escape the solar system and penetrate into the galaxy.

On the Air.

chapter

17

In ninth grade English I was required to give a speech on the poet Gerard Manley Hopkins, and when my turn was called I stood mute before the class. All those faces hoping to hear something interesting. I stood there a full thirty seconds, a long enough pause that Mrs. Lepinsky told me I could start whenever I was ready. Was she kidding? I would *never* be ready. The intersection of *Elle* and *ready* was a logical impossibility. We were parallel lines, like train tracks, if we ever met there'd be disaster.

I focused on one kid in particular, Robbie Pollard. Can't believe I still remember his name. He sat smack in the middle of the classroom, the first of many high school crushes who never seemed aware that I existed in a love-fogged state for him alone. Or, technically, that I existed at all. He was doodling, so he didn't realize I was staring for another ten seconds. Probably only looked up, because I *wasn't* talking. When he did, he kinda snorted in disgust, and that was enough to break the spell. I recited the first lines of the poem I'd memorized: The world is charged with the grandeur of God. It will flame out, like shining from shook foil.

"Like shining from shook foil." I loved that line, and for a while called anyone who destroyed the grandeur of my world a "foil shaker." Which is not as effective an insult as you might hope.

There's the sound of crickets. Back in the radio station, Blake is playing a Crickets sound effect.

Sarah laughs. "Didn't you start working for some psychic phone bank?"

Maya is gesticulating in front of me, miming words coming out of her mouth, as if the problem is I don't realize I'm supposed to speak. You take your tongue on faith, that this wibbly slab of flesh knows where to go to make the right sound. I am here to tell you, do not disregard the tongue. Do not disrespect the tongue. Honor the tongue, for without assistance from the tongue, you appear to every single human within the 805 area code—and, fainter, to those throughout the galaxy and beyond—to be a sub-moronic mouthbreather. I simply cannot operate the complex speaking machinery that is my mouth.

"Dionne Warwick?" Sarah says, not laughing. "Miss Cleo?"

With tremendous effort of will, I say, "Uuh-guh."

"Uuh-guh?" Blake says.

"I'll think that's a yes," Sarah tells him.

"Who calls you for advice, Cro-Magnons?" Cue Man

Grunting sound effect. "The Neanderthal psychic line, Elle speaking."

I say, "Gah-gu."

Even I don't know what that means. But I'm stuck, hypnotized by the On the Air sign. I stare like a...like one of those animals who gets hypnotized by things.

Sarah laughs. "Advice to the lovelorn caveman…"

"They ask how to find a woman," Blake says. "Elle tells 'em to drag her by the hair back to the cave."

Sarah laughs some more. "Sounds like my ex-boyfriend."

Maya saves the day. Somehow sensing I'm caught in the headlights, she whips off her sweater and covers the sign. The spell is broken and my tongue springs into action—

"Let's not talk about ex-boyfriends," I blurt, giving Maya the peace sign. "Mine left town for two weeks and came back married to someone else."

Cue Woman Screaming.

"Isn't a psychic supposed to see that coming?" Blake asks.

"That's the whole 'why don't you pick the lotto numbers' question. I'm an intuitive, really—and I'm hardly infallible. Yes, my intuition was screaming for attention—" Cue Woman Screaming again. "But I was a woman in love, and women in love are masters at ignoring their intuition—that's why they need to call me. Get a second opinion. I wish I'd called someone before my ex ran off and married an Iowan floozy."

"Now we're getting somewhere!" Blake says. "Some might consider you a floozy yourself. Caught stripping on the Internet."

Sarah laughs. "I haven't seen it, myself, but I hear it's quite the show."

"I thought *everyone* had seen that," I say. "Santa Barbara Grrrls dot com. G-R-R-R-R-L-S."

"From your article in the *Permanent Press,*" Sarah says, "I got the impression that you were the victim here, caught on tape without permission. An invasion of privacy. But here you are, *on the air,* promoting the site. What's that about?"

I pause a moment, stricken by the phrase "on the air." But the sign is still covered, so I'm okay. "That's right, Sarah, I was filmed in a dressing room without my knowledge. But who hasn't heard about Paris Hilton's sex videos? And who cares? The more people know, the less titillating this is—and the less shameful. These guys, the Vile Voyeurs who run this site, they're afraid of women. They're afraid of women's sexuality. They have to hide cameras to see a girl naked! Screw them. I'm not gonna let them scare me, or shame me. I'm not proud of this—it's just some greasy Peeping Toms—but no way a bunch of little boys are gonna control *this* woman. Men look at women all the time, fine, they've got horny toad lizard brains telling them if they miss a jiggle they've failed in life. But I'm not about to stop wearing what I want, where I want, and when I want because I'm afraid some man's gonna ogle me. These guys aren't even men, they're boys. Well, I'm a *woman.* Hear me roar."

"Well, that's interesting—" Blake starts.

He doesn't get further because Sarah's clapping and saying, "Preach, sister!" and "Damn straight!" and "Horny toad brains!"

Blake furiously taps his screen, and in a second we're surrounded by the sound of bullfrogs. "Sounds like the horny toads are out in force," he says, once Sarah quiets.

I flush with success. "It's a toad's world," I say.

Blake laughs. "Now, that's no surprise—but the real mystery remains. Who are these Peeping Toms? The—what do you call them?—Vile Voyeurs? You're psychic, can't you divine who they are?"

"I consider myself more of an intuitive—"

"But you solved the mystery of the 'Missing Bitch' with your intuition," he says. "Why not this?"

"Well, I wouldn't want people to get the idea that any mystery is solvable simply by dialing my number—" and here I give my number, twice "—however, let me see if I get anything…"

"Let's give Elle a little intuition music," Blake says into his microphone, "and we'll be right back with her exposé of…"

Sarah intones, "The Vile Voyeurs," and Blake puts a kind of hollow echo on her words.

Then he cues up "Hotel California" and turns to me. "You're good," he says.

"If I remember how to talk," I say.

"Even *that* was good. Nothing draws them in like the chance to hear someone fall on her face. You know they all got riveted," he tells Sarah, "wondering if she'd *totally* fuck up."

She nods. "And then got an earful of horny toad."

"She's a natural," he says. "You, Elle have the gift—you can talk about nothing like it's something."

I beam. "That *is* my gift."

We chatter for a few more minutes, then he cues up some groovy sci-fi noise and says, "We're back in the studio with Elle Medina, psychic counselor and online stripper—ouch! She just threw a bottle at my head."

I've done no such thing. "A whiskey bottle, Blake," I say. "From your desk drawer."

Sarah laughs. "So, Elle, during the break you focused on the mystery, did you have any luck?"

I grab a stack of takeout menus from the console and riffle

the pages. "I'll read the cards, now that I'm focused, we'll see if anything comes together."

Sarah mouths, "You liar!" Then laughs.

"What is that you're doing there?" Blake asks. "That layout?"

I glance at the top menu. "This is a Thai layout, Blake—but the cards are just tools, the real work happens inside. Let me see…this card shows, um, Spring Roll…spring rolling in, the end of winter, the beginning of spring. Land of spring—wait, I'm getting something." I pause dramatically. "Barbalicious!"

"Barbalicious?" Blake says. "Sounds like some sort of Santa Barbara bubble gum."

"Barbalicious is the name of the corporation behind the Vile Voyeurs," I explain. "I'm really getting a strong feeling, here. Barbalicious. That's the name."

"One of those Harry Potter flavors," Blake says. "But southern Californian."

Sarah laughs. "Tastes like saltwater with sandy grit."

Blake taps his screen. "Okay, I'm getting a call, my producer actually, from the other room. Yes, Matt?"

"She's right," a deep voice says in my headphones. "I searched Barbalicious—they're a local company with a handful of Web sites."

Cue the sound of the Correct Answer Bell on a game show.

"Give us some names, Elle," Blake says. "Preferably with phone numbers."

Sarah laughs. "We'll give 'em a call, see if they're not your Vile Voyeurs."

I flip the menus again and am completely uninspired. What made me think I could just give them Barbalicious and be done? "Uh, these things come in pieces, so I—"

Cue "Wipeout" sound effect.

"Hey, we're out of time anyway. Well, you heard it here first, folks. Barbalicious, coming soon to a candy store near you."

Sarah laughs. "When we come back, Elle Medina—filmed stripping in a dressing room—we'll hear more about this infringement on her freedom to change clothes."

Sarah takes off her headset and I say, "Wait a minute. Why'd you say I'd be here when you get back? My fifteen minutes of fame were up three minutes ago."

"We're getting phone calls for you," she says. "Stay and talk to some callers?"

"Well…" I look at Maya. She's curled on the couch reading a magazine. "Sure."

They both appear pleased that I'm staying, which I must say is a novel feeling. When the commercials are done, Blake takes the first call.

"Oh, hey, this is Scott—" he's kinda whispering "—big fan of the show. I wanted to ask her a question, the psychic."

"I'm here, Scott," I say. "What can I do for you?"

"It's about a woman," he says, sounds like he's speaking close into the phone.

"You have a crush on her," I say. "Are you at work?"

"Yeah."

"She works with you?" I ask. "Same office?"

"Holy sh—"

Cue the sound of fireworks. "Down, boy," Blake says.

"Sorry, Blake," the caller says. "But that's incredible. That's all totally right, the same office."

I figured that's why he's whispering. Still, I *am* good. "Small company?"

"Yeah, and we listen to the show every day. It's never been this good, this is unbelievable."

"Scott, can you see everyone from where you're sitting?"

"No, I'm in the break room."

"Is it possible that your girl's listening right now?"

There's silence as this sinks in. Blake cues a hollow, ghostly moaning sound.

Sarah laughs. "Scott?"

"He's there," I say. "Listen, Scott, you think she hasn't noticed you, but she has. Believe me. Now, maybe she's hoping you'll make the first move, maybe she's not, but don't worry—she knows you exist."

"You think?"

"This is what you're gonna do," I tell him. "Hang up right now and ask her to go to dinner at Emily's. They've got an artichoke appetizer right now that's to die for. I mean, this thing is—"

Cue the Meg Ryan orgasm scene from *When Harry Met Sally.*

"Yeah," I say. "And the appetizer lasts like ten minutes." I talk to Scott for another moment, then he hangs up.

"You think this is going to work?" Blake asks me. "She's going to say yes?"

"Hey, you can't ask for a cuter-meet than this. A crazy psychic lady on the radio got you together. Is it gonna be long-term? Doesn't matter. He asked a girl out and next time it'll be easier, until he finds the right person. It's all about taking those first steps."

"We've got another caller," Blake says. "Hello, you're on the air."

"Hi, I'm calling for Elle? This is Allison. I'm graduating from UCSB and my mom wants me to go to graduate school, but—"

"You don't want to go," I say, without thinking.

"Yeah!" she says. "I totally don't."

"You want to…travel?" All college grads want to travel. Or move in with inappropriate boyfriends or girlfriends. "I'm getting *moving*…"

"Travel, definitely travel."

"Where?" I ask, because why should I do all the work?

"Um. I don't know. I was sorting hoping you might…"

"Gotcha. Let me meditate on this…I'm getting Greece." Which is where I'd go, if I could afford it.

"Greece? That's hot!"

But another thought occurs to me. "Wait, no, that picture is fading. I'm seeing travel, but with a purpose. Like Peace Corps or one of those international volunteer groups. You ever thought of that?"

"Like…maybe?"

"Check the UCSB career center. I see travel, education, helping people—plus looks great on a résumé, for your mom."

"That kinda makes…scary sense."

I wish her a bon voyage—cue Fog Horn—and we're on to the next caller.

Forty-five minutes later, I'm still answering phone calls. Cindy wants to know about Lasik eye surgery, Martha needs a raise, Peggy has to dump his sorry ass and Donald wants to know where he can download more mpegs of girls stripping in dressing rooms. Blake beeps out my answer, then this happens:

"Hi," the caller says, a girl's voice. Then nothing.

"Hello?" Blake say. "Still there?"

"Yes."

"Honey, this is radio," Sarah says. "We require sound."

But I can tell from the tone of her voice this isn't a fun call: this is a crisis hotline call. I shake my head at them and say, "I'm here, there's no rush. I know it was hard for you to call—do you want to talk to me off the air?"

"Were you really on Santa Barbara Grrrrls?" she asks.

"I still am, as far as I know."

"Well…so was I." The words tumble out—"I heard what you said about Paris Hilton and nobody caring she's a scag, but she's Paris Hilton, she's a billionaire, I mean it's different, isn't it? With me, I'm not—nobody knows anything about me, except what they see. That's not the same. That sucks."

"What's your name?" Blake asks. "We need to call you something."

"Um…"

Obviously, she doesn't want to give her real name. "Well, gee…" I say, "could you—"

"You *are* psychic!" she says. "The first letter of my name is G."

What? *G?* "Oh! Well, G, that's what we'll call you, then."

"But what you said, about telling everyone to show it's no big deal, I guess that means I have to tell you my real name."

"No! No, that's not for everyone. Let's start slower than that, G. Can you tell me what happened?"

"Were you in a dressing room?" Sarah asks, a bit salaciously.

I scowl at her—poor G doesn't find this funny. Sarah raises her hands in apology, and gestures for me to go ahead.

"That's what's so vile about the voyeurs," I say. "The invasion of privacy. For me it was a dressing room, other women have gotten caught falling out of their bikinis at the beach or exposing themselves climbing in a short skirt out of a car. Mostly, though, the Vile Voyeurs like the bar scene. Women who have a little too much to drink, and either pull a Tara Reid—"breast hanging out of her dress "—or worse, are targeted by drunk guys pulling up their skirts."

"Or down their tops," Sarah says quietly. She's finally getting the picture.

"That was me," G says.

"At a bar?" I ask.

"My friend's twenty-first birthday. I guess I got really wasted. I don't even remember anything happening, but the next day I'm at school, and these two guys I don't even know come and say they saw my…breasts. I thought they were just being jerks, but when I got to class this other guy had his laptop open and was showing people pictures of me."

Sarah and I both groan. "I'm so sorry," I say.

"I hate men," Sarah says.

"Me, too," I say.

"Yeah," Blake says. "Me, three."

"Shut up," Sarah says.

"I just felt so bad," G says. "Like I never wanted to go back to school, and—just really, really bad."

"I would, too," I say.

"But I heard you before, you act like it's nothing, like it's funny."

"It's not nothing, and it's not funny. The thing is, with me it's different, because—" my whole life is based on humiliating myself "—I'm older, and at least I remember being in the dressing room, and—and, if you knew me, you'd know this is my life. This kind of thing happens to me all the time. Like there was this neighborhood kid bugging me, so I got all these water balloons, and the next time he came around I beaned him…except it wasn't him, it was my landlord! And they weren't water balloons, they were condoms."

Sarah laughs. Blake laughs. Even G laughs.

"The thing is, G, either I laugh at everything and move on, or honestly, I'd be in tears just about every day of my life."

"I don't know," G says, sounding better, but dubious. "I don't think I can laugh about this."

"You don't have to. We all deal with bad stuff differently. What works for me doesn't necessarily work for you. I don't want you to laugh it off, it's not funny. But you do need to find a way to deal with it, and that might mean talking to somebody. Stay on the line, and we'll talk some more."

"I'm sorry, G," Sarah says, gently. "But our time is up."

"Okay. Thanks. And my name is Gabrielle."

Maya and I look at each other: Gabrielle was the daughter of the saleswoman at Petticoat Junction. As Blake and Sarah wrap up the show, I talk with Gabrielle off air, until she says, "I just feel better, talking to someone else, knowing they weren't only after me, you know? Thanks. I dunno. Thanks."

She hangs up and Maya and I say goodbye to Blake and Sarah, who just finished reading my 900 number on the air. We get into Maya's car and she looks at me and doesn't start the engine.

"Oh, God," I say. "I have food in my teeth, don't I?"

"You were terrific," she says. "I mean—you were *terrific.*"

Maya has been my best friend since the seventh grade and because neither of us have siblings we've always been more like sisters. We love like crazy and make each other crazy— and I can always count on her to tell me the truth.

"I had no idea," she says, turning in her seat to face me. "You were funny and smart and helpful. Sure, you talk crazy psychic stuff, but nobody takes that seriously. I mean, it's ridiculous, being a fake psychic, but you're *good.* You really helped those callers."

"God, I hope so. That Scott guy seemed sweet, and I was too nervous at the beginning to get a sense of him, maybe the girl is totally out of his league. And Cindy…what if she goes blind? But Lasik has totally improved, I read an article in *Allure* last month. And she *sounds* like she'd be so much happier without glasses, you know, like she thinks she'll be prettier, so she will be. Do you think I should call Gabrielle back? Well, I'll talk to her mother, and give her my number. I hope I didn't fuck that up."

Maya looks dumbfounded.

"Don't worry," I say. "I'll call my contact at the crisis center, she'll recommend a good counselor—she knows everything."

She nods slowly. "That's how you do it?"

"Well, *I* can't handle the serious stuff. I can't even remember to water houseplants."

"No, I mean…you really care. You get a bunch of weirdos on the phone, and you treat them like friends. You want to help them, make them happier. You really care what happens to them."

I don't get it. "Well, sure. What else would I do?"

"I don't know," she laughs, shaking her head. "I thought…I don't know what I thought. I'm just really proud you're my friend."

"You just made my day."

"Good," Maya says. "Now, let's make mine. I haven't bought my dress yet." She starts the car. "Petticoat Junction should be open by now and you can ask the saleswoman if that was her daughter."

"Oh, wait—no!" I say.

"What? You've got to be somewhere?"

"Well. I…sort of."

Maya looks at me strangely. "Okaaay. Speaking of weirdos, where should I drop you?"

Must tell her about the Johnny and Weldon couture dress.

There will never be a better time—she's happy with me for once. But how best to tell her? Preferably from within some variety of reinforced concrete bunker, or...ah-ha! "My apartment."

"And wake Sleeping Beauty? It's not even noon yet—you know someone's snoring naked in your bed."

"I can't live my life avoiding Wicked Tad," I tell her. "Anyway, there's something I need to do—it'll only take ten minutes, then I'm all yours."

Maya parks outside and settles comfortably into the driver's seat.

"Aren't you coming inside?" I ask. She has to come inside.

She pulls a *New Yorker* from the back. "Nah, I'll wait here. Take as long as you need."

"Don't you want to say hi to Merrick?"

She scans the parking lot. "He's not here."

"Oh," I say, dejected. "Yeah. Well, come say hi to Wicked Tad."

Maya gives me a look. "I don't know how you put up with him. Good thing the two of you get along, or he'd be sleeping on my couch and I'd have to set him on fire."

"Yeah," I say, because I don't want to admit that I'm this close to chasing him from my apartment with a battle-ax. "Well, come inside anyway."

"Why?"

"Maybe I need your help moving something."

"Do you?"

"I might."

"What?"

"I don't know." I frown. "Something heavy. Would you just come inside?"

She raises her eyebrows but unbuckles her seatbelt and follows me inside. In the foyer I say, "Oh, look—the tailors are open! Let's say hi!"

"What is it with you and saying hi?"

I open their door and hip-check Maya inside. She slides to a halt, rubbing her bottom. Johnny looks up from the corner where he's hemming pants and Weldon finishes a seam or something on the sewing machine. "This is Maya," I tell them.

"The blushing bride," Weldon says.

"But she's adorable," Johnny says, standing from his chair.

"I told you so," I say.

"We heard you on SB's a.m. FM," Weldon says. "Johnny cried."

"I had something in my eye. Shut up." He turns to Maya. "Let me see you," he says. "Spin."

Maya smiles. "You first."

Without a moment's hesitation, Johnny executes a perfect jazz spin, hands extended, one foot tucked into his knee. Maya laughs and returns a modest pirouette. Even in faded Levi's and a white T-shirt, she's graceful and elegant.

"And she knows how to *move,* too," Johnny crows, then explains to me, "You're a clumper. The dress isn't all that matters, you know—one must *wear* the dress. You plod. You stomp. You galumph."

"She does not—" Maya starts.

Johnny presses a finger to her mouth and shushes her. "Shh! I'm thinking. Genius at work—silence in the gallery." Maya presses her lips together, looking more like she's trying not to laugh than to keep quiet, and Johnny removes his finger from her lips and presses it to his own. "I'm seeing Degas," he says. "The ballerinas, the quick pastel sketches, catching the movement and the light."

"Deconstructed," Weldon says, standing from behind his machine with a spiral-bound notepad. "Reconstructed."

Johnny cocks his head at Maya. "Ethereal, but grounded."

Weldon sketches furiously. "We need to find the right white."

"Pearl," Johnny says. "Or seafoam."

"For a wedding dress?" Weldon says. "With that peaches-and-cream complexion? Traditional—"

"A *what?*" Maya says.

"A peaches-and-cream complexion," I say, too quickly. "You really have lovely skin."

"A wedding dress?" she says.

I say, "Surprise!"

chapter

18

"No, no, no." Maya shakes her head. "I already picked a dress."

Johnny looks at Weldon. Weldon looks at Johnny. They both say, "Petticoat Junction."

"What's wrong with Petticoat Junction?"

"Are you getting married, or gettin' yer wagons hitched?"

"There's nothing wrong with Pet—" Maya starts.

Weldon shows her his sketch. "This is what we're think-ing—roughly."

Her eyes widen, and I step forward to peek, but can't see around Weldon and Johnny, who are rapid-fire explaining and brainstorming and enthusing. I step around and they whirl Maya the opposite direction, chatting about fabric and drape.

I finally get positioned to see the notepad, and Weldon snaps it shut, looking to Maya. "Tell me that's not gorgeous."

"It's gorgeous, but…how much does this cost? More than ninety-nine dollars?"

The tailors fix me with an expectant look.

"Not that much more," I say. "You pay a hundred and the rest is my wedding gift."

"Elle, you know you can't afford this."

I sidle toward the notepad, because this sketch must really be something for Maya to even consider it. "Of course I can. You *know* I'm gonna drop more on your wedding than I can afford anyway, it's not like *not* spending too much is even an option."

"I guess," Maya says. "They're gonna do your bridesmaid dress, too?"

"I'm the bridesmaid?"

"Of course you're the bridesmaid, you little weirdo."

"Well, you didn't say anything."

"I didn't say anything because *of course* you're the bridesmaid."

I've almost completed my sidling, but Johnny grabs me and starts measuring, tutting under his breath, while Weldon and Maya chat about the Bruins, or the Bears or something. I'm pretty sure one of them is gonna mention how much more fabric my dress will require—*seven times as much!*—but nobody does.

Maya and I get pastries and coffee at a French bakery on State Street. All in all, that went pretty well. Maya's nervously excited about her Johnny-and-Weldon couture, and now I only have to worry about paying for everything, and whether a couple beer-guzzling, sports-talking, steak-grilling tailors can make a nice dress.

Well, and if they like me. At least they're warming up. Maybe. "The Gay Tailors hate me," I say, biting into my *pain au chocolat*.

"Maybe because you call them the Gay Tailors," Maya says.

"Not to their faces."

"It could get back to them."

"But they're gay and they're tailors, both good things. What's offensive?"

Maya shrugs and sips her skinny latté.

"It's like calling you the blonde skinny," I say. "Or Pixie Six."

"Pixie Six?"

"For size six, and being pixie petite. I kind of like that." I lower my voice. "'We are gathered here today to join in holy matrimony, Perfect Brad and Pixie Six…'"

She doesn't quite smile.

"What? Is it the wedding dress? You're already having second thoughts?"

"Not about the dress, no."

"Not Brad!" I say appalled.

"Of course not Brad. The wedding. Everything's twice as complex as it should be, and ten times as expensive, I can't even find a place to have the damn thing. Anything cheaper than $5,000 is booked until next year, I thought maybe a restaurant, but most don't take wedding parties, or they cost more than hiring a hall. And do you know what they charge to rent tables and napkins and everything? And—" she swallows "—I haven't called a single caterer."

"Oh. Dear."

"I know," she squeaks. "And my mom set aside a fund before she died—she knew Dad's too cheap—and I could spend that, but it's such a waste, blowing everything on one night. The bar needs so much work, if we got married at the justice of the peace we could pour that money into the bar, but I don't want to get married at the justice of the peace, and I don't know what to do, I'm gonna end up getting married in a beautiful dress in some administrative office with three guests, and I want a real wedding!"

"Okay," I say. "This is what we're gonna do—"

"Wait." She holds up her hand. "I know I need help, but you have to promise no gospel choir, no confetti canon and no Statue of Liberty cake."

"We don't need a canon, we can toss the—"

"Those are the rules," she says. "And no monogrammed napkin rings. Otherwise I'm open."

"I can live with that." I pop the last bite of my *pain au chocolat* into my mouth. "Okay, here's the plan. You have the ceremony on the beach, right before sunset."

"Can you *do* that? Don't you need a permit?"

"What, walk on the beach? Say a few words? You're fine as long as there aren't any chairs or food or anything—this is just the ceremony. Plus, you think the ranger is going to interrupt a wedding in progress? They're all totally sweet, they don't even like telling people to leash dogs."

"On the beach," she says, in epiphany. "That's so Santa Barbara."

"And free. All you need is maybe something to stand under."

"A *huppah.*"

Sounds like she's choking on her latté. "Wrong pipe?"

"No," she says. "That's the wedding canopy Jews get married under."

"Well, then we're already ahead," I say. "After the ceremony, we have the reception at Shika."

"At the bar? Have you *seen* the bar?"

Exactly the response I was hoping for. I smile in triumph. "Not the *old* Shika—the *new* Shika, after you redecorate. Put the money for the wedding into the bar, have the reception there—deduct everything as a business expense, and end up with a way better bar. Shika's a great space, high ceilings and the skylights and the art deco bar. Just cosmetic stuff needs changing. Fresh paint, new lighting fixtures and furniture. Merrick says he'd love to do some designing for you, as a wedding present." Or he will, once I tell him about the idea. "We nuke the booths, maybe put in a couple couches and a coffee table."

She brightens. She glows. "My God, Elle, that's brilliant!"

"I'm on a roll."

"What about the food?" she asks. "No caterer, remember?"

"Think Provence. Casual French chic—fresh heirloom tomatoes and olive oils, artisan cheeses and bread. Olives and little delicious delicacies, mozzarella draped in basil and drizzled with balsamic. Nothing hot, nothing complex— good, elegant, rustic fare."

"But who's going to do it?"

"I'll call Valentine," I say simply. "She'll know."

"And the rentals?"

"Don't rent, buy—you'll need new everything for the bar, anyway. You know how pretty you want your wedding to be? Imagine the bar like that, all the time. You make a pretty bar and women'll come—and where drunk women go, men follow."

"How about flowers and invitations?" she asks. "Those don't count as remodeling."

"For invites, you're on your own. Talk to Ray Flood in my building, I bet he can get you a deal. Other than that, I dunno, think simple elegance. I hate all those extra sheets people put in invitations—tacky and expensive and bad for the environment."

"And flowers?"

"Hmm, tricky. What about the Flower Show? We could find someone there."

"It's the weekend of the wedding."

"Oh. Well, there are all those flower wholesalers in Carpinteria." The city just south of Santa Barbara. "I'll see what I can come up with, leave flowers to me."

A tentative smile tugs at her lips. "Sounds perfect, actually."

Now if I can only make it all happen. But I smile confidently, because confidence is the first step. At least, that's what I tell my clients.

Two halcyon hours discussing decorations, renovations and innovations with *Maya* looking to *me* for advice. Kill me now. I'm done. Nothing will ever surpass this moment. But we finally part, with Maya enthused and me enthusiastically overwhelmed.

I head to Merrick's house, and am staring into his fridge when I remember to check my messages. I turned the ringer off on my cell for the radio show, and have heard nothing. Wonder if Merrick called. He wasn't at the office, he's not here, could he be at the courthouse, getting permits? Or the planning commission? I hope not. He always comes back in a foul mood after dealing with the planning commission, and it would mean he'd missed my radio show.

I call voice mail. I have twenty-eight messages.

Twenty-eight. Messages. For me.

I have twenty-eight messages. Well, unless the guy from Lompoc got my number. Then I have a twenty-eight-part phone sex story.

Message one: "I'm calling for Elle, I heard you on the radio this morning? Is this the number? Anyway, if this is you, I want your advice. I'm starting my own business, but I think maybe this is a really bad idea. Could you call me back? What are your rates again?"

The next message is a woman who's afraid her fifteen-year-old daughter's doing drugs, because she's sullen and moody. Then there's two "advice for the lovelorn" calls, then Carlos, then five people who want my advice but don't mention a problem, then a guy calling to say he saw me online and my tits are too small, then another lovelorn, and three more people without specific problems, and so on... twenty-eight messages.

I can't believe that worked. One morning on the radio and I'm in business, baby! But how am I going to call all these people? That's a lot of phone calls, a lot of hour-long conversations. Maybe I should offer half-hour consults for fifty bucks. Or sixty, that's how you price, right? Some of these problems are definitely fifteen-minuters. I mean, how much can be said about warts, once I look up all the home remedies online? But the key to making a living in this job is repeat business: you don't just answer the one question, you establish a relationship. I'm not just an intuitive counselor, I'm a life coach. Well, you know what they say: those who can't do, coach. I'm wondering what advice I'd give me when the phone rings in my hand.

"Elle Medina," I say, in my professional voice.

"Elle, it's Teri."

"Teri! Hello…" Which one is Teri? The one with the cheating husband. "Um, shall we start from the beginning?"

"Your editor," she says.

"Right! Teri, yes, I—there's a lot of noise, here. I'm getting static."

"How's your column coming?"

"I finished the first draft, everything's done but a little polishing."

"So you haven't lined up an interview yet?"

"Um…yeah."

"Doesn't matter. You're off the twinkle-twinkle beat. I want another voyeur column."

"But I wrote everything in the first column."

"You wrote eight hundred words. Watch that video again, there's four thousand words worth of humiliation there. Were you on the radio this morning?"

Sounds bad. "Um…yeah."

"Elle, you have to tell us these things. Synergy sells this paper."

"Nothing sells the paper—it's free."

"Sells the ads. That's what sells the ads. Which pay for your column. Did you mention your column?"

"Um…" I try to remember. "The DJs did."

"Good. And if you need a new angle, why not talk about your promotion, from *Grrrl of the Week* to *Our Slutty Sponsor?* You saw the new caption, no?"

I sputter.

"Yeah," she says, "since the article ran, they put you on their home page as a sponsor, they say you're doing a great job promoting them."

"I'll get you that column tomorrow," I say. "You'll want to wear lead gloves."

★ ★ ★

I'm thinking of synonyms for *vile* (*craven? loathsome?*) when Merrick comes home. I'm also ignoring the phone, which hasn't stopped ringing.

"Hey, girly," Merrick says, dropping his keys on the kitchen counter. "Your phone's ringing."

"You perhaps heard I was on the radio this morning?"

"Oh, right."

Ah, well. That means he didn't listen to the show. "Well, I'm getting calls up the wazoo. To hear me is to love me— they all want consultations."

"Beer?" he says, opening the fridge.

I nod. "You know how I'm always bitching that nobody ever calls, and I'm stuck on the twinkle-twinkle beat for my column?"

He laughs. "The *what* beat?"

"I thought you'd like that. Well, now I have like forty clients waiting, and my editor wants a column about something other than colonic color therapy. But am I happy? No. I'm overwhelmed. How can I return all these calls *and* have time to write my column by one o' clock tomorrow?"

"So don't return the calls," Merrick says, loosening his tie.

"Since when did you start wearing a tie?" I ask. He prefers open-collar button-downs.

"Planning Commission."

"Ooh," I tiptoe away from him and join Miu on the patio.

"What?" Merrick says, joining us.

Poor unsuspecting Miu has no idea where he's been and rubs her head against his thigh hoping for some love. He absently scratches her and the phone rings.

"Let the machine pick up," I say. "Probably another client. Tad gave out your number a few times."

"What if it's for me?" Merrick asks. "I do live here."

"It's not for you."

"I didn't get any calls?"

"Oh, your niece called." This is the beauty college student who dyed Merrick's hair bright orange by mistake. "She wants you to take her to lunch on Friday. Don't let her near your head."

We hear the machine engage through the patio door.

"Anything else?" Merrick asks.

I shrug modestly. "Said she caught me on the radio and I was good."

"I mean any other messages," he says mildly.

"Oh," I say. "No. So you missed the whole thing?"

"The meeting started at eight."

"Well, how'd it go?"

"The usual."

"Make it smaller with more Spanish elements?"

Merrick laughs. "So you *do* listen."

"More than you, apparently."

"Sorry," he says. "I couldn't reschedule. Went pretty well, huh?"

On cue, my cell rings. "I'm a star," I tell him, airily, then glance back at my column. "Do you prefer 'loathsome hobgoblins' or 'craven toad-lickers?'"

chapter

19

My second piece on the e-Peeping Toms is composed of one hundred percent habanero. It requires one of those protective welding faceplates—as seen in *Flashdance*—to read. Let me just say that "underwear-sniffing, mother-fixated jelly-vendors" was my way of attempting to bury the hatchet with the Vile Voyeurs, and letting bygones be bygones.

The weeks pass in a blur of unprecedented—and fairly disorienting—success. I am a tsunami of advice, inspiration, and love. For example, the phone rings with an appointment as I'm having a pedicure. I counsel Amy about her relationship troubles as I try to decide between two colors from OPI's Canadian Collection: Polar Bare and Nice Color, Eh? Amy supported her husband for ten years while he went to graduate school, but now that he's a professor, she's decided she can't stand him.

"What's the problem?" I ask.

"He wants me to call him 'doctor.'" she says.

"Ooh. That's wrong."

"You're telling me."

Actually, I'm not telling her. I'm telling the nice woman who's applying polish to my toes, because the Polar Bare looks insipid. I motion for her to switch to Nice Color, Eh? "Right," I tell Amy. "And he's not even a medical doctor? Just a Ph.D.? That is pretty irritating, but…tell me what's going on with you."

She hesitates a moment. "Well, there's this guy at work. He asked me out."

"Does he know you're married?"

"He says it doesn't matter, he can't help how he feels."

"His feelings? Women feel with our hearts, but you know where feelings are located on a man, right?"

She laughs. "Well…"

"Let me ask you this—are you annoyed with your husband because he wants you to call him 'doctor,' or because you're considering having an affair and you feel guilty?"

Silence. Sounds like "yes."

"Do you love your husband?"

More silence. Still sounds like "yes."

"What do you do?" I ask.

"I'm a paralegal. I wanted to be a lawyer, but we couldn't afford for both of us to go to school."

Ah, now we're getting somewhere. "Your husband has a job?"

"He got lucky. Tenure-track position at a community college."

"Let your husband play doctor, Amy, while you go back to law school."

"Law school? I'm too old. By the time I finish I'll be forty."

"If you don't go, you'll *still* be forty. Plus, it's not like you're changing careers, just improving the one you've already started. Your husband had his chance, now it's yours."

"Law school," she says. "You know, I'd really rather *be* an asshole attorney than work for one."

"That's the spirit. And Amy, the affair at work? That's the wrong path to take. Start applying to schools and things'll soon be getting better with the doctor. And if they don't, hollaback." Which has become my standard sign-off. A little hip-hop in the psy-ops.

I shut my phone and examine my toes. Don't know why I was so sure going back to school would solve Amy's problems with her husband, given it's not solving my problems with Merrick. I'm such a fraud. My phone rings as I'm paying for my pedicure.

"Yo, it's Elle."

"Why are you on this hip-hop kick, again?" Maya asks.

"Everyone needs a shtick. Mine is pulling together New Age and O.G."

"Do you even know what O.G. stands for?"

"Um, Old…Ghetto?"

"So basically you're a fake psychic with a fake hip-hop shtick."

"Can I at least say 'hollaback?' I'm no whiter than Gwen Stefani." She's way skinnier, though. I think she's a size zero. If she loses a pound she'll be in the negative digits.

Maya says, "You want to hit some furniture stores tomorrow? I'm shopping for the bar."

Since I'd suggested investing her trousseau money in re-decorating, Maya had been a whirlwind of activity, organizing painters and contractors. The first step had been stripping the walls of pictures of Jews on the lower east side of New York, circa 1940. Maya's dad and I had watched, tears in our eyes, as Maya placed each ancestor in a crate marked Bushmill's Irish Whiskey. "You could have at least used a slivovitz box," her dad said. Merrick, of course, has been a prince, stopping at Shika, most nights after work, drinking Manhattans and instructing Maya to paint the walls Moroccan-blue, pull up the linoleum and polish the concrete underneath, et cetera. I once suggested tea lights, and Maya told me my beer cost $4.50.

"I can't go tomorrow," I say, getting into my car. "My column's due. I can go today if you want."

"Why can't you write your column today and go shopping tomorrow?"

"Because I always write my column right before it's due."

"But—"

"Hey, that's the process. It's like pulling all-nighters in college. There's no fighting it, Maya."

She sighs. "Can you really write another piece about being one of the lead Santa Barbara Girls?" Her trill on the *R*s is sadly lacking.

She means a third article about the Vile Voyeurs. I wrote the New Age column for five months and never got a call. I write about sex twice in two weeks and my phone hasn't stopped ringing. So some of them are sexual deviants—they still pay the full fee.

"I interviewed Gabrielle," I tell Maya.

"The one who called you on the radio? From Santa Barbara Girls?"

"*Grrrrls,*" I say. "And yes. She's gonna remain anonymous, though."

"What are you going to write?"

"It's a think piece," I say.

"In other words, you have no idea."

"Exactly."

Three hours later, we're examining barstools and my phone tingles.

"*Elle,*" Maya says. I'd promised to shut off my phone.

"I thought you just meant in the car," I say, turning my back on her and putting a finger in my free ear to block out her fuming.

"Elle, it's Blake from—"

"My favorite a.m. FM DJ."

"That's right. Listen, we're still talking about you." A short pause. "Good things. When're you coming back on the show?"

"Any time," I say. "I'd love to come back."

"How about three mornings a week for three hours. Open phone lines."

"Three mornings—is this a *job?*"

"Yeah, of course."

"I see. Hold one moment." I put my hand over the phone and tell Maya, "I got a call about a job." Maya's disappeared, but I keep talking. "*They* called *me.* I didn't call *them.* They called me. About a *job.* For a job. They called me." I take my hand off the phone. "Blake, I'm not sure."

"I heard all that, Elle."

"Oh. Then what's it pay?"

A paltry sum, but he says the exposure is invaluable.

"Invaluable," I agree, then tell him okay, but no sound effects when I'm talking to callers.

"That's part of my shtick," he says.

"Yo," I say. "Limit it to Sarah and me—not the callers."

He agrees and we settle the details and I snap my phone shut with a good deal of wrist action. I boogie through a display of coffee tables toward Maya, and only resist the urge to tap-dance my way across the tabletops because a) I cannot tap-dance and b) Maya hates being kicked out of stores. Even after knowing me for fifteen years.

"Guess who has her own new radio show?" I call out.

"Janeane Garofalo," Maya says.

"No. Well, yeah, but not her."

"Ben Affleck. Giovanni Ribisi. Mindy Cohen."

"From *Facts of Life?*"

"Yeah, she played Tootie."

"She played Natalie and I loved her. But, no, not Mindy Cohen."

"Then could it possibly be…" Maya switches into announcer voice, "ELLE MEDINA?"

I hold my hands high. "Thank you, thank you very much. I want to thank all the little people."

"That's awesome," she says.

"Three times a week. *And* they're going to pay me."

"How much?"

"Um, like minimum-wage much."

"Oh."

"Yeah, but it's good for business, so basically, I'm getting paid to advertise."

"That's true. Now focus—turn that phone off and help me pick out some tables and chairs. What do you think of these?"

"Merrick said no wicker."

"They've got metal arms."

I scan the floor and see low, black wooden platform sofas with black cushions. "You don't need chairs. The walls are Moroccan-blue, right? Go with low couches, low tables. Like something out of *InStyle*. One of those bars the stars go to. A star bar. Why isn't there a candy called that?"

Maya wanders over to the sofas, settles her mini-bum into one. Bounces a moment, then mimes sipping a cocktail and flirting with men. "These might work." She stops miming and looks thoughtful. "This is so weird."

"What?"

"You. You're all—"

I strike a Wonder Woman pose. "Invincible!"

chapter 20

Let me say that I don't believe stepping on a crack will actually break your mother's back. I don't think black cats are bad luck, or there's any danger in walking under a ladder that doesn't involve someone on top of the ladder dropping things on you. And there's no such thing as "tempting fate." Fate's not mooning around her living room waiting for the phone to ring. Fate's not a waffler who heaves a sigh of relief when someone finally brags, thinking, "Ah! Thank goodness, I had no idea what to do next. Now I'll grind *them* into paste!"

So crowing about my invincibility wasn't, strictly speaking, tempting fate. Still, when I write my memoirs, *A Gentlewoman's Advice from a Life Well-Lived,* on page one there will be a small disclaimer. "I'm still horribly a mess, actually. Nothing to see here. Move along." Just in case.

The fateful moment, however, didn't occur immediately. I escaped the furniture store without incident and even thrived for a time, still secure in my sparkly new karma.

I wake early the next day and pound out my eight hundred words. I figure the whole Vile Voyeurs thing is spent—despite the fact that I'm still getting the occasional obscene phone call—so I take the next step. I write about some of my callers, disguising their questions of course, and about my answers, and what I wished I'd said, and what I hoped they'd do.

Teri loves it. Well, she tells me to stop bolding every other word, but she still loves it. Is there *any* stopping me? Then, a couple days later, Wicked Tad moves out. He got the job with the clean-cut computer guys and can, as he put it, "Afford something better than this dump." And he's right, it *is* a dump, because he's been dumping there for weeks now. Although it's Saturday afternoon, Merrick's heading for work, so Miu and I ride in with him and start cleaning. Well, Miu mostly lounges on her cashmere throw and chews a rawhide bone—but that needs doing.

By seven, I've scrubbed the floors, polished the cabinets and scoured the bath, and am officially exhausted and starving. Miu trails me downstairs to knock on Merrick's door and see if he wants to order Chinese, but there's no answer. I try the knob. Locked. I check the parking lot. Merrick's car is missing. Hmm.

Back in my apartment, I call his cell.

"Hey," he says. "Where are you?"

"I'm still here. Where are you?"

"Still where? I'm home eating dinner, I made pasta. When are you getting here?"

"Are you kidding me?"

"No. It's capellini with tomatoes and basil, I even grated extra Parmesan for you."

"Merrick, I'm in my apartment. You dropped me here, remember?"

A pause. "Oh, shit."

"You *forgot?*"

"No. Well…" He clears his throat. "Yeah."

I don't know what to say. I know I'm often irritating and demanding, but forgettable?

"I'm sorry, Elle, I was totally in my head, you know how busy I've been. I'll come get you—then I'll grate even *more* Parmesan. Be there in ten. Less than that."

"Actually…" I'm sitting in my chair, talking on my phone, watching my Miu in her corner. Fresh sheets sing their siren song in my bedroom. "I'll stay here tonight."

"But I have capellini!"

"I'm just happy to be here tonight."

"You don't want to come home?" he asks.

I sigh. "Merrick, I *am* home."

By morning, I'm all twitchy for Merrick. We did not bid each other a very good-night. He didn't understand why I'd want to sleep alone. And in the warm light of day, neither do I. Sleeping alone sucks, even having cuddled with Miu through most of the night. The good news is this: I can move in with Merrick.

I just needed to be sure I didn't *need* to move in with him. But now my career actually exists, with phone clients, a regular radio gig and a column for the *Permanent Press*. Not to mention the whole wedding coordinator thing. Okay, maybe none of that actually comprises a *career* career, but it's pretty good—for me, it's fantastic.

Plus, with the money I save in rent I can contribute to Merrick's mortgage. And, um, I missed him last night. I love him.

I call him first thing. My plan is to have a nice romantic day, and let him convince me to move back in with him by nightfall. He arrives early, to romance me over breakfast, then suggests we check out the Contemporary Arts Forum, which is a sort of gallery upstairs at Paseo Nuevo, the outdoor mall. Contemporary art is a hobby of Merrick's. He likes to read books about it, and gets very intense when we come here. I, on the other hand, know nothing about it, but it's sort of my style: the artists are trying to convince people that whatever they say is art *is* art, and that their off-kilter ideas are worth paying for—just like me.

There are usually two exhibitions at the CAF, one in the main room and one in a little side gallery. Today, the main exhibition is apples and twigs. McIntosh pierced with white birch, Golden Delicious enmeshed in oak, that kinda thing, and the small gallery has a projector shooting random images of Web sites on the wall. The apple/twig thing is pretty neat, organic decay and fermentation, but the Web shots are just lame. Even I wouldn't have the nerve to call that art.

It's the end of my first week as SB's a.m. FM advice dispenser, the Emily Post of the airwaves, and Merrick considers a grid of Granny Smiths extra closely after admitting he's a terrible boyfriend.

"You didn't listen *once?*" I say. "Is this true?"

"I know, I'm sorry," he says. "You started so soon, I already had appointments every morning."

"You couldn't have listened during your fancy appointments?"

"I promise—next week, I'll listen every day."

"And you'd better enjoy yourself, too!"

He kisses me. "I bet you're great. But what're you gonna do once you start school?"

"Oh. About Laverna…"

"You don't have to worry," he tells me.

"I don't?"

"I remember how much textbooks cost—it's outrageous. I thought I'd buy your books for you because I kinda pushed you into this."

I *must* tell him I'm not going to grad school, but he'll be disappointed, and I don't want to ruin the romantic day of reconciliation with disappointment. But what's romantic about lying? And why should I be ashamed? I'm a fake psychic, yes, but I'm helping people and doing the only thing I do well. I was hoping Merrick had loved me on the radio, to make this easier, but I'm tired of putting off the inevitable. I take a deep breath to confess that I won't be attending Laverna and my cell buzzes in my purse.

Oops. Merrick told me to turn it off when we came in, I must've set it to vibrate by accident. "This art makes me have to pee," I say, and head for the restroom.

God, I'm such a coward.

I click my phone open the moment I swing through the glass door into the sunlight.

"Did you know it was me?" Blake says—because I'm psychic, I should know.

"Ha ha."

"Have you intuited the news?"

"They're replacing you with a talking dog?"

"Missing Bitch and the Talking Dog—we can go on the road. No, this is even better. They heard your show on tape, down in L.A. The parent station."

"No!"

"Yep."

"They love me?"

"They love you."

"They really *really* love me?"

"Don't push it, Elle."

"No, right."

"They want to talk with you about a show in L.A."

The gates of heaven swing open on well-oiled hinges, and pearly light billows forth. L.A. is big and famous and glitzy and offers unlimited opportunity to appear on billboards. That's when you know you've arrived. My giant face on a billboard. My giant *airbrushed* face, on a billboard.

"On the radio in L.A...." I say, in a hushed voice.

"Not the radio," he says. "TV."

By which he means: television. I shit you not. Not local access, either, actual TV with cameras and makeup and bottled water, for a five-minute advice segment on a morning show. The producer, Shelly Pitts-Jones is coming to Santa Barbara in a month, Blake told her that I'm TV-friendly— which he says means "not a total goblin"—and she'll come to make sure I have the right look.

The right look? That sounds like seventeen sleepless nights and six thousand dollars in pore cleansers and hair products.

I thank Blake and when I stop hyperventilating, canter back into the gallery and find Merrick heading toward the side gallery. I tell him the news and he says, "So, what did you say?"

"What do you mean, what did I say?"

"I mean, what did you say?"

"I told them no, I don't want to be on television."

"So you said yes."

"Of course I said yes!"

"You'll be driving down to L.A."

"Twice a week, if this works out. The producer's gonna in be in town next month, she wants to check if I'm a total goblin before offering anything. If not, this thing's in the bag."

"But you're not a total goblin—"

"Thank you."

"—which means you'll get this job—"

I beam.

"—and you're not going to Laverna."

I stop beaming.

"You're not, are you?"

"No," I say, squaring my shoulders. "I'm not going to Laverna. I'm not going to any grad school." No reason to explain about the other program, getting certified as a psychic, as am afraid his head would explode. "I don't want to be a psychologist. I hate the classes, I hate the teachers, I hate the theories. I get sick thinking about giving real advice to real people with real problems."

"So you're giving them fake advice?"

"I don't give fake advice! I just—I pretend to be a psychic instead of pretending to be a wise and caring therapist. They're all full of shit, too."

"And that makes what you're doing better?"

"It's no worse—and costs a lot less."

"But you're lying."

"And you're being an asshole."

He rubs his face. "This whole co-op thing in New York is falling apart. I've been working my ass off for three months,

working late—that's how I forgot you—I'm redoing everything two dozen times. My career is on the line, Elle. Either
I ace this or I'm just some small-town architect doing condo
conversions. Now I've got to fly back to New York, and the
co-op board is screwing me, and you've been no help."

"No help? You never told me any of this! You're always
reminding me I'm not psychic, but I'm supposed to read
your mind?"

"You won't move in with me—you won't get yourself
settled, not where you live, not what you do. I just need
something settled, I'm sorry, but it's like I'm doing all the
work in this relationship, and you don't even try."

"What, at Laverna? That's not who I am, or what I want.
I'm sorry if I embarrass you, but this is me."

"You? You're living a lie, Elle. And you know people are
gonna find out you're not a psychic—and in the most public
way possible."

"Why would you say that?"

"Because I know you."

"That is so untrue," I say.

And I become aware of a high school art class whispering and giggling and staring at me from the side gallery with
the projections of Web sites. I think because we're fighting,
but no: on the wall, *Santa Barbara Grrrrls* is running a video
of me naked in the shower, soaping myself, then applying
body butter as the bathroom door opens and Tad enters.
Thinking Tad was Merrick I'd shot him a sexy grin. The
video ends and loops back to the beginning.

"Okay," I say, staying calm. "That's another video of me."

"Don't," Merrick says.

"It's not what it looks like."

"Just don't," he says.

chapter

21

Four days later, and Merrick and I still haven't spoken—I
don't even know if he's in town. I haven't called him because
I'm embarrassed about being caught by the Vile Voyeurs
again, humiliated and angry. And he hasn't called, I guess,
because I'm not the woman he wants me to be.

Today, this letter runs in the *Permanent Press:*

Dear Permanent Press:
If your columnist, Elle Medina, is really psychic she'd
know who the Vile Voyeurs are. If they were animals,
I, as a pet psychic, would know exactly who to hold ac-
countable. In case you didn't know, she was caught again
naked on video, this time in her own shower. You have

to ask yourself how she could have been filmed in her own dinky apartment without knowing the camera was there? Is she responsible? Is this a publicity stunt? I think your readers deserve the truth.

Sincerely,

Crystal Smith

Pet Psychic

Goleta

At first, I thought, who cares? She's even faker than I am. Who's going to listen to some Goleta-living whack-job pet psychic?

Turns out a lot of people.

My editor, Teri, calls to tell me they've got an office pool going about how long before my boyfriend leaves me.

"What are the odds?" I hear myself ask.

"Jimmy's giving three to one that he's staying with you."

"That's not too bad."

"Actually, it means most people think he's already dumped you."

"Oh. Right."

"Has he?"

"Is that why you're calling, Teri?" Because I don't know the answer. Has he dumped me? And which is worse, being dumped by Merrick or not knowing if I'm dumped?

"I'm calling because I want to know who these guys are, the voyeurs. You've got a week. I want names, Elle. You ferret out these jerks, I'll even let you bold their names in your column. Give me fifteen-hundred words, a week from Tuesday."

"Fifteen-hundred? That's twice the size of my regular column. Are you going to pay me twice as much?"

"No," she says. "But if you keep me informed about your boyfriend, we could make a little profit on the side."

"Terri, do you think I would bet *money* on the outcome of my relationship with the man I love? The man I want to spend the rest of my life—"

"Two hundred bucks."

"I'll call you," I say, and hang up.

I'm not really gambling on my future with Merrick, because I'm confident we're still together, so there's nothing wrong with a little inside information on the office pool. This is entirely ethically defensible. Emily Post would agree.

Anyway, I have a more immediate problem: how am I supposed to figure out who the Vile Voyeurs are? What does Teri think, I'm an investigative journalist? Nobody knows who these guys are.

I dial Carlos. "Did you find anything out about Barbalicious?"

He says he didn't. "The site is free, so they don't take plastic. There's no credit trail." I hear him clicking on his keyboard. "At least, not that I can find."

"Thanks anyway. I guess I'll…I'll…yeah, I'll…"

"Hey, you're not crying, are you? You've never cried before. You're a liar, not a crier."

I break down and explain about me and Merrick and school, about Maya getting married before me, about the office pool and how a vindictive pet psychic is out to get me. Then I tell him to stop laughing, it's not funny—and I was videoed naked and projected against the museum wall in front of pimply art students as I fought with Merrick. I sniffle. "And I don't even know how they got a camera in my bathroom."

"Who else has access to your apartment?"

"Miu, but she wouldn't betray me. Merrick. My landlord, Monty. Neil, the—"

"Yeah, I know Neil—we spoke on the phone, remember? He wouldn't dare, his wife would kill him. How about your landlord? There've been cases before, Peeping Tom landlords."

"Monty's like my fairy godfather, no way. Who else? Just Wicked Tad."

"Who?"

"Maya's fiancé's brother. Hey, maybe it *was* him. He could've hooked that up no problem. He was crashing at my place." I don't know why this possibility didn't occur to me before. Probably my reluctance to associate anything negative with Perfect Brad.

"For how long?"

"Oh, a while. Wait, no—he wasn't even in town the first time I was filmed."

"Anyone else?"

"I don't know. Crystal Smith? She could be masterminding the whole thing."

"The vindictive pet psychic? Who else?"

"I dunno, anyone Tad invited in. The Gay Tailors. Anyway, Carlos, thanks for listening."

"I'm always here for you, Elle."

I smile. It's nice someone likes me. "Even if I miss a payment?"

"Don't push it, missy."

I camp outside Ray Flood's apartment until he agrees to use all his Internet prowess to unearth the identities of the Vile Voyeurs. This takes about five minutes, as he's clearly afraid I really will camp out there, and he'll have to live with me on his doorstep.

He reports back the next afternoon: he found nothing. So I call Neil, and tell him Kara will be furious about him posting nudie pictures of me on the Internet. I figure the accusation will unsettle him, if he's responsible, and he'll reveal his guilt by acting nervous. So I listen very closely as he says, "The Internet? That's just the first step of DARPA's plan to monitor all communications, not only on computer but your cellphone, your landline—I'm talking Big Brother, here. Thought Police. Only thing—"

Okay, it's not Neil. I call Monty, but don't have the nerve to accuse him of planting a secret camera in my house. I'm afraid he'll actually physically bust a gut and have to go to the hospital. Besides, I know it's not Monty.

Could be Ray Flood, though—he gets all shy around me, and I'm pretty sure his libido is bound up in his CPU. But then why would he have told me about Barbalicious?

I'd definitely suspect the Gay Tailors—I think Johnny would really enjoy persecuting me—except, frankly, I imagine he'd flee in horror at the very thought of my naked body.

Which reminds me, I need to prod him and Weldon into putting the finishing touches on Maya's haute-coutailored dress. Her wedding is in two weeks, and while I've gotten no further with *Santa Barbara Grrrrls,* I've had plenty of time to help with the wedding plans. Too bad I'm doing this for love and not money, because it's going stunningly well. The bar is gorgeous, and will actually be completed on time, the rabbi inspected my cleavage and agreed to perform the ceremony on the beach, Valentine arranged a cheap caterer (no one's cheaper than a cheap Montecitan) and I just confirmed the flowers from the wholesaler in Carpinteria.

Everything is perfect.

Well, except I'm going to lose my job at the paper, and it's been eight days since I spoke with Merrick. I called him this morning and got his voice mail, saying he's in New York on business. I knew he wasn't coming to the office, but thought he'd been working at home. His message says he's not sure when he'll be returning. So he left and didn't tell me. That's actually good news, because it means we're only fighting. If we'd broken up he would have told me. And the chances he'll actually meet Scarlett Johansson are totally slim. I think she lives in L.A.

I don't manage to completely convince myself that a man leaving town without telling his girlfriend is good, so I tamp down my remaining anxieties with a chocolate-chocolate-chip muffin on my way to the station. Amazingly, I've still got a job. Three days a week as SB's a.m. FM…oh, whatever the fuck I am. People call and I give them advice. Unfortunately, despite blasting my 900 number every twenty minutes, I'm getting no calls at home. Why would anyone pay when I'm available for free, nine hours a week? So instead of making $100 an hour, I'm getting minimum wage. Even a *fake* psychic deserves more than that.

God, it'd be such a relief to stop pretending, to just give advice without all the gibberish. And when I think about it, what's holding me back? Nobody *actually* believes I'm psychic, do they?

So this is it. I'll admit I'm not psychic. What's the worst that could happen? I mean, besides getting fired, never getting another call, living in a trolley, and not being discovered for six weeks after I die of éclair poisoning?

I make a trial run with the first few calls, no astral planes, no pretend tarot cards, just straightforward advice to Angela that yes, she should quit smoking, and to Samantha that no, her husband having a two-hour lunch with his ex-girlfriend doesn't necessarily mean he's having an affair. It means he's acting like a jerk. Call him on it, don't divorce him. Yet.

Nobody seems to notice that I've dropped the psychic mumbo jumbo. My third call is Stuart from Solvang, who wants to know if he should move out of his mother's house. I ask about his finances, his relationship with his mother, and I think: all right, this is it, I'm free to be me, what's the worst that can happen?

"Move out," I tell Stuart.

"Why?" he says.

"You're thirty-two, it's time to do your own laundry."

"But why?" he says.

"Because you have to decide if you're a boy or a man. You need to separate from your mother and—"

"Yeah, but *why?*" he says.

I sigh. "Because the cards say so."

"Oh. Okay."

The cards are wise. And I am a fraud.

I'm on the way into my building, wishing I'd stopped for a second chocolate-chocolate-chip muffin, when Johnny hails me from his shop. I brighten. Here I am minding my own moody business and one of the Gay Tailors wants to talk to me! This is a watershed moment. If only I'd known moodiness was the key—I can do moody.

"Hi," I say, extra moodily.

"You have something in your teeth," he tells me. "The dresses are ready."

I pick my teeth and follow him into the shop, wondering what other aesthetic affronts I'm committing. Are my toes hanging over the ends of my flip-flops? Are my split ends showing? Is my goiter visible? The place is cold and empty, and Weldon is not in his usual spot behind the sewing machine.

"Where'th Weldon?" I ask, still digging between my teeth.

"His name is Weldon," Johnny says.

"I thaid *Weldon!*"

"You said Waldo. Where's Waldo? Not funny."

"I thaid Weldon! I know what hith name ith!"

He heaves a pained sigh. "Maybe if you take your thumb out of your mouth."

I stop digging between my teeth. "It wasn't my thumb. Where are the dresses?"

"You mean the dretheth?"

"I don't have a lisp! I could be a newscaster. I work on the radio, you know—do you really think they'd let me—because I don't—" I take a deep breath, and enunciate carefully. "The dresses?"

He gestures to a rack. "Over there. Don't ruin anything. I've got calls to make."

So much for my watershed moment…but who cares? The dresses are ready! I skip to the rack and flip through plastic-wrapped hangers, looking for the ones marked Elle and Maya. There is no Elle but there is a Maya's (Old) Maid. Very funny.

I slip the plastic off with a delicate touch, hold the dress out. It is exquisite. Champagne silk with delicate embroidery, flowing skirts and slight shimmer to the fabric when you turn it sideways. I'm gonna look fairy-tale beautiful—in a good way, not in the elementary school make-Elle-play-the-wolf-in-both-*Red-Riding-Hood*-and-*Three-Little-Pigs* way. It's sleek and lovely, the best bridesmaid dress I've ever seen. I'm frankly amazed: I half-suspected that the Gay Tailors would sabotage me, but I guess I underestimated their professionalism. In fact, the dress is so perfect that if the bride were anyone but Maya, I'd be afraid of outshining her—an entirely novel fear for me.

But considering the bride *is* Maya, I'm impatient to see her dress: if this is what they made me, she'll be radiant in hers. I flip though the rack, checking every bit of white. Maya's name is not there.

I flip again, increasingly frantic. They can't have forgotten the wedding dress? I flip a third time, and there's no wedding dress here, so I wait until Johnny hangs up between calls and accuse him of not finishing Maya's dress.

He dials again. "It's there," he tells me, then turns his back, talking on the phone.

I check again. Slower this time, dress by dress—she didn't exactly specify white—and my hand stops at a sickly green dress with Maya on the ticket. A puffed, pleated, ruffled, seasick-green bridesmaid's dress. This cannot be *my* Maya's dress. I sort through the dresses again. There is no other Maya. My stomach turns. I hiss to Johnny—surely he'll scoff and tease me for thinking even momentarily that this was for Maya.

He turns and sees the dress and nods. He mouths "Maya's gonna look fabulous" then turns back to his conversation.

I close my eyes and clutch the dress to my chest. The room sways but I manage not to faint, praying for a miracle, promising my soul to any power that will transform this dress. I finally peek, and it's worse than I remember. What was I thinking, promising my soul? I close my eyes and promise my hair, my new drapey suit, and my Sean Bean fantasy.

No luck. This thing is hideous. I toss Maya's floofy puke-dress onto the worktable, grab my dress by the hanger, and retreat to the fluttering of plastic and champagne silk. I charge upstairs and throw myself on the bed. Miu prods me comfortingly with her cold nose. "You'll still love me?" I ask, wiping drool from her black velvety jowls.

She eyes me sadly, as if to say, "Yeah, but I'm the only one."

How am I going to explain to Maya that I've ruined her wedding just to get the Gay Tailors to like me? She looked great in that $99 sample dress, too. Oh, God, and my dress is so perfect, she's gonna look like the bridesmaid and me the bride. Why am I such a terrible friend?

I no longer have Merrick. I'll lose my *Permanent Press* job when I can't unearth the Vile Voyeurs. Despite all the self-promotion, I'm getting *fewer* calls—and if I quit, the TV gig will definitely vanish. And anyway, there's no way I'm gonna be on TV: I mean, really. And now, after ruining Brad's conversion, I've ruined Maya's wedding—and once she sees her dress, I'll no longer have a best friend.

I lay my head on Miu's side and listen to her breath and the arrhythmic beat of her heart. I wish I were a dog. Then I wouldn't have to—

Wait a second. What if I buy the $99 sample dress? Maya loved that thing. "Then everything will be fine," I tell Miu. Doesn't solve my problems with Merrick or the Vile Voyeurs, but at least I'll still have Maya. I kiss Miu on the head, clip her leash to her collar and say, "Let's go buy a wedding dress."

Exactly sixteen seconds later, my car screeches to a halt in the red zone outside Petticoat Junction. I tell Miu to guard the front seat, and look pathetic at anyone who tries to give me the boot, and race inside.

The same saleswoman is there, Gabrielle's mom, and she smiles at me. "Thanks so much, Gabrielle's feeling a lot better. Said she owed it to you."

"Really? I'm so glad." I should give her Merrick's phone number—I could use the reference—but instead say, "But listen, the dress my friend liked so much, the $99 one? I want to buy it."

"The sample dress? It sold weeks ago."

I clutch at my forehead and moan.

"But I can order you one," she says.

I unclutch. "Oh, great! Yes, please, let's order one."

"But it'll be full price, since it's not the sample."

"That's fine. Money is no object, I'm saving a wedding here." Besides, I remember Maya telling me the dress cost $279 new. I don't actually have $279 after paying too much "way" to Johnny and Weldon, but I'll make this work somehow. I have no other choice.

The saleswoman and I find the dress in the style book, agree the new version is slightly different, but Maya is unlikely to notice the pin-tucked pleats and seed pearls added to the buttons. If anything, it's cuter than the old one. The saleswomen fills out an order form, then looks up the price. Looks back at the style number, looks at the price again. Looks at me.

"I'm sorry," she says. "Apparently it's $800. They raised the price."

I swallow. "No problem." With a prayer to Carlos, I hand over my credit card. "Money is no, um…"

The saleswoman swipes the card. Nothing happens. The tension is thick in the air. The saleswoman waits. I wait, watching storm clouds gather in the distance, as bolts of lightning flash in ominous fashion. Somewhere, a thousand bats swarm screeching around a decrepit bell tower.

The saleswoman glances at the machine. "Oh," she says.

That's all I need to know: denied. She tells me she's sorry,

and I slink out to my car and find a day glow traffic violation pinned by my windshield wiper. I toss Miu a cookie
from the glove compartment so she knows I don't blame her,
and lay my head against the steering wheel.

Now what?

No boyfriend, no best friend, no career as a wedding coordinator. Still lying about being a psychic—all that's left is
my fantasies about escaping to L.A. where my fake psychic
TV spot turns into a nationally syndicated show, with me interviewing celebrities on the red carpet, culminating in Clive
Owen proposing to me on live TV when I ask him who he's
wearing at the Oscars.

My cell rings as I'm wondering if I'd say yes. On the one
hand, I love Merrick, despite everything. On the other, *Clive
Owen.* "That'll be the TV people," I tell Miu. "They're no
longer interested." I answer by saying, "Hey Blake."

"Maybe you *are* psychic," Blake says.

"Yeah," I say morosely.

"I'm calling about the TV deal."

"I know."

"So, next Saturday?"

"Next Saturday, what?"

"Your powers are failing you, Elle. Next Saturday the
producer is coming to Santa Barbara. She wants to meet you."

"It's not off?" I say.

"Off? No, she's totally eager to meet you."

"But…that's fantastic!"

"So next Saturday at—"

"Wait a minute—*next* Saturday?"

"Seven o' clock."

"I can't. My best friend is getting married. Possibly in the
nude, but she's getting married."

"A nude wedding? Why wasn't I invited?"

"Can't we arrange some other time?"

"You don't know Shelly Pitts–Jones. She's not what you'd call flexible. Plus, she flying to San Francisco right after meeting you."

"I could go to L.A. during the week, anytime."

"If you're serious about this job, Elle, meet her on Saturday, or not at all."

chapter
22

I should have said, "Not at all," but this is the only thing in my life that hasn't crumbled into dust—I need this job. If I get this job, I can salvage everything else. I mean, a job on TV? That justifies anything. So instead of telling him no, I told him where the producer can meet me.

At Shika. During Maya's wedding reception.

And I'm actually feeling pretty pleased with myself for this wonderful save—I'll meet the producer in a lively party-type atmosphere, wearing a gorgeous dress. She'll love me. I'll get a regular job as a TV chatty person, which will show Merrick how reliable and steady I am. Maya will forgive me for ruining her wedding, because I'll name drop Shika on the set all the time. And I'll finally be able to stop pretending, because nobody cares if you're psychic...once you're a star.

★ ★ ★

I'm not entirely complacent about the "Maya forgiving me" part, though, so I spend three days searching for another one of those sample dresses. Well, first I try to raise my credit limit, but Carlos puts me on speakerphone so all the guys in his office can laugh at my request. He agrees I can spend $300 on a dress, though, so I search online, and call all around the country, trying to find one of these things on sale.

And on Day Three, I succeed! Except the soonest they can ship the dress to me is in two weeks. I beg, I plead, to no avail. So Maya's gonna look like a girl-grinch at her own wedding, because I had to interfere. I spend a few days hating myself, trying to pretend I'm not only psychic but cheerful to the occasional client, and not talking to Merrick.

Finally, overwhelmed by both my metaphorical and literal funk, I take my laundry to the basement—and that's when he calls. The message from New York, from my loving boyfriend? "We need to talk. I'll see you at the wedding."

I curse my clean sheets, then weep into them.

I dial his cell several hundred times, but every time the voice mail beeps I don't know what to say. I'm afraid if I leave a message, I'll somehow blurt something inappropriate, which will escalate into us breaking up by answering machine. This doesn't stop me from dialing—on my way to the radio station, the grocery store, coffee with Darwin and Adele, to walk Miu—I like to hear his voice. Of course, if he calls again, I won't pick up, as I'm avoiding Maya. Haven't had the guts to tell her about the dress. She leaves me daily wedding updates on my cell, and keeps mentioning she needs to stop by Johnny and Weldon's, but hasn't had a chance. Is it because she's so beautiful she can afford to lack vanity? Anyway, she still doesn't know about the catastrophe that is her dress, so I'm living in a sort of terrible half world, where everything appears fine but just below the surface all the horrors of hell are bursting at the seams of reality.

Then, late Thursday afternoon, two days before Maya's wedding, Miu and I return from splitting a burrito for lunch to find Maya exiting the building. Her dress, covered in white plastic, hangs from two fingers over her shoulder. She smiles and says, "Elle? What're you *doing?*"

I step from behind the Dumpster. "Oh, I thought there was a, um…I thought I saw a quarter on the ground…"

She approaches, still smiling, like a soft-spoken psycho in a movie who grins as he eats human hearts. "Why haven't you called me?"

I shove Miu behind me to protect her from Maya's wrath. "I have," I lie. "It's always busy. I guess with the planning and all…"

"Everything's all done," she says, brightly. "Thanks to you. Shika, the beach, the dress—"

I can't take anymore. I snap. "I'm sorry! I'm so sorry, I know I fucked up, and I should've called, but I didn't know how to tell you, and Merrick and I aren't talking, and I'm making no money at the radio, and I *tried* to buy the Petticoat Junction dress, but my credit card was denied, and Carlos wouldn't help, and I couldn't find another dress, and I totally fucked up and ruined *everything*. And I only did it so the Gay Tailors would like me, which they don't anyway, and why do I need them as best friends when *you're* my best friend, or at least you were, now I wouldn't blame you—"

"You and Merrick broke up?"

"What? No. We're just not talking."

"Why not?"

"Because I'm so…*me*. But that's not the problem. I mean, Maya, your dress?"

She cocks her head. "What about it?"

"You haven't tried it on, have you?"

"Sure, just now. It's gorgeous. You were so right, it doesn't even compare to that sack at Petticoat Junction—"

"Wait, wait. Stop. This can't be the same dress." I move the plastic aside to peek at the dress. Yes, this is the green floofy excrescence. "Um…you tried *this* dress on?"

"It's like a fairy tale. It's—"

"And you looked in the mirror?"

She pauses. "What are you saying, Elle?"

"This thing is *fugly*. You can't wear this, it's what the frog princess wears in some Tim Burton film, it's—"

She laughs. "No, seriously."

"Would I *kid* about a wedding dress?"

Now she frowns. "You really don't like it?"

"You really do?"

"I love it! It's perfect. The best gift you could've given me."

Is this possible? Maya is not fashion obsessive, because she's so naturally cute she doesn't have to be, but she's never given any sign of being completely lacking in taste. Until now. "Um," I say. "So I didn't ruin your wedding?"

She laughs. "Not yet!"

I don't know what to say. On the one hand, she doesn't hate me. On the other, she's gonna wear this butt-ugly dress, and for the rest of her life, in all her wedding photos, she'll have to say, "I'm the one in the Ms. Kermit costume."

"Well, I love the dress, and I don't care what you say." She checks her watch. "I've gotta meet Brad at the jeweler's.

We're picking up the rings." She pats Miu and heads for her car, then turns. "Oh, the flowers are all set, right?"

"I confirmed last week."

"And you're coming for dinner tomorrow night? We're not doing a rehearsal, it's just family, so I want you to be there."

"Okay, great. But Maya, you might want to check that dress with Brad when you get home—"

"Before the wedding? No way! He's not gonna see me in this until I'm walking down the sandy aisle. We've been living together so long, I want there to be *some* surprise."

With that dress, he's in for more than a surprise. He's in for a shock.

Twenty-four hours later, after much pizza eating and contemplation I still don't know how I'm going to save Maya's wedding. She actually liked the dress. And worse, mine is gorgeous—for once in my life, I'll totally outshine her…and for once in my life, I don't want to.

How will I ever find the Vile Voyeurs by next week? How will I find them at all? I don't even want to *think* about them. My response to my second appearance on *Santa Barbara Grrrrls* has been total repression—simply too humiliating to even consider, especially because of Merrick.

Speaking of which, what will I do when Merrick dumps me? Is he going to dump me at Maya's wedding? Is he going to dump me in front of the TV producer woman? Is he going to tap his wine glass with a fork, and make an announcement to the whole gathering, explaining why he's dumping me?

The phone rings, and I reluctantly answer, expecting a client. It's the florist calling about the wedding arrangements.

"We always call a week in advance," the florist says, "to make sure we've got the right number of centerpieces and bouquets."

"Well, a day," I say, because I'm in a pissy mood.

"What?"

"The wedding's tomorrow, so technically it's not a week." I take a deep breath. "Anyway, for the centerpieces—"

"Wait. Tomorrow?"

"Right, Saturday, like I told you. We'll need—"

"We have you down for *next* Saturday."

"No, you don't."

She assures me that they do.

"Well, then I'm glad you called. You've still got plenty of time to—"

"I'm sorry, I'm so sorry but the Flower Show is this weekend—all our stock is tagged for the show."

"Start un-tagging," I say.

"I can't—we can't. They're cut, they're in the truck, half of them are already at the show. We don't have anything."

I remain calm. "You've got to have something. Roses?"

"No."

"Lilies? Irises? Orchids?"

"I've got nothing. I'm sorry. This is just a complete mix-up."

"This is *your* mix-up and you're going to fix it. This is my best friend's wedding, and I'm not going to let you screw it up. I write a column for the *Permanent Press,* you know. I'm gonna write about this whole thing, and I'm gonna put your name in bold."

She starts to cry, stumbling over herself to apologize, saying how she always messes up, and she's so sorry, and she's just trying to make this whole business work, but it's tough when you're in charge of everything. "Sometimes I want to chuck the whole thing and get a job as a waitress."

So I forgive her. Because she is me, right? And I try to encourage her, and give her some free career advice without pretending to consult the cards, or the stars or the etheric spheres. But I also demand the numbers of all the other wholesalers in the area, and tell her that her company's gonna foot the bill. She tells me, sniffling, that the Flower Show is so big around here, she doesn't think anyone's gonna have flowers, but gives me a dozen phone numbers.

An hour later, I'm done with her list and deep in the florist section of Merrick's Yellow Pages, when Neil bursts in. "You've got to flush it!"

"What?"

He charges into the kitchen and starts going through my cupboards. Miu skirts his heels, aquiver with suspicion and delight. "The cops are downstairs!" he calls. "You gotta flush it, Elle!"

"What? I don't have the slightest—flush what?"

"The pot." He continues to ransack the kitchen. "Where's the pot?"

I stand in the kitchen door. "You want a pot? That cabinet, there." I point to the cabinet that holds my cookware. "Big or little?"

He jerks open the cabinet. "Where?"

"What?"

"Where's the pot?"

"All those metal things in front of you? With handles? Those are—"

"Not *a* pot, *the* pot!" He whispers frantically. "The marijuana, Elle. The chronic, the ganja, the reefer, the dope. Mary Jane, weed, the fucking pot!"

"Oooh, that," I say. "You never gave it to me."

"I left it on your kitchen counter, where did you put it? Oh, God, the cops are downstairs."

"Neil, you never gave me the pot."

"You weren't here," he says. "I left it on the counter."

"Was Wicked Tad here?"

"Who?"

"Brad's brother."

"No—c'mon, help me look. The fucking cops are downstairs, man."

"How'd you get in?" I ask.

"I hold the keys for Monty, so if anyone needs a repair. Would you shut up and look for the—"

A door slams downstairs.

"Are the cops really here?" I ask.

"Oh, God, they're going to bust us. Prison's okay for *you*, but I can't handle that kinda thing. Find that pot, Elle. Did Brad's brother put it somewhere?"

I'm so anxious about screwing up Maya's wedding that this hardly phases me. "I'll check the bedroom," I say.

I rifle through my bureau doors and the closet and turn up empty-handed. Well, except for a pair of Wicked Tad's boxers, a few photos of him with his clean-cut buddies and some pay stubs. I use a pen to drop his boxers in the trash and toss the rest on the bureau.

I head for the bathroom to check the toilet—because in the movies that's where people always hide things—and see Neil in the kitchen, eating something long and drippy.

"What *is* that?"

"Ice cream burrito."

I glance at the remains on the counter. Neil wrapped

three-month-old chocolate frozen yogurt in a stale flour tortilla, and is wolfing it down with a dippy grin.

"You're *stoned!*" I say. "You idiot!" There are no cops, there's just Neil's paranoia.

He savors the last bite and washes his hands in the sink.

I take a deep breath and say, "Do you know where I can find eight floral centerpieces, five boutonnieres and two bridal bouquets by tomorrow?"

"'Course I do," he says.

He sounds so confident that despite his mental state I feel some measure of relief. "Where?"

"The Flower Show."

"Yes, but once they're in the Flower Show, they're *in the Flower Show!* I can't get them, they're no good to me, I can't bring them to the wedding."

He ambles toward the front door. "Flowers? Is that all you're worried about?"

"Yes, Neil, silly me—I'm worried there aren't any flowers for Maya's wedding."

"Well, all the flowers in the county are at the Flower Show," he explains.

I resist the urge to throttle him. "I know. That's why there aren't any for the wedding."

"Yeah, so no problem."

"How is that no problem?" I ask through clenched teeth.

"Because all the good flowers are at the show."

"Get out!"

"What? I'm just saying, all the good flowers are at the show, so there won't be any fancy non-crap flowers showing you up. Everything is relative. I mean, it's like when a pretty girl hangs out with a plain girl—"

"Shut up! Maya just likes me, that's all!"

He blinks. "Huh?"

"Nothing. Anyway, I've been calling all the local florists, and there aren't even any old moth-eaten flowers to—" I stop, struck by a thought. "Everything's relative."

"Huh?"

"You're a genius, Neil. Give me your keys."

"What? No—"

I pat his pockets. "Give 'em."

He rears backward, but I'm too quick. I hear a jingle in his right pants pocket and pull his keys out. A bit personal, but effective. I trot downstairs, Neil and Miu at my heels, and flip through the key ring until I find the one that'll open Merrick's office door. Neil mumbles curses and protests, but I ignore him.

I slip inside Merrick's office and shut the door behind me. Everything is relative. My Johnny and Weldon couture is gorgeous, but I'm the bridesmaid. I can't look better than Maya at her own wedding, which wouldn't be a problem, except her dress is so horrible.

Drastic measures are required. I press speed dial on his phone. "Hi," I say. "We actually haven't met. This is Elle. I'm desperate."

Late Friday night, after returning home and trying *H* through *Z* in the florist section of the phone book, I call Maya and forget to mention there are no flowers for her wedding. Instead I say I have stomach flu and won't be able to attend the rehearsal dinner.

She says, "Stomach flu?"

"I'm very sick," I tell her.

"But you'll be better by the wedding?"

"Oh, definitely! Of course. In the pink of health."

There's a short pause. "Okay, Elle. I don't want to know. Just...don't hurt yourself."

I cough in what I imagine is a flu-like fashion, and say goodbye. I've got until five tomorrow to sort out the flowers and the "everything's relative." No problem. No problem at all.

At eleven p.m., I think I actually *do* have stomach flu. God knows I don't have anything else: like a clue. I've called everyone who can conceivably help, and now start calling the inconceivable. I call Valentine, my most loyal client, and tell her that this time *I* need advice. She tells me to come right over and I'm in the car and halfway to her house before I realize I have no idea how she can help.

Nothing is blacker than Montecito at midnight. No street-lights, no street signs. If you don't know the way, you don't belong. And, as it happens, I *don't* know the way, and I *don't* belong. But I eventually find Valentine's cobblestone driveway, the cast-iron gates open against my arrival, and I follow the curved drive toward the house. Feel like I'm missing my cloak as I bang on the ancient wooden door, the sliver of a moon disappears behind a cloud, and Valentine hushes me inside. She gives me twelve small crystal vases, pale pink French ribbon, a handful of American Beauty...and an evil plan.

That's all I need.

Armed with a Maglite and pair of kitchen shears, I hit a few of Valentine's neighbors before moving on to my favorite gardens in Santa Barbara. The cottage on Olive Street, the municipal building with the profusion of pink iceberg floribunda around the chain-link fence. I pass Maya and Brad's place on my way to the Mission Rose Garden—their bedroom window is dark, getting a good night's rest before the big day. At least, some of us are sleeping. I've got miles to go.

chapter

23

I collapse into a dead sleep at six in the morning. The phone rings, and I fumble toward the noise, half crawling onto the floor, and find myself three inches from my alarm clock. 12:15. I panic—I don't even know what day it is. Did I miss the wedding? Am I in jail?

I clutch at the phone and Maya's voice says: "Elle?"

On my third try, I croak, "Hi."

"You *do* sound sick."

"Well, I'm not," I say.

"Then where the fuck are my flowers? Hell, where's my bridesmaid? I'm here at the bar, and the flowers are not. Gimme the florists' number."

"It's still early, you can't expect—"

"It's three o'clock!"

I look at my alarm clock. Still 12:15. No. The little hand is on the three. I've slept for nine hours. "Shit."

"Shit? What shit? We'll have no shit today, I'm getting fucking married. Don't you say shit. I'm going home to change then straight to the beach—where are the flowers?"

The bride is a wee bit stressed. "They're all ready." True. "They're fantastic." True. "I talked to the florist yesterday." True. "I'll go to the bar and get everything ready." Also true! "I love you—now go change and don't worry about anything."

I stagger to the bathroom, and a devil-clown lurches at me, hair crazy and eyes ringed, face a cartoonish horror. I shriek before realizing it's me in the mirror. I avert my gaze and step into the shower, bathe and dress and head for Shika, my car overflowing with my ill-gotten gain.

The bar has been transformed. The dingy walls are now an iridescent blue, the old linoleum pitched for polished concrete and the vinyl booths burned to make room for low uphol-stered benches and leather chairs. The space appears to have doubled in size and shines with afternoon light coming in from the skylights. There are little built-in shelves where rusty grates used to be, and a half hour after I arrive those shelves are cor-nucopias of overblown garden roses in pink and yellow. Valen-tine's crystal vases are placed on the black-lacquered tables, twined with ribbon. The trunk of my car was coated with rose petals, and as a finishing touch I scatter them on the floor.

"Looks like Snow White lives here," Kid says, from behind me.

"Not bad, huh?" I say, turning to him.

He's resplendent in a tuxedo. When he sees me, he says, "Holy shit! I mean—holy shit. Well, the *bar* looks fantastic."

And that's all that matters. I put the guest book near the front door, place a few disposable cameras on the tables, check the stereo and the food and the drink. Maya's dad is behind the bar, which has been utterly refinished and looks gorgeous. He winces when he sees me, but gamely kisses my cheek, and we chatter as I put the finishing touches on the room: the vintage silver champagne glasses I found when looking for a conversion gift for Brad and the framed picture of Maya's mom.

When I step back and look at the bar, I get a little weepy. Not from jealousy, though, from happiness. Sure, maybe I'm a little sad about myself—Merrick, grad school, my job, my column, my naked appearances on the Web, my whole personality and future—but at least I did this one thing right. I made a wedding for Maya, as beautiful and loving as she deserves.

Mr. Goldberg puts his arm around me. "I don't know what Maya would've done without you, all these years. Before Brad, you were the only person who really made her laugh."

Okay. Now I get more than a little weepy.

The front parking lot at Hendry's Beach is full, so I park a little farther away and walk, my dress whipping around my ankles in the ocean breeze. Three surfer dudes head for their Jeep, boards under their arms, laughing and talking—then grow silent as I near, eyes averted like I'm some awful medieval Medusa who could kill them with a stare.

I head past the Brown Pelican restaurant, kicking off my shoes and going down the steps onto the beach. The sun hovers over the Channel Islands, orange-yellow in the clear blue sky, and touches the crests of waves with shimmering light. The tide is low, so the beach is wide and open, and a flowery scent comes off the cliffs and mixes with the tang of salt air. The wedding is a ten-minute walk from the parking lot, in front of a little cove. The *chupah* is made of bamboo polls set into sand, covered with Maya's grandfather's black and white *talis,* or prayer shawl. Simple but elegant— even kind of romantic on the beach before sunset, rippling in the wind.

Twenty or thirty people mill around, mostly barefoot or in sandals, except for some of the older generation who prefer to get sand in their shoes. Brad's family is there, and Monty and Mr. Goldberg and a bunch of friends and cousins. They all grow quieter as I approach, and slowly turn to face me as if choreographed. It's a scene from *Frankenstein,* where the lurching monster approaches from the gloom. Usually, on a scale of one to ten, I'm a strong seven. With makeup, I'm an eight.

Today, I'm a .03.

Last night, after taking Neil's keys, I'd hit the speed dial in Merrick's office to call his niece—the one in beauty school who dyed his hair a shade of orange never seen in nature. She'd heard the desperation in my voice, and agreed to dye my hair the same unnatural Chernobyl red and cut it into Little Lord Fauntleroy ringlets.

Why? Because everything's relative.

I couldn't look better than Maya at her wedding, and given my dress was spectacular…well, I sabotaged my looks. I made myself so hideous that Maya'd look better than me even if she wore an Astroturf muumuu. I'd stick close to her all night, and ensure that, by comparison, she looked beautiful.

Only one problem. I finally tried on the dress this morning

to discover that the cut, while gorgeous on the hanger is a nightmare when wrapped around my lumpy, fleshy self. Even the color looks horrid, given my new hair. My legs are two sausages, my waist—which actually *does* exist—disappears and my hips are two rolling hillocks.

So the hair sabotage was hardly necessary, but at least I can be *sure* that Maya will outshine me, despite her dress.

Oh, and one more problem: Maya's gown, hideous on the hanger, is perfect. She is an ethereal sea nymph. What appeared sickly green in the tailors' shop is a stunning seafoam in the warm sunlight, the abundance of ruffles like waves of fabric flowing in a train from Maya's miniscule waist. Serene and gorgeous, Maya looks like she's stepped from the pages of *Vogue.*

Until she gets a load of me.

One minute she's twenty feet away, laughing—the next minute, she's twenty inches away, not laughing. "If this is some kind of joke…"

"It's no joke!" I say. "It's, um—would you believe it's bozo chic?"

"Elle, this is my wedding—you're my bridesmaid. Look at you!"

"I did this for you," I tell her.

This gives her a moment's pause. "Do I want to know?"

I take a deep breath and blurt out everything. About how I tried to woo the tailors by having them design her dress, but they clearly hate me anyway. That I tried to buy the sample dress but couldn't, her god-awful dress turned out divine, my divine dress turned out god-awful, the flowers I had to poach from Santa Barbara homes and gardens, Merrick's niece and—

"You *stole* the flowers for my wedding?" she says, missing the point.

"Well, it's not really stealing. Nobody owns Mother Nature, Maya."

"But if caught, they'd throw you in jail?"

"Oh, sure. I mean, trespassing was the least of it."

She laughs. "And how does—" she gestures at me, head to toe "—this have anything to do with my dress?"

"I was afraid I'd outshine you at your own wedding—" Some expression flickers on her face and I say, "You'd better not laugh! It was a real possibility, at least if your dress was horrible, and mine was beautiful, instead of the opposite. It's *your* day, I didn't want to look better than the bride."

"You did all this for me?"

I shrug. "Any half-assed friend would've done the same."

"You look like Krusty the Clown's transvestite brother," she says, reminding me I've also gone overboard with the blue eye shadow and cherry lipstick. "That takes more than a half ass."

"Hey! My ass is not—"

She hugs me. "I can't believe you uglified yourself for me—that's the nicest thing I've ever heard."

"But I'm gonna ruin all your wedding photos."

"Are you kidding? We'll still be laughing at those when we're ninety-seven and sharing a room at the nursing home." She brushes a Little Lord Fauntleroy curl from my forehead. "You're the sweetest person I've ever met."

She sounds so sincere that I'm speechless for a moment. But I'm not good with sincerity—or speechlessness—so I say: "You're missing something."

"No honey," she eyes me up and down, "I think I've seen it all."

"No, *this.*" I pin a pale yellow rosebud behind her ear. "Yellow's for remembrance. For your mom."

Maya gets teary, which I cannot allow for reasons of mascara, so from my bag I pull her bouquet. "And for you."

"It's so simple," she says.

White roses tied with creamy French ribbon. Took me fourteen tries and thirty minutes to get the bow right. And it's not simple, it's elegant. It's classic. I can't believe she doesn't like it. Well, I can believe, but somehow in the wee hours I'd convinced myself this was going to work. "Um—"

"I don't know how I ever doubted you." Maya weepily beams. "It's perfect."

Maya drifts off in a haze of happy to show Brad and her father, and I consider running through the sand to the bathroom back at the parking lot, to minimize the bozocity. But it's a ten-minute walk and a thirty-minute fix, so I drift toward Monty and try to blend. Be easier if we'd gone with a Halloween theme. Monty sees me coming, and I'm pretty sure that only a lifetime of gentlemanly behavior keeps him from yelling, "Back, foul creature, to the depths from which you sprang!"

Instead, he raises an eyebrow. He's looking even more dapper then usual, and I'm about to comment on his resplendence when I see the Lusty Rabbi arriving through the sand. I'm extremely glad to see him, as I'm in desperate need of an ogle—even a casual checking-out will do, anything to bolster my ego. So I step forward with a smile, and he shakes my hand and asks if we've met.

"Um," I say. How can he not recognize me, he's totally hot for me!

"You look familiar," he says. "But I meet so many people. You must be Mrs. Nesslebaum's, er, daughter?"

Her *"er, daughter?"* Do I look like I've been through gender reassignment surgery? "No, I—I'm Elle? Maya's friend?"

There's a gleam of horrified recognition in his eyes. "Oh! Of course. I'm—" He struggles for a word. "I'm so sorry."

I simper politely and slink over to stand with Maya and Brad and Wicked Tad—who is Brad's best man—at the *chupah*. Brad kisses me on the cheek without recoiling, which means Maya filled him in, and Tad says, "And I thought your purple sweatsuit was bad."

I'm about to explain to him the merits of Juicy Couture, while dunking his head in a tide pool, when I see Merrick. Past the *chupah*, past the closest crowd of people, standing on the sand, gorgeous in beige silk suit and bare feet. Neil's beside him in khaki cargo pants and a black button-down, and for some reason the sight of the two of them together makes me smile. Maybe because Neil is living proof that Merrick's taste in people isn't as uptight as you might think.

We haven't spoken since the fight, but he returns my smile across the crowded beach, and time stops. I've never really believed in all that soulmate crap, that someone out there is the other half of me—there's plenty of me already, probably too much—but Merrick just...works. We have our problems, and our disagreements, and I know I disappoint him and maybe sometimes he disappoints me, but we...well, we fit. We're better together than apart.

The thing is, even looking like I do right now, there's nothing in Merrick's eyes I don't want to see. And I don't know what he sees in my eyes, but there's nothing I don't want to share.

And time starts again, and everyone gathers, and the rabbi says, "We're not gathered here to marry Maya and Brad. That's not our job. In the Jewish tradition, Maya and Brad do all the heavy lifting. Nobody marries them to each other except themselves. They're the ones who begin a new relationship, one of consecrating and exalting. They say to each other, before witnesses, *harei at mekudeshet li,* which means, 'Behold, you are made holy to me.'" He pauses for a moment, and the sun shines a little redder over the ocean, bathing us in rosy light. "They don't say, 'I love you' or 'I need you' or 'I want you.' They say, 'You are holy to me.' Many of us don't believe in holiness, or we think it's something far away, on some distant mountaintop. But what we're saying today is, the mountaintop isn't so far away. The mountaintop is across the breakfast table. The mountaintop is in the other room, brushing its teeth. There is something holy in the car with you, in bed with you, arguing with you, loving you—even frustrating and disappointing you. Most of us don't consider our spouses holy, but this is what Brad and Maya promise each other today—to see each other as holy."

They drink wine and say a prayer that means, 'I am my beloved's and my beloved is mine.' They say the Seven Blessings, each of them shatters a wine glass underfoot, and I am beaming and crying and looking at Merrick as the Lusty Rabbi says: "I now pronounce you husband and wife."

chapter

24

I really should slip home after the ceremony to change into something nicer than a ruffled clownsuit, wash my face and fix my hair, but Maya hasn't seen the finished bar: I want to be there when she opens the door and sees how amazing Shika looks. Well, plus I got waylaid by Brad's parents after the ceremony, and Merrick volunteered to drive some relatives to the reception, so we haven't had the chance to say hello yet.

Anyway, I figure I can watch Maya's thrilled amazement, repair some of the damage in the bathroom and sweep to a romantic conclusion with Merrick, no problem at all.

Well, one tiny problem.

Yes, Maya loves the new Shika. Her eyes go wide and her

smile wider. She's thrilled with Brad, with the wedding, with me. She laughs at the rose-petal-strewn bar, she *oohs* at the candles and the flowers. For once, the bar is packed; music plays and laughter sounds and glasses clink. Maya spins, taking in the whole scene, then stops to look at her father. They share a moment. I don't know what it means, but they're both smiling and teary when the moment ends.

And yes, Merrick stands by the bar, and he turns when he sees me. There's something warm and excited and hopeful in his expression, probably a mirror of my own. I've already planned that when I see him I'm gonna say, too, "Let's get holy together."

But that tiny problem?

Blake Conahy and the L.A. producer, Shelly Pitts-Jones, are waiting just inside the doors.

"Elle," Blake starts, enthusiastically, until he gets a closer look. "Holy mother of Dog."

"What?" I say. "Omigod! This is a, um, it's a costume wedding, ha ha! We're all supposed to come as, er, um—"

"Lepers?" Blake suggests.

"Yes?" I say.

"Her?" Pitts-Jones says, aghast. She is blonde and severe looking in a red silk suit.

"She doesn't really look like this," Blake explains.

"You said she was pleasantly plain," the producer tells him.

"You said I'm *what?*" I say.

"Pretty," Blake says. "I said pretty."

"Unthreateningly pretty," she says. "Listen, I love love *love* your show, Elle. Love it."

"Thank you," I start. "I feel that—"

"But you have a face for radio." She checks her watch. "I don't have time for this. C'mon, Blake."

Blake shoots me an apologetic look over his shoulder as he follows her outside, and Merrick whispers in my ear, "Lucy."

I forget my clever lines and fall into his arms. It's nice there. Warm and comfy, and nobody can see my face.

"That *asshole!*" Maya says, behind me, a fury in a stunning seafoam gown.

"Which asshole?" Merrick says.

"'A face made for radio!'" Maya says, glaring toward the door. "I oughtta kick her ass. I should've kicked her ass out of here. It's my bar, she can't come in here and say—"

"Well, you have to admit Elle has appeared to better advantage," Merrick says, kissing my awful ringlets. "I'm trying not to imagine what cataclysmic events led to—"

"She did it for me," Maya says. "She thought my dress was ugly, so she—"

"But your dress is beautiful," Merrick says.

"Work with me, Merrick," she says. "This is Elle. She thought it was horrible, okay? That's why she decided to make herself even uglier—so I'd look good by comparison."

He glances from her to me and doesn't say anything.

"Because that's the kinda girl she is," Maya says. "And Elle— you're *always* the good sister, I couldn't ask for a better one."

Brad comes then and swoops her away to dance.

I stay in Merrick's arms and we don't really dance, we just hold each other. He says, "I heard you on the radio."

"In New York?"

"I had Neil tape your shows and FedEx them."

"Even though you hated me?"

"Yeah," he says.

"Um—" I want to ask if he liked the shows, but I'm afraid.

"You're fantastic," he says. "You're tremendous. You're really really good at that."

"What about the whole 'thou shalt not tell a lie' thing?"

"I'm sorry. I guess we both—I guess I like making pronouncements, and you like pretending you're a lost sheep, but you—" He swallows. "All I could think, the whole time I was in New York, is how lucky I am to have someone who shines so bright in my life."

There's a brief pause during which my heart expands to fill the bar, then the block, then the county, and so on and so on until…well, you get the picture. Then I say, "So the co-op thing went okay?"

"Not how I planned it," he says. "But, yeah." And he kisses me into next week.

When the kiss finally ends, the reception is in full swing. Monty's pulling a sexy fifty-something from Brad's side of the family, Wicked Tad is sitting with his Clean Cut bosses—who must've crashed the reception—drinking heavily, and the Gay Tailors, who also just showed up, are dancing about as gracelessly as any two straight men. "Maybe they're not really gay," I murmur. "Maybe that's why they didn't want to be my best friends."

"Maybe you have enough friends already," Merrick says.

Yeah. Maybe so.

We sway to the music for a few minutes, in our own little world. Then Neil materializes at my shoulder. "Here's the stuff," he says, and hands me a bulging plastic grocery sack.

"The stuff?" I hiss, picturing a ten-pound brick of marijuana, and the resultant arrests and convictions. Maybe I can just cop a plea to "flower poaching" and hope for house arrest.

"Your new clothes," he says.

"I asked Neil to run to your place for a change," Merrick tells me. "He has the keys, you know."

"Oh, that's a relief. Except…you had *Neil* pick out my clothes?"

"Kara came with me," Neil says.

"Is she here?" I ask.

"Sure that's her, right there." He points. "In the blue top."

I spin, but too late—all I see is a shadow disappearing behind the shifting crowd. "I think your wife is Keyser Soze," I tell Neil. From *The Usual Suspects.*

"Hey, I liked that movie, and you don't know how right you are. She's Kara Soze," he says.

We laugh, and I kiss Merrick and tell him I'll be back in three seconds, after I repair some of the damage. I head to the bathroom, rummaging around in the plastic bag. Kara did a good job: she grabbed my makeup and my new drapey suit from Element. I dig for eye makeup remover, but get a wad of paper that I must've shoved in my makeup case by mistake: the photos of Tad with his buddies and some pay stubs. I figure I'll swing by his table, scare his bosses, and give them the photos. Then I look closer. The party swirls around me, and I look closer still. It can't be. I check the pay stubs. Oh, God, it is.

"What's wrong?" Merrick asks.

I give him the pictures and pay stubs.

He flips through them and frowns.

"What should I do?" I ask.

"First, never let my niece touch your hair again. Second, move in with me."

"Done and done," I say. "But what about *this?*"

"I'm gonna go kick their asses," he says, matter-of-factly.

"All of them?" I ask, wanting to add *my hero!*

"Sure," he says. "They're so drunk they can't see straight."

Must admit this is very manly and exciting, especially as he clearly intends to barroom brawl for me—which still counts even if the bar in question is festooned with roses. He takes a resolute step forward, and I lay a hand on his arm. "Not at their wedding," I say. "Besides, I have a better idea."

As the reception roars into the evening, I wash my face and change into my drapey suit and Victorian bustier and pin my tangerine curls back, to minimize the visual impact. I dance with Merrick, make a few phones calls, invent oddly named drinks for Kid to mix, and try to keep everything moving, so Maya can simply enjoy. Judging from her glow of pleasure, that's working pretty well.

Ray Flood steps in, looking deeply shy, and I chat with him for a moment before he escapes out the backdoor—where there's a sort of concrete "garden" with a few tables. I think he's getting used to me, and maybe liking me a little, too. Monty busses me on the cheek and leaves with the fifty-something hottie, Neil gets in a big fight with Kara, who has locked herself in the bathroom so I never even catch a glimpse of her, and even Darwin and Adele, my friends from the phone-psychic business, show up for a beer and an herbal tea. That's the nice thing about having a reception at a bar: you can invite *everyone*.

Must be almost midnight when Jenna, my friend the stripper from Café Lustre, slithers through the crowd toward me, still looking like the cover of *Maxim*. She thinks she owes me for getting the previous bouncer fired, so she's happy to help. I flick my eyes toward Tad, Clean-Cut and Cleaner-Cut, and Jenna winks at me and sways in their direction. Even stone drunk, they perk up at her approach, with stunned, glazed looks at her fishnets and cleavage.

I follow behind, and hear her say, "This place is dead. You wanna come out back and have a *real* party?"

I can't believe how clunky and obvious she is, but then I remember: They're men. And, sure enough, all three of them instantly rise, like stupid muffins in a warm oven.

I let Clean-Cut and Cleaner-Cut pass, then put my palm on Tad's chest and shove him back into his seat. "Not you."

The honeymoon is over.

Or maybe the honeymoon has just begun. Maya and Brad are back from Maui, and Merrick and I are living together. Making the commitment really changed things—I'm not just staying at his place anymore, I'm living there. I'm not worried about becoming clingy and desperate, either. I'm not the same Elle I used to be. Now I know even if I *do* become needy and desperate, I can handle it. We can handle it. Plus, this isn't all on me—Merrick's an anal, controlling perfectionist, so I'm not the only nutjob in this relationship.

Bottom line is, I trust him. I trust me. I trust *us.*

Speaking of trust…turns out Wicked Tad was more than a *tad* wicked, and I never should've trusted him at all. In the photos of him with his clean-cut friends, one of the guys was wearing a T-shirt with the barely visible logo Santa Barbara Grrrrls. And his pay stubs were issued by Barbalicious.

They'd just happened to catch me in the dressing room, but after my column appeared in the *Permanent Press,* and they saw that I was driving more traffic to their site—because of the controversy—than they'd ever had, they found where I lived and offered Tad a job. His first duty? Putting a camera in my shower.

Fortunately, revenge is sweet.

I push through the doors into the new Shika, which is fast becoming, if not a trendy young bar, at least middling-popular among the Sting-loving set. The usual crowd is there, along with the Gay Tailors and Ray Flood, and I marvel for a moment that I have a "usual crowd." Then I fire up my laptop (well, fifty percent mine) and log on to *Santa Barbara Grrrrls*.

"Not *another* video?" Brad says.

He's been out of town, he doesn't know what's coming. "Yeah," I say. "Another video."

"Oh, sweetie," Maya says, from where she's pulling a few beers.

"This one isn't of me," I tell them, and click.

The lighting is pretty good, so I turn and smile at Ray, who arranged the lighting and webcam. Never say that eBay isn't a good investment.

"Hey," Brad says. "That's here, at Shika. Out the back door."

And for a moment, that's all it is. Then a woman sashays into the frame. Jenna. Followed by two drunk clean-cut men, stumbling and leering, then looking around nervously to be sure they were alone before undressing. It takes Jenna—now off-screen—about two minutes to convince them to bark like naked dogs. At the five-minute mark, I have to turn the video off. Revenge is sweet, but ugly, and even I can't stomach the sight of a naked Clean-Cut playing dead while a naked Cleaner-Cut balances a beer coaster on his nose.

There's silence for a moment, then Brad says, "Ouch."

"That's my girl," Merrick says.

"Those guys," Maya says. "They weren't—I mean, they just met Dustin at the bar, right?"

"Who's Dustin?" I ask.

She sighs. "Tad."

"Oh! I forgot he has a real name. No, they hired him. To put the camera in my shower. And they—"

The rest of my words are drowned out by the combination of Brad's cursing and Maya's angry howl.

"How come he's not on the video?" Neil asks. "He's the one who betrayed you, like Karl Rove selling out—"

"Yes, we know how you feel about Karl, Neil. But I couldn't," I say. "He's family."

"I'm going to kill him," Brad says.

"Get in line," Maya says.

"Oh, we're even," I tell them. "He's the one who hooked this video up on the site—"

"On pain of death," Merrick says.

"—and anyway, he's in a better place now. With a positive role model. Learning important life skills."

"Lompoc, I hope," Maya says, meaning the prison.

"Better," I say. "Sedona."

"Not with—"

I nod. "Living with my mom. She finally got someone to take the busboy job, next door. Not that he had much choice—I threatened to release all the videos of him in my shower. And one time he—"

"Stop!" Maya says. "Brother-in-law! Too much information!"

"Yeah," Merrick says, "I think that's the *real* reason she agreed to move in with me."

I haven't told him yet that I've kept the apartment—but only for use as an office, upstairs from his. Because sure, I'll never see the inside of a TV studio, but Blake's producer was as good as her word. She said I had a face for radio, and hooked me up with a big L.A. station. They refuse to put me on the billboards, but that's okay…for now. It's steady work, and rewarding work, and I'm so damn good at it I actually need a real office to handle everything.

Oh, and the name of my show? *Straight to Elle: Fake Psychic, Real Advice.*

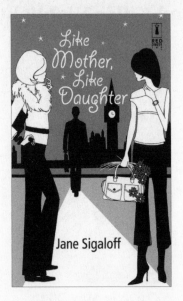

25 stories from the
hottest female writers on the scene

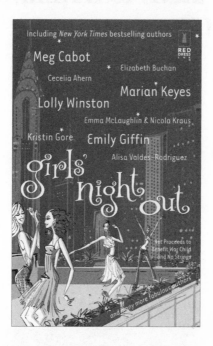

On sale June 2006

Too tired to doll up and head out for a night
on the town? Just dip into this year's must-read
collection for a Girls' Night Out to remember!

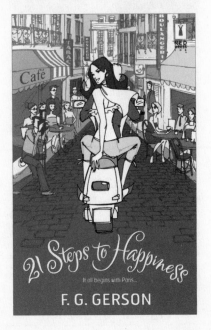